"*Salvagia* delivers nostalgic mystery, adventure, and climate punk all in one package. This is a miss-your-subway-stop, keep-listening-in-your-driveway, hide-it-in-a-textbook, read-it-during-a-Zoom-call level of superb."

—MUR LAFFERTY,
author of the Midsolar Murders series

"This near-future novel weaves together elements of murder mysteries, thrillers, and found families into a propellant-fueled, page-turner of a plot. Along the way, Chawaga's debut presents a critique of many present-day issues while avoiding a descent into total dystopianism, leaving the reader with a satisfyingly bittersweet finish."

—S. B. DIVYA,
Hugo and Nebula awards finalist
and author of *Meru*

"A sharp and inventive debut, *Salvagia* is a full-throttle trip that doesn't let up until the last page. With deft worldbuilding and compellingly noirish characters, Chawaga's future Florida crackles with intrigue and danger at every turn."

—VICTOR MANIBO,
author of *The Sleepless* and *Escape Velocity*

"*Salvagia* is a wonderful debut from one of the best new writers we have. If you love smart, exciting science fiction, this one's for you!"

—JONATHAN STRAHAN,
World Fantasy Award–winning editor of
*New Adventures in Space Opera*

"*Salvagia* makes the climate apocalypse look cool. From the depths of sunken Miami to the heights of atmo-breaker races, Chawaga zips through post–climate change Florida, taking his characters through a thrilling murder mystery that unravels into a set of corporate and personal entanglements that serve as a neat mirror of our own world's issues, magnified and extrapolated into the future."

—ISABEL J. KIM,
Hugo and Nebula awards finalist
and author of *Sublimation*

# SALVAGIA

# SALVAGIA

a novel

# TIM CHAWAGA

DIVERSION BOOKS

Diversion Books
A division of Diversion Publishing Corp.
www.diversionbooks.com

Copyright © 2025 by Tim Chawaga

All rights reserved, including the right to reproduce this book or portions thereof in any form whatsoever. No part of this publication may be reproduced or transmitted in any form or by any means, electronic or mechanical, including photocopying, recording, or any other information storage and retrieval, without the written permission of the publisher.

Diversion Books and colophon are registered trademarks of Diversion Publishing Corp.

For more information, email info@diversionbooks.com

First Diversion Books Edition: August 2025
Trade paperback ISBN: 979-8-89515-038-2
e-ISBN: 979-8-89515-037-5

Design by Neuwirth & Associates, Inc.
Cover design by Steve Thomas

Printed in the United States of America

1 3 5 7 9 10 8 6 4 2

Diversion books are available at special discounts for bulk purchases in the US by corporations, institutions, and other organizations. For more information, please contact admin@diversionbooks.com.

The publisher does not have any control over and does not assume any responsibility for author or third-party websites or their content.

*For Mom, who read every draft*

# 1

The prize was a single shoe.

A Keds Champion Original canvas sneaker, discovered on its side thirty-five meters down, half-buried in the calcareous ooze outside the wreck that Kohl and I had come to dive. Size 8, circa early 2050s, treated with that special wear-resistant chemical that degrades slowly and so artfully in salt water, one side of the white canvas prismed into a psychedelic rainbow pattern, the other side pristine, preserved by silt, the laces calcified against the tongue like icing on a cake.

Half what it had been, half what it became. Life transitioning toward death, loss transforming into beauty. The prize was the most on-the-nose dictionary definition of nostalgic salvage that I had ever seen. Salvagia exquisite enough to deliver me—maybe, finally—from my own transitional existence.

After a tense and endless decomp, Kohl and I surfaced and climbed back aboard the *Floating Ghost*, the pearl-white, luxury CabanaBoat that hitherto I could afford only to charter. Myra lounged on the deck, sipping rum on the rocks. We showed her the prize. She was thrilled to hear that it might be worth enough for me to buy the *Ghost* and stay in the state.

"Next year at the Inner Boca Boatel!" she exclaimed. I was a rare find for her. She hoarded peculiar Florida characters as fiercely as the salvagia market was hoarding sneakers then, and now she might just get to keep me.

My peculiarity just then was my trepidation in the face of salvation. Myra frowned at my thin, humorless smile, and watched me slip my Knuckles on. Kohl headed for the master stateroom belowdecks, probably to catch the first shower while the water was hot.

"Triss, you're armed," Myra said, when Kohl was gone. "Are we expecting trouble?" Her tone was conspiratorial, semi-hopeful, like she was asking if a secret celebrity was coming to dinner.

"Always," I replied, not just because it was the kind of answer Myra liked. I was expecting trouble, though not pirates or any kind of problem my Knuckles could really solve.

SuperCane Isha had made landfall a couple weeks ago. SuperCanes were common enough, but this one had hit all the right places, deploying devastating daughter tornadoes, building up speed and power along the coast, before cutting inland just south of the Astro America and wreaking so much havoc that I'd heard the feds were abandoning the state entirely.

Isha had severely shuffled up the yoreshore, the aquatic area between where the shore used to be and where it was now. So we needed the *Ghost*, whose real-time hazard charting could sense a way through the new sandbars and churn up piles of ancient concrete.

But on the way down, the *Ghost* kept shifting too close to shore, sniffing around sandbars for too long. Near Fort Myers she sped straight for a reef and got so close to it I had to run her emergency stop routine. The jolt threw Myra and Kohl from the couch in the lounge. I told them my finger had slipped. For some reason it was important to me that Kohl thought I knew what I was doing.

The truth was that I could neither sail the *Floating Ghost* nor speak to her, beyond telling her to stop and to go, along a pre-planned route set by Charlie, her owner. She was semi-sentient, but she spoke a dead language. The company that built her had folded many years ago and kept its secrets.

I wanted to get back to Charlie with all haste, tell him I had the money so he wouldn't search for other buyers. I went through the lounge and to the little cockpit and told the *Ghost* to go, running the routine several times, like "Go, go, go," to communicate urgency. But she took her time pulling up her anchor, shook herself from side to side for some reason, and only then, leisurely, did she begin to putter back to the yoreshore.

I gripped my Knuckles. They'd belonged to my Gamma. I wore them when I needed to feel the illusion of control over my life, which I'd built out of tightening loopholes and fading fine print. With luck, it would soon rely entirely on a boat I couldn't understand and wouldn't listen.

I wore them almost all the time.

The *Ghost* kept a good pace, up until we passed old flooded Key West, where only the cemetery remains above water.

Someone was throwing a party there. A small armada of yachts was anchored in the bight. A colony of pastel people flossed themselves among the bone-white teeth of the headstones.

"We should crash it," said Kohl. He'd found me on the sundeck. He smelled like sweat and brine, sea industry. He hadn't taken a shower after all.

"We don't know who they are," I replied. They looked too fancy to be pirates. I thought it was probably one of the corporate mafias, who controlled most things in South Florida outside of OrlanDome, which was run by the feds. They could be just as dangerous as pirates to outsiders.

"Don't you want to see what it's for?" said Kohl. "All the way out here?"

"They're building something," said Myra, pointing. Anchored on the other side of the yoreshore, behind the cemetery, was some giant and mechanical thing, squatting in the water on huge metal legs, the shadow cast by the setting sun behind it long enough to almost touch the shore. "That's a construction titan. I've never seen one on this side of the Gulf. I bet we'll be seeing a lot more of them down here once the feds leave."

"Do these titans make nice buildings?" Kohl asked.

Myra snorted. "No. Cheap housing, usually for people who've lost their homes but won't go to the domes. They are glorified storm barriers, sandbags filled with people instead of sand. They go up fast and they go down first. But I'd love to see a titan up close."

"Well, shoot," said Kohl. "I think I'd like to see that, too. Get us closer, Trissy."

I had been warming to him somewhat, perhaps as a byproduct of our profitable dive. I was even considering letting him take a turn holding the diving bag that held the prize, which he kept eyeing and which I kept clutched to my side. His unsanctioned nickname cooled me off again, and the hoarding instincts honed in childhood kept my charity in check.

"I heard a story someplace that the graves say funny things on them," he added.

"Ooh!" squealed Myra. "Triss! Funny things! I brought my birding binoculars, maybe we can read them."

"And toast our success," added Kohl.

"It's just like Inner Boca, don't you think?"

"Inner Boca doesn't exist," I reminded her, but it dampened her mood not a bit.

I could feel the *Ghost* listing toward the bight. She wanted to check out the party, too. It would be easier to let her sniff her fill from a distance, so I went down and told her to stop. She threw her anchor but inched forward, tightening the slack. Myra went inside to get her binoculars and Kohl went with her to raid Charlie's rum cabinet. I threw my legs over the railing and tried to relax.

It was easier than I thought. The evening breeze draped peace and distant laughter over me like a warm, breathable blanket.

Florida sunset, beautiful boat, stable weather, cold drinks, and good friends; it *was* uncannily similar to Myra's description of her fictional Inner Boca Boatel, which was just a fable, a manifestation of her theoretical Third Way of Florida living, which she hoped either to stumble upon or put into practice herself once she'd collected enough Florida characters.

And I had to admit, leaning on the deck of the *Ghost*, feeling the breeze, it all felt exactly the way I thought it would, in the rare moments when Myra convinced me that I really would find a way to buy the *Ghost*, and I forgot that I knew better, having witnessed some Third Ways myself.

At some point I set the bag with the prize down next to me.

A Go-Fast boat went fast by us, too close, churning up a massive wake, stopping on a dime near the rest of the armada. The wake hit us portside and the prize pitched over the edge.

I lunged for it and missed.

I pressed the top button of the Knuckle in the palm of my left hand, extending the baton. It caught the end of the drawstring. The baton bent. The drawstring slipped.

I heard sprinting steps behind me. Kohl reached over the side and grabbed the bag.

"Close one," he said. I looked up at him with a sheepish grin, and went to take the bag, to feel the comfort of its weight.

He didn't let go.

His wetsuit was on again. He held an oxygen tank in his other hand, a little one, light but dense. His smile was cold. He wore his gogs tinted, like always, and they blinded me with reflected sunset. It occurred to me that I had never seen his eyes.

The blow should have smashed my skull. Instead my hand came up in time and the baton caught him by surprise. The tank cracked off of it and glanced my nose. I cried out. The force sent me to the deck and my head bounced off the TeakLike with a wet smack. He jumped over the side.

The *Ghost* began to shake, whirring her outboards in an unfamiliar and disturbing way. It kept me down and made me nauseous. She pitched forward, rolling me all the way to the edge. I brought my hands up just in time to protect my nose from the railing, retched through the bars and over the side. There was no sign of Kohl in the water, not even a ripple. The yoreshore here was all ruined streets and buildings and other little hidey-holes for him to bide his time in.

But he probably had a timeline, otherwise he would have stuck around to finish me off. He was the one who wanted to stop here.

Which meant that he was heading for the party.

I struggled, pulled myself up. I had to get the prize.

The *Ghost* turned hard in the other direction, which spun me around to face the lounge.

There was a lump on the floor. Myra hadn't come running at the sound of me hitting the deck.

I stumbled into the lounge. Kohl had done a better job with her. There was a lot of blood from a gash in her forehead. The shaking of the *Ghost* smeared it like a sudden angry brushstroke.

She was breathing. I rolled her over. Her eyes were open but unfocused.

I should have stayed with her and told the *Ghost* to take us back to Charlie. I probably needed a doctor myself. I was having trouble moving steadily.

But Charlie lived in Lakeland, up the gulfside yoreshore, almost all the way to OrlanDome. I couldn't predict how long it would take the *Ghost* to get back. Holding Myra's head, hoping the *Ghost* could stay on course for half a day would be unbearable.

And Kohl was escaping.

I squeezed my Knuckles again. This was a problem they *could* solve.

I mopped Myra's wound with a clean towel and bound it and put a pillow under her head. I left her on the floor. I was afraid to move her.

"The party's our best hope," I muttered. If I said it out loud it might make it true.

"For what?" Myra's voice was barely a whisper.

"A doctor. A hospital. Help."

"In the Keys? Good luck. The hospitals sank in the 2080s. Same storm that drowned all the Hemingway cats. Do you know what makes a Hemingway cat?"

"Is this a joke?"

"Six toes. His cat had six toes. A dominant gene. A hundred and eighty-seven documented polydactyl cats."

"How many toes?"

"Six!"

"No, total. I need to know. You should count them for me, one by one, just to be sure. All four paws. All hundred and eighty-seven. Out loud. Don't fall asleep. Maybe do it twice. When I get back there'll be a quiz."

She put her hand on my head and told me to stop shouting.

The *Ghost* was agitated. She made it difficult to grab the equipment I needed: diving mask and fins, oxygen tank, regulator. I leapt over the railing, but the *Ghost* shuddered, and I stumbled and flopped into the water, scraping myself on the ruins of the old world.

There are those who feel more comfortable in the water than on land. I am not among them. I had a landlocked childhood. Diving does not come naturally to me.

It is the disorienting wrenching of all the senses being sucked into a hostile dimension. We evolved to escape this place. We are not meant to be here. Big sky is a comfort to me. Open ocean is a terror. My dive earlier today had been in open ocean.

The yoreshore, however, is shallow and nearly devoid of life, which makes it a little easier on my nerves.

I found the remains of a street that led to the shore. I hoped Kohl had used it, too. I knew him from the Federal Hydrofluorocarbon Disposal Depot where we both waited in line with the other junk divers to drop off the air conditioners and other assorted hazards salvaged from the yoreshore. I didn't know anything about him at all, except he told me that he had deep water diving experience, which was what I needed to dive the wreck the *Ghost* had found for me.

Wreck diving something that big at that depth is essentially cave diving, very deadly. Attempting it alone is ill-advised. But I also needed Kohl so he could go into the wreck for me, while I stayed out.

By sheer dumb luck I found the prize in the mud, so it would have happened the same way if I had gone alone. But I was too afraid. The split in the hull was a jagged mouth that spoke to me of utter darkness, disorientation, constricted space—the particular horrors from my past that make it so I cannot find sleep in any windowless space, like my assigned hab in OrlanDome. On the *Ghost* I slept in the lounge, with its wraparound glass windows, instead of the master stateroom belowdecks. She'd started opening the windows in the middle of the night to let the breeze in for me.

I swam down the street, past a crumbled concrete wall to a flat and open field, possibly an old backyard. I caught a steady, fluid movement through murky water and streaks of my own blood.

I moved closer, over the foundations of a house, big enough maybe to have been a mansion. The floating shape sprouted out of a big rectangular silt-filled hole that might have once been a swimming pool.

The shadowy shape resolved itself: feet bound with taut chain leading into the pool, hands and arms unbound and floating grotesquely above the gray-blue maskless head. The hands were black and bloated, swelling out of the neoprene at the wrists, the skin of the palms so dark they looked stained.

The face in front of me was disfigured yet familiar.

I got as close as I dared, enough to see the corpse of a man with a widow's peak and a neat goatee. His face was dark blue, almost purple, a once-deep tan drained by the chill of death and the sea. The silver in his hair and the light crease of wrinkles ironed out by bloat or cosmetic adjustment put him in his early sixties, maybe. The eyes and mouth were wide, in an expression of abject horror so convincing that I turned to see what he was looking at, half-expecting to find a giant squid or other sea monster.

It was the eyes that placed him for me, finally. Bright orange, tinting beautifully but unnaturally toward gold. Genetically modified, the color copyrighted. I had seen it many times on camera, so bright that they attracted the gaze no matter where they were in the frame. Down here, in the dark and drained of life, they still glinted a little.

This was the body of Edgar Ortiz, probably the most famous man in South Florida.

I recoiled in surprise, and so the corpse couldn't touch me. I had the urge to tell Myra, and my shock gave way to guilt and despair. A celebrity had come to dinner after all.

The chain wrapped around his feet and clipped to itself. The other end was attached to a heavy chunk of metal on the ocean floor.

Something struck the ocean floor on my left. Another chain, an anchor. I looked up. A hundred feet of hull hovered above me, spotlights illuminating the surrounding surface without revealing what lurked below. Party people treaded water, oblivious to the woman and corpse close enough to tickle their toes.

I should have kept moving. I shouldn't have involved myself in whatever this was.

But I knew what it was to be alone, in the dark and sure of death. I could do for Edgar what it taken hours for anyone to do for me: return him to the world.

And I itched toward action. If Edgar Ortiz had been at this party, alive, then I had a good idea of who was throwing it. His discovery might be a good distraction, hopefully enough to give me the cover I needed to crash and blend in.

## SALVAGIA

Once unclipped, Edgar hungered for the surface. I recalled some poetic thing I'd heard about the buoyancy of corpses, how the purifying sea removes the ballast of their earthly burdens.

I pressed on, back to the ruined road leading to the shore. My burdens kept me under, deep enough to graze the swollen asphalt with my fins.

## 2

When the sand gave way to pebbles I broke the surface, sloshed two steps and then froze.

A woman stared at me from the shore.

The sun had dipped below the horizon while I was underwater, and I could imagine how I looked, sloughing out of the sea like a swamp thing. I approached slowly, with my hands out to show her they were empty, palm-side toward me. From the back my Knuckles looked like rings, three on each hand—gold on the left, silver on the right. I was wearing a pink swimsuit with a cute windmill pattern, casual enough. My nose was the bigger problem. If it wasn't broken then it was certainly swollen enough to look it.

The woman appeared to be somewhere in her fifties, though if you were rich enough you could pass for that decade for decades. She could be rich enough. She wore a pair of designer gogs, possibly Chanel. She was smoking one of those rejuvenation cigarettes, so maybe she was older. I could smell it from the water. It smelled like deep-fried eucalyptus.

She wore a black fedora and a skirt of pastel colors in an abstract floral pattern. I recognized them as the uniform of Mourning in Miami, the most powerful corporate mafia in South Florida and a movement, made up of members of the Miami diaspora and their descendants. Their goal was to bring Miami back, though Miami was uninhabitable, having bled its population for decades before collapsing with great finality at the turn of the century.

The Mourners were led by Edgar Ortiz. Until very recently, anyway.

"They're for my health," the woman said, indicating the cigarettes, as if we were mid-conversation. "I need a breeze, otherwise my clothes stink for hours."

I found her stillness disquieting. She was just an elegant woman, smoking alone. We were surrounded on all sides by mausoleums and headstones, blocked off from the rest of the party. She seemed entirely unafraid.

Maybe I didn't look as bad as I thought.

"I need a doctor," I said. My throat was tight, and my voice came out hoarse.

"It's too late for that," she replied, not unkindly. She nodded behind me. I glanced back and saw the flurry of activity around the large yacht, Mourners in the process of discovering Edgar's body. "I'm pretty sure he's dead."

So much for blending in. I realized I was holding my breath. I exhaled through my nose and snorted a clot of blood into the surf. The woman made a face. I decided to not even bother playing dumb.

"It's not for him," I said. "My friend and I were attacked."

"By who?"

"A man. He wears tinted gogs. Have you seen him?"

"One of us? A Mourner? That's my yacht out there, but my people are usually well-behaved."

"No," I said. "He's in a wetsuit, he's not wearing the uniform."

"There are lots of people here tonight that aren't in uniform. Grifters, drifters. Atmo-breakers, too. Do you know what those are?"

"Of course," I said, feeling somewhat patronized. Daytona and NASA had drowned along with Miami, but atmo-breaking was both, reincarnated: a deadly race through the debris field that permeated the atmosphere. It was the most famous Florida-specific pastime, and its home was the Astro America, a luxury hotel built on stilts in the yoreshore over Cape Canaveral, that ancient source of all our early, more sacrosanct space activities.

Edgar Ortiz had been generally famous and interesting—he'd bought the floundering Miami Dolphins, moved them to Orlando, and won a Super Bowl in less than five years—but developing the atmo-breaking circuit was what he was most known for. He was, for example, the only atmo-breaker I knew by name.

The woman kicked off her flats and stepped into the sea. I fingered the trigger of my Knuckle, and felt slightly ridiculous.

She pulled the scarf off from around her neck and handed it to me.

I took it, careful not to show her my palms. She watched me splash seawater on my nose and wipe it clean. Despite what she'd said about the breeze, I smelled her cigarette on the scarf behind my own blood.

"What's your name?" she asked.

"Triss."

"Triss. I'm Maria. Here's the deal. I'll tell you where you can find a doctor if you promise not to speak to anybody about what you found down there."

She was unnervingly calm for someone who had just found out about the death of the most famous man in Florida. So she had probably already known about it. Or she had killed him herself. He'd been chained to the bottom, as in, someone had put him there after he died. I had the urge to interrogate her—Why was he in a wetsuit? Why were his hands stained black?—but I sensed that an unspoken part of the deal was to remain incurious.

There was one question, though, that I thought I should ask: "How do you know you can trust me?"

She considered this. "I suppose I don't," she said, finally. "I didn't kill him, but I would like to be the one to break the news. I have my own little vision of how I'll do it. But I'm not too precious about it. If your silence were essential, I'd just have you killed."

"I see," I said, glancing at the shadows behind the surrounding headstones. I felt less silly about being on my guard.

"And I have a feeling you want to stay out of it."

"I do."

"Then it's a deal?"

I hesitated.

It wasn't just that I didn't trust this woman, who was not afraid of me and probably *had* just killed the leader of her own movement, despite what she said.

I was expecting to have to search the entire island for help, which meant that I had an excuse to keep an eye out for Kohl at the same time. If I knew exactly where to find a doctor, then looking for Kohl became a distraction. Helping Myra should be priority one.

"Well?"

I nodded, curtly, keeping my eyes on the shadows.

"Good," said Maria. "The atmo-breakers are doing time trials here tonight. They keep a medic. Not sure why—in a drag race to space, you're either fine or you're vaporized. They're setting up the breakers on the other side of the cemetery, near the construction site. The medic is wearing blue. He'll be the only one without ads on his clothes. Tell him that I sent you."

"Thank you."

"You should hurry. The race is starting soon."

I tried to hand the scarf back to her, but she waved it away with disgust. I took off my fins and stacked my equipment near the rock I'd almost tripped over. Turned out it was a headstone. I glanced at the epithet—"Gloria Russel, 1926–2000, 'I'm Just Resting My Eyes.'"

Kohl was right. The graves did say funny things.

The safest, most solitary route to the other side of the island would probably have been around the shore, which looked deserted and concealed by mausoleums in both directions.

I cut straight through the party instead, sneaking through the mobile golf course while the front nine reorganized itself into a new configuration, moving toward the lights and the siren sound of "Margaritaville," that classic Mourner anthem, which they were playing on repeat.

To actively search for Kohl would be to prioritize revenge over helping Myra. I couldn't quite bring myself to do that. So, as was my nature, I made a loophole; I decided that if I happened to come across him while on my way to the doctor, he would become an obstacle to helping Myra and it would therefore be necessary for me to engage him. All I had to do was find a route that increased my odds of running into him.

This ended up being more difficult than I thought. The construction titan looming in the distance was my north star, but heading straight for it kept me on the outskirts of the dance floor. I wanted to keep listing toward the center, toward the higher density of people. I felt like the *Ghost*, sneaking at a sandbar, addicted to the crowd the way she was addicted to the shore.

I was forced to admit to myself that it wasn't just about the money. I needed to punish him, for me and Myra. Kohl had taken more than the Ked; he'd popped the pipe dream. He'd gotten Myra talking about the Inner Boca Boatel again. He stoked her obsession with the Third Way with stories of a commune he knew called Coral Castle, where he swore he'd seen a great Lost Cause: the almost certainly extinct Florida panther. Myra believed him, perhaps because he looked a little like a panther himself—sharp-angled and lean, with big tinted gogs that made his eyes huge, reflective, and unblinking.

He'd done all this, built up all her hopes (and mine). Then he snatched them away.

Those gogs bounced the laser lights from the dance floor drones into my eyes and that was how I spotted him, slinking, sneaking a gun from the holster of a Mourner at the edge of the AutoBar. He and I were two of the only people not wearing the Mourner uniform: black fedora and blazer, bright pastels, like hard-boiled detectives that had suffered an accident in the "vibrant" section of a paint swatch. He spotted me, too, and darted off.

I pursued. The crowd pushed against me, forcing me to zigzag, off the dance floor and past the bar, and down the cramped and crowded cemetery street I wasn't even sure he'd used. I lost sight of him but I kept moving—deafened by the 3-DJ drones flitting around like mosquitoes on a stagnant pond, shot at near the firing range, nearly pancaked by drag-racing muscle cars; before I knew it I was lost and panicking, the mausoleums too high for me to see over, no hope of doctors, atmo-breakers, or escape, gripped with the sudden certainty that Kohl had got around me somehow, that if I went back the way I'd come he would be there, poised with his stolen gun to finish the job. The only way to make sure he wasn't behind me was to keep him in front of me, so I lunged at a Kohl-like shadow, leaping over a freshly printed fence and slipping in ankle-deep mud, landing on my tender face and bringing tears and stars to my eyes.

"Are you all right?" someone asked.

I grabbed out blindly and touched metal, cool and curved. I used it to pull myself up. I rubbed my eyes and gazed upon twelve feet of jagged steel and squat hydraulics.

It was a mechanical gator.

Deactivated, thankfully. Turned on, it was only a lightly dangerous dive bar pastime. To beat it you had to reach right into its mouth, unhook its jaw hinge, and push the top half of its head up, perpendicular, like a lever. I had never beat it, but the last time I had tried was the night I had met Myra, in a bar along the lakes outside of OrlanDome. She'd coached me, and by the end of the night I wasn't winning, but I was definitely losing slower.

To find it here, nestled against a particularly tall mausoleum, felt like a sign.

A man was standing next to me. He was short, and like me, he wasn't in uniform. He wore a ratty old soccer jersey with sponsorship logos that glitched out in a distracting way. "The technicians said it just shut down. They can't figure out why, but—"

"Either give me a boost or vamoose," I replied. The man hesitated, but then obliged, and I stepped in his hands and clambered on the back of the gator. But he didn't go away.

"Name's Félix," he said. "Félix Martí. I'm looking for recruits. I'd love to tell you about it."

"Not interested," I grunted, pulling myself up the side of the mausoleum, but for the moment I was a captive audience.

"It's called the Florida Aquatic Co-op," he said. "A new community. When the feds pull out we'll need something other than that hideous Conchipublican, or whatever they're calling it out there. And I say that as a personal friend of Edgar Ortiz."

He seemed like someone Myra would love to talk to, standing in front of something Myra loved to watch pulverize me. I considered breaking my promise to Maria to keep my secret about Edgar, just to get him to shut up. "Another Third Way," I muttered.

I expected Félix to be confused, or insulted. "What're the other two?" he asked.

I spun around and spotted the high stack of cargo containers and construction materials. A long barge bobbed in the water, with half a dozen rockets lined up like champagne glasses teetering on a tray—the atmo-breakers.

"First is the federal domes," I said. "Second's corporate mafias. Third is . . ."

Near the barge, I saw little groups of people with glowing sponsorship ads all over their bodies, the same as Félix's soccer jersey but bright and steady, and another figure walking away from them, alone. I probably wouldn't have noticed them, except they walked past a group of pilots. Their silhouette dimmed the other logos out, which meant they didn't have any. And they appeared to be wearing blue.

The medic.

They walked toward the stacks of construction materials and would soon be hidden behind them.

"Third is what?" asked Félix. His sincerity surprised me, and pulled my attention back to him. He really wanted to know. I tried to remember how Myra described it. She had two master's degrees, so most of what she said was academic and went over my head.

Except for the Inner Boca Boatel. She described it as a little mom-and-pop establishment, still mostly overgrown, nestled along the as-yet-undeveloped yoreshore, where groups of like-minded folks would come and go, or stay forever. Perfect for me and the *Floating Ghost*. Neon-pink sunset parties on the decks with lots of ice-cold drinks and the perfect number of attendees (fewer than ten), lasting into and through the perfect hours of the night (after two, before six). With lots and lots of visits from a good friend, who would lecture the jolly crowd about the two artificial, top-heavy structures that had so restricted the ways to live in this world, but in a soothing voice that would make them appear, for that brief and perfect time, distant and comprehensible.

"It's nothing at all," I said.

Kohl had reminded me what really made Inner Boca a fantasy: the other people. Late-night impromptu parties required a certain amount of trust between all party members, and trust was hard to come by in the Florida yoreshore. Anything worth building down here would also be worth taking, and any party would be derailed by a little battery. Let alone, say, a murdered floating corpse.

"Hey, you got a boat?" asked Félix.

The question woke me like salt in a fresh wound. "CabanaBoat," I said, thinly.

"CabanaBoat?" said Félix. "That's perfect! Wait right there."

He hurried away, and I left him as soon as he was off, jumping over the crowded street to the nearest mausoleum in the direction of the party. Smoke billowed from the atmo-breaker engines. I had no time for Third Way pitches or pipe dreams anymore.

I had to save the last remaining dreamer I knew.

I caught the medic just before they disappeared into the stacks. They walked down a spit of shore, between the construction materials and a crop of pylons rising out of the water. The sand on the shore was pitch-black, like tar.

The medic walked toward two figures at the end of the beach. I got close enough to make out more specific features: he presented male, had dark hair, and a too-perfect tan. He wore something like blue scrubs, but they were made of some ultralight material like luminescent silk. Shapes of gold stitching peppered the blue suit, like treasure at the bottom of a silt-free pool.

I had almost caught up to him, but then I sank a foot into the black sand, which had a consistency more like wet concrete. I had to pause to shuck it out.

The medic, however, moved over it deftly, almost running.

He was heading toward two figures at the end of the shore. One of them was approaching the other. I saw moonlight glint off the tinted gogs of the one that was moving: Kohl again, holding the salvagia bag like a shield.

There was something wrong with the silhouette of the other one. The proportions of the head and arms were too big. And they were rippling.

Kohl spoke. I wasn't quite close enough to hear what he was saying, but when he pulled out the Ked from his diving bag I squeezed my Knuckles and triggered my batons.

The other figure reached for the Ked, their arms stretching out, impossibly long, impossibly thin . . . I had just pulled my shoe out of the sand, but I stopped, open-mouthed, and let my foot sink in again.

Kohl tapped his gogs and the other person burst into a thousand pieces.

The medic took cover behind a stack of pipes. I saw a bit of scrub running along the containers and jumped to it, moving forward and crouching right behind him. I was loud, but everyone was distracted enough by the disintegrated person not to notice.

The medic looked just as confused as I was. He must have gotten lost. When the time was right, I could grab him and get him out of there.

Unless, of course, there was a chance to grab the Ked.

The pieces of the person flitted around and then congealed again. I was close enough to see that they were micro-drones. They formed a rough sheet and were poised to strike Kohl in a wave shape like the hood of a cobra.

"Repulser field," I heard Kohl gloat. "See? I'm not so stupid." But he sounded nervous, and I didn't blame him. He expected a human being underneath the drones and was unnerved that there wasn't one.

Kohl was trying to sell my prize, so this must be a fencer, one of the middlemen that dealt in the salvagia market, buying from freelance divers and selling to collectors. They came in all sizes, from peddlers of disaster tourism trinkets to the shadow cabals that acquired pieces by more dubious means.

I had a feeling this one lurked closer to the cabal. Kohl was prepared, but this was out of his league. As much as I wanted to take the prize back, I found myself frozen, hesitating.

"We must examine it more closely," said the drones. Their voice was modulated, low and slow and calculating. "To assess its value."

"Not until I see the kiloDollars," Kohl replied. "You can look at it from where you are."

"We must scan it."

"No chance," laughed Kohl.

"Then no deal."

Kohl considered. "You can send five," he said, and adjusted the field.

A group of little flies broke free from the swarm and quickly penetrated Kohl's personal space, flitting around the Ked and taking up strategic positions, making mechanical noises.

He didn't see the lone one, circling behind and above him. I counted the detachment and confirmed that there were only four. Soon, it shot over his shoulder and buried itself in his arm.

Kohl screeched, put his hand to his gogs, and turned up the field again. All the drones shot out of his personal space.

But the drones on the Ked had taken up the right positions, and when Kohl pushed them all back, they took the shoe with them. There weren't enough to hold it up. It fell into the sand. Kohl scrambled to snatch it again, but he was a magnet turned the wrong way. The drones kept pushing the Ked away from him, toward the full swarm.

More drones came to reinforce, until a quivering metal bubble enclosed the Ked, anchoring it to the sand and keeping Kohl out.

He pulled his gun and pointed it in the general direction of the swarm, which made some noise approximate to laughter.

Directly in front of me, the gold-stitched shapes on the medic's shirt began to glow. Images flickered to life inside of them—ads for US Lunar Steel, Tres Equis Beer, and a brand of rejuvenation cigarettes that might have been the same ones Maria had been smoking. His arms glowed with words too. On the left side *Ortiz*, on the right, *Orbitals*.

So not a medic at all. And the ads were bright enough to give away his position.

The atmo-breaker and I both said "Shit" at exactly the same time. Fortunately he didn't seem to hear me.

"Who's there?" said Kohl, pointing his gun at the stack of pipes. The atmo-breaker stepped out with his hands up while I crouched down as low as I could.

"Sorry fellas," he said. "I'd've let you figure this out, but it looks like I'm short on time."

The swarm made an interesting noise, like a sigh of frustration.

"We met earlier," said the atmo-breaker.

"We know," said the swarm.

"I wanted to speak with you."

"We're busy."

The atmo-breaker glanced at Kohl. "Maurice says the presentation's about to start. Shouldn't the Church of the Invisible Hand be there, too?"

"We are very much still there. Enough of us anyway."

"Enough of you? Way it was told to me, the Church and the Mourners are equal partners. I think we deserve the whole hive."

"Do you speak for Edgar Ortiz? Or Maurice Thibodeux?"

"Nah, I speak for me." He grinned and spat into the sand. "But they like to keep me happy."

I expected them to swarm him, but they just hovered there, agitated.

"If Edgar Ortiz can't be bothered to appear, we see no need for us to commit our full resources," the swarm said. "Already we can see that you are squabbling with each other. We find that tedious. This is interesting."

At this point Kohl seemed to realize that the atmo-breaker was probably a more effective target for his gun than a bunch of metal insects, and pointed it at him. "Tell it to get off my Ked," he said.

"What?" said the atmo-breaker.

"Tell it to get off my Ked!" Kohl screamed.

"Can you, um . . . can you get off his Ked?"

"We cannot."

Kohl yelled some more.

I took this as my cue to leave, and I had maybe just enough cover to do it. But when I moved back a few steps I became aware of a small hovering presence beside me.

"There is something in the water," a single micro-drone whispered in my ear. Its voice was different from the other one, different from the swarm. Softer, reedier. "In a few seconds, he'll be distracted, and you'll have your chance."

"My chance to do what?" I tried to keep the fear out of my voice.

"You want to hurt him. I can tell. And it would be inconvenient to us if he killed this person, even accidentally."

I blinked. "Why should I trust you?"

"You shouldn't. But look. There *is* something in the water."

I peered over my stack. I saw a ripple in the surf, big and fast, slithering silver.

The mechanical gator burst out and launched itself onto shore and scrambled toward Kohl.

I sprang up from my hiding place.

Kohl did a double take at me, then the gator, wasting time he could have spent shooting one of us. I brought the baton of my left Knuckle down on his gun arm and tackled him to the ground. I punched him across the face with my Knuckled fist. His tactical gogs flew into the water, taking their repulser field with them.

The drones fell upon him then. Somehow, Kohl kept his grip on the gun. He fired and clipped one in front of the barrel, so the rest swarmed his hand. Their mandibles burrowed up his fingernails and he screamed. He yanked the gun out with his other hand and tossed it into the sand, and clawed at his fingers.

The gator came right up to us. I gasped and scrambled off of him, tried to put Kohl's body between us, but it went for the atmo-breaker instead. Faster than I could blink, his foot was in its mouth, and it dragged him back, toward the black quicksand muck around the pylons.

Kohl and I went scrabbling. I got the gun first. The drones were at his eyes now, he had no gogs to protect them.

He picked himself up and ran inland, tearing at his hands and face, back to the stacks of construction material. I heard a crash, a stack of metal falling.

And I saw the Ked. It was exposed again. I clawed the sand on all fours toward it. I was so close. A micro-drone appeared and hovered, its thin sharp mandible just inches from my eye. I froze.

"Don't get greedy," it said, in that reedy modulation.

Suddenly, they were all around me, the whole swarm. Hovering, stock-still. I tossed Kohl's gun into the ocean and put my hands up, fingers away from my batons. They didn't move.

"But I helped you," I said, a pointless argument. I had heard of the Church of the Invisible Hand. Not much, but I knew they would need a more profitable reason to keep me alive.

I braced myself. The burrowing never came. Instead they hovered there, muttering indecipherably among themselves. Someone had accidentally left the mic on.

And then they all flew off at top speed back in the direction of the party.

The atmo-breaker scratched the sandy ground for purchase, his foot in the gator's mouth. If he didn't break free soon the gator would death-roll him, which didn't typically kill you in mud, but it was pulling him into the ocean, toward that black sticky sand that would suffocate him if the gator kept him face down.

I considered the Ked again.

But only the atmo-breaker could bring me to the medic. And the gator beckoned me. I was eager to take the rest of my rage out on it. Smashing Kohl's face hadn't been enough.

I leapt forward and hammered my Knuckled fist onto the top of its snout, and overshot. By a lot. Landed with my head and neck over its snout, my arm caught in an exposed piston in the crutch of its elbow.

Now it was dragging both of us into the water. My trapped arm dug a trench through the black muck. My upper body pushed down on the head of the gator, and water filled my mouth and nostrils. I sputtered and twisted, flipping myself off the gator and wrenching my wrist a little too far. It was still caught, and now my foot was in the black sand, but at least my head was above the waterline, and I could only sink so far down if my arm was in the gator's jaw. My palm turned outward, with my Knuckle nestled inside it, baton-side out. It was useless there. Not that bashing it in the head would do anything.

The gator's head bobbed back above the water, the bumps of its eyes and snout clearly visible even as the rest of its body disappeared into the muck. I felt the piston near my caught hand lengthen and then contract. Preparing to roll.

I spotted a glimmer of red inside its mouth, right below the slit of its eye. The jaw hinge. I focused on it, twisting so that my free hand could find its snout and grab the lower half of its jaw. I pulled the lower jaw open easily enough, but once it sensed that motion it engaged, and snapped back.

This had always been my downfall. I had the nerve to reach into its mouth, but I didn't have the speed to open the jaw and pull the part out before it grabbed my hand.

When I asked Myra, in that Orlando bar, what it was about me, out of all the gator wrestlers that flailed about that night, that compelled her to give me unsolicited advice, she said that I was neither the strongest nor the fastest. Simply the most surprising. I later understood that to be my coronation as a peculiar Florida character and, to this day, I try to live up to it.

Just then it gave me an idea.

"Hey!" I shouted. The atmo-breaker did his best to turn and look at me.

"Don't pull your leg out," I said.

"What?" The words sputtered out with seawater.

"When I free you, flex your foot."

"Why?"

"Because! I—"

The gator's head jerked back suddenly then, pulling both our heads underwater.

I had no idea what he'd do. If I opened the jaw and he pulled his leg out, he would be free but I'd still be stuck.

I pulled the jaw down again, jammed in my right hand, and pulled the baton trigger. It extended with a spring-loaded hiss. The gator's jaw hit the muck with enough force to stick a little bit, and then it engaged its snapback. The baton held. Then it gave a little. I couldn't see anything through the murk, so I felt my way deeper into the gator's mouth.

My thumbnail pressed down on a delicate little spring, inside of a silicon wrapper. I tried to peel that away and it all sprung back together.

The jaw mechanism was still engaged. It was bending the baton too far.

I peeled the silicon wrapper away and tried again. And again. And again. My lungs burned.

The baton cracked in half.

I tensed, waiting for the rubber treads to come clamping down on my forearm, but they didn't. I prodded around with my elbow and felt the profile of a human foot, vertically pointed just like I'd told him to. I peeled the wrapper away and felt two pieces hooked together. I clawed desperately, with my one free finger. I felt a moist snap, like a wet twig bent too far.

The gator rose up on its pistons, all of them. But without the joint, its lower jaw remained slack on the bottom. My wrist was free. I shoved the foot out with one hand and wrenched the gator's upper jaw to the night sky with the other.

It shuddered and went still.

The atmo-breaker got his leg free. He was covered in black sand. I pulled myself out of that same muck, using one of the pylons for leverage. It took a while, and I coughed up a lot of water. I glanced up and searched the shore. A small crowd of Mourners had gathered there.

The Ked was gone.

I retched again.

The pilot bent over me. His gogs had fallen off. For the second time that night I saw orange-gold eyes.

"Shit, your nose looks terrible." he said. "I'm Riley."

"Triss," I said, between burps of water. "It was already like that."

"So you were after that old moldy shoe too?" asked Riley. "It was like . . . what did that guy call it again? A Ket?"

"A Ked."

"Was it what I think it was? Nostalgic salvage?"

"Salvagia."

"That's it. That's exactly it." We stared at each other. They were the exact same eyes. He broke his gaze, wrung water out of his sleeves. "Well, this is a first," he said, winking. "Never kissed the Karman all wet before."

I didn't know what that meant. "I need a doctor."

He stuck out his hand to help me up. "I gotta get to my breaker. C'mon, I'll get you a kickass seat in the bleachers. And then—"

A woman grabbed Riley's shoulder and yanked him toward her. She wore a sleeveless black jumpsuit that somehow looked casual, professional, and tactical all at once. "No," she said. "Maurice sent me to secure you. We're leaving."

He shook her off. "Deena, I've got a race. They won't wait for me."

"You're going back to the *Marino*." She glanced at me briefly. "Maria Feinstein-Reyes made her move."

"You said you had that covered."

"She caught us by surprise. She tanked the deal. She probably sent this thing after you."

Maria. She had said she wanted to break the news of Edgar's death in a particular way. This must have been part of it.

"You're not safe," said Deena. "We need you safe."

"Nowhere safer than fifty miles up," replied Riley, sloshing toward the shore.

"Maria found your father."

That stopped him. Also briefly me, from retching into the sea again.

"Well," sighed Riley, son of Edgar. "Shit."

He sounded sad, but not particularly surprised.

# 3

"Go to the dock the long way," Deena told Riley. "Along the shore. Don't go through the crowd. The tender will meet you there."

Deena pointed in the opposite direction of the barge with all the atmo-breakers on it, which was, we all noticed, moving out to sea now. The lights were on in the cockpits of all the rocket ships, their pilots fiddling around with various instruments, their exhausts simmering red. Only one ship was still dark at both ends.

"What about her?" Riley pointed at me.

I sat in the water and plucked the pieces of my broken Knuckle from the gator's treads. I glanced at the shore again, just to make sure the prize was really gone.

"I'll deal with her," Deena said.

There is authority in stillness. I saw it often in my Gamma. The older Mourner, Maria, reminded me of her.

Deena was jumpy. She stepped toward me.

I flicked the little primer on the stunner of my working Knuckle and jabbed it into her forearm. The sea sprayed it a little and it shorted out, but she yelped and swore and jumped back, then reached into her jumper for a weapon of her own. Riley stepped between us.

"Hold on," he said, then looked at me. "You said you need a doctor. What for?"

"My friend's hurt," I said.

"Where'd you come from?"

"My boat's out in the yoreshore."

"We got a medic. He ain't much but if it'll do some good I'm happy to lend him to you." I nodded. He turned to Deena. "If we help her I'll come quietly. Okay?" She glared at me but did nothing but shake out her smarting hand.

"Can you point your boat out to me?" Riley asked.

I was about to say that the *Ghost* was back on the other side of the cemetery, but when I looked up at the water in front of me I found her, to my surprise and alarm. She was much closer to the shore than she should be. It looked like she was trying to get closer.

"There."

Riley squinted.

"I don't see it. Come on, show me again."

He pulled me up onto the gator's corpse and we walked the length of it.

"Salvagia," he said, loud enough for Deena to hear. "You ever hear of that, Deena?"

"No."

"The Perezes have a collection. Pre-flood relics, pulled out of the yoreshore. Shoes or toys or silverware. Anything, really. Anything with a good story. That's what makes the most money, right?" This he said to me.

"Sure," I said, not really interested in extrapolating. The narrative of a salvagia piece was important somehow, yes. So was the way it decayed. Part of the reason I knew the Ked was so valuable was that it had only decayed on one side. There were both "before" and "after" elements to it, and I knew collectors liked that. But, truthfully, I just tried to keep up with the trades, I had no secret insight. Sneakers, for example, were hot right now, but I had no idea why.

"Sounds like trash," said Deena.

He squinted. "I still can't see it." The surf came up to our knees. He climbed one of the big concrete pylons and pulled me up. "Show me again."

I pointed at the *Ghost*. He leaned close, as if to see where I was pointing from my point of view. A big wave, big enough to swallow the pylon, hid the *Ghost* for a couple seconds.

"I have a job for you," he whispered.

I did my best to remain still. "I have to get back." I stepped away. He grabbed my arm. I heard Deena sloshing toward us.

"Sixty-five thousand kiloDollars," he said.

"Sixty-five?" I wasn't sure I heard him right. That was enough to buy three *Ghosts*.

"At least. Could be more. You're the expert. I'll send the doc. Come back with him."

"I can't—"

"Bet you're a strong swimmer. Odds are she'll go for me, but if she can catch you she might try. Better get a move on."

And with that he dove off, deftly hitting the middle of the big wave. He came up in knee-high water and started running parallel to the shore in the direction of the barge. He kicked up water like a sprinkler and moved much faster than I would have thought possible. He waved to the crowd and they cheered.

35

It did not take me very long to swim to the *Ghost*, because she had gotten so dangerously close to me.

She was rubbing her side against the ruins of an old building, screeching her fiberglass hull on the concrete. I climbed it and tried to nudge her away. Charlie would kill me for letting her make a mark like that on herself.

"I'm here, girl," I said, patting her side. "I'm back."

But she kept scraping.

I pulled myself aboard, and saw that her security measures were already disabled, and there were two strangers in the lounge.

Myra was lying on the couch instead of the floor, her head swaddled in white cloth. I recognized one of the strangers. His fingers were in his ears. The other one was at the helm looking helpless. I went to the aft deck and opened the glass door and pushed him aside and ran the routines that told her to "go."

She pulled away and briefly resumed her return route, back up the yoreshore to Charlie. I told her to stop as soon as she was clear of the hazards, and she listened to that, too. I allowed myself to feel some relief, though she had moved a little closer to the breaker barge and its surface had just begun to smoke with priming engines. It was several hundred feet away, at least, but I had no idea what constituted a safe distance. If I told her to go again she would get even closer. So I tried not to think about it.

I turned my attention to the intruders. They were feds. The one I recognized was Gomer Afti. He wasn't supposed to be in the field. He was supposed to be at the front of the fed disposal queue, waiting for me to drop off my air conditioner quota so he could make the same quietly sad remark about how much paperwork I generated for him. He looked seasick.

The other one had the feeling of a fed about him, too, straight-backed and clean-cut. He also looked uncomfortable. Feds that spend all their time in the hyper-filtered Consolidated dome climate develop a kind of allergic reaction to the outside. His brow was moist and his shirt had stains around the armpits. They both wore the free federally provided ocular implants that marked you as a member of the placidly Consolidated: clear contacts with a visible barcode around the iris.

Myra took up the whole couch. The feds were nestled together on the loveseat. They were both drinking water. The great recliner in the corner lay empty. They'd chosen to be less comfortable and to be closer to each other. Interesting.

"She followed you," croaked Myra. Her voice was weak. She'd moved from the floor to the couch. Gomer stood up and handed me a towel from the bathroom. I was dripping all over the TeakLike.

"Strangers make her antsy," I replied.

"She liked Kohl," said Myra. It was true. I tried not to dwell on the pipe dream again.

"Everyone likes Kohl," said Gomer. "Except me. I could have warned you about Kohl."

"What are you doing here?" I asked him.

"I let them in," Myra said.

"We saw your boat almost running aground," said the other agent. "My partner recognized it, said he knew you. We thought we could help."

"But you didn't," I said.

"No. Turns out neither of us know how to operate an unlicensed semi-sent."

"And neither of you are doctors either."

"We did what we could," said Gomer. "She tried to stand up. She almost passed out, but I caught her and we got her to the couch. I think she might have a concussion."

"Can you take her somewhere?" I asked.

Gomer shook his head. "We're undercover." The other agent cleared his throat. "Maybe I wasn't supposed to say that."

"Well, Mourning in Miami promised me a doctor as soon as the race is over." I hoped it was true. "So you'll probably want to get going."

I took Myra's ice pack and went to the bar to refill it. The one who wasn't Gomer stood in my way. "Agent Andy Somer," he said. He flashed a badge of some kind, then stuck out a sweaty hand.

Gomer flashed his badge, too, as an afterthought.

"Gomer and Somer," I ignored his outstretched hand and chewed their names like cud while grabbing ice from the little freezer. "Andy and Afti."

"We'd like to ask you some questions. Quick ones, I promise."

I looked at Myra, who was trying to get up again.

"If Gomer can keep playing nurse," I said. "Then fine." I gave Gomer the ice pack. Then I sat in the recliner, next to the open glass door. "So what are you agents of? Change? Real estate? Are you here to sell me one of those Alaskan time shares I see ads for everywhere?"

"We're with the IXS," said Somer.

"What's that?"

Somer opened his mouth to speak, but Myra interrupted him. "The Internal Exchange Service," she said. "They monitor big wealth transfers."

"Is there a big wealth transfer going on here?"

"We were hoping you could tell us that," said Somer. "How long have you been associated with the Ortizes?"

I blinked. "What time is it?"

Somer gestured to Myra's birdwatching binoculars on the table. "We saw the whole thing from the shore." said Somer. "Did Riley Ortiz mention what the construction titan was building?"

"No," I replied.
"What is the nature of your relationship to him?"
"I met him tonight."
"And he's lending you his doctor?"
"I saved his life."
"Did you see Edgar Ortiz?"
I hesitated. Too long, I knew.
"No," I said.
"But Edgar was there?" he pressed.
"I don't recall."
"Recall harder. Like it's your civic duty."

I already regretted the lie. Giving them Edgar Ortiz's death could have been my out. They must not have known he was dead yet, and it would certainly interest them. And now Somer could tell I was hiding something.

But he was also making me angry. He was that self-righteous flavor of fed. And he was being mostly polite, but confident. That was a bad sign.

"I wasn't there to socialize," I said. "I went to find a doctor, and I went to get back what was stolen from me. I wasn't paying attention to the rest of it."

"We're not here to arrest you," Gomer added. "If that's what you're worried about."

"What are you here for, then?"

"Andy and I just want to know everything we can about that construction titan."

"Please call me Agent Somer, Agent Afti." Somer's voice was tight, like this wasn't the first time he'd had to remind him.

"Why?" I asked.

"Like your friend said," said Somer. "We like to keep track of who has what."

"Well, I have nothing. You can even write that down."

"You know," Somer said. "I'm surprised."

I fingered my Knuckle. Here it came. "By what?"

"I expected you to be a little more cooperative. You're smart, Triss Mackey. I didn't think you'd make us spell it out for you, the ways in which we can end your life."

"Andy," said Gomer.

"End the life you've chosen for yourself, I mean. Not the life you owe your country, the, what was it, Agent Gomer? Two years? Of service still deferred. We can help you live that life tomorrow. Tonight, even. At any moment."

Just then, the race began and drowned out my colorful reply with an ear-splitting roar, a bright white light that burst from the barge.

Myra yelped and clutched her head.

I leapt out of my chair. Somer stood up. I brushed past him, but before I even got to the helm the *Ghost* had picked up her anchor. She puttered away from the breaker barge, back toward the building she'd been scraping. I wanted to tell her to stop but Myra looked like her head was about to explode. Gomer smothered her ears with a pillow in a strangely maternal way.

The *Ghost* avoided the wall she'd beat herself on before and took us around the other side. The building's three remaining walls made a little cove. She nestled herself inside of it, turned herself to face the building and the barge. The walls buffered us from the noise enough that we could hear each other, and Myra relaxed a little.

The *Ghost* dropped her anchor far enough away from the walls that she couldn't reach them, even if she strained. An admirable bit of self-control.

The roar subsided a bit, enough for Myra to whimper, but put her head back on the pillow. Not enough for us to hear each other yet. Somer got up and went to the window and watched the race.

He didn't even bother to keep an eye on me. He had me leashed and he knew it.

The breakers pushed into the air and were soon out of sight, their exhausts like large twinkling stars in the sky. I went back to the recliner and sat down and got up again. I looked out at the water. No sign of a doctor yet.

"Have you ever been to the Astro America?" asked Somer, pensively, gesturing to the atmo-breakers slowly rising into the night sky.

"I can't afford it," I said.

"It's beautiful," said Somer. "But it's just a mirage. We don't know how it exists. It honestly shouldn't. No structure that tall can last long in the yoreshore. The storms are getting stronger every year. Wind pummeling it from above, water surging and seeping up from below. OrlanDome is aerodynamic and a hundred miles inland, and still it costs us millions of kiloDollars to maintain it. We spend more on waterproofing in one year than New York does in ten. And if *we* can't make it down here . . ."

"You don't think anyone can."

Somer was a card-carrying Consolidation Democrat. I'd known lots of people like him. I'd fled to Florida to get away from them, in fact. Myra calls the feds the First Way. They think of themselves as the only way.

"I mean they obviously *can*," said Somer. "The Astro America is there. For now. The question is the cost. To build something like that, to maintain it year after year, to get a construction titan all the way out here, these things require vast sums of money, with transactions between parties that don't like to be watched. The IXS needs to know who has money like that down here. The best time to find out is when they move it. Much more possible to do it now than try to piece it together after the fact."

"After what fact?"

"Gravity, weather, chemical spill. Salt water in the aquifer. Pick one. Whatever fact comes around first and annihilates their unsustainable fantasy. Their pipe dream."

The choice of words made me wince.

"Maybe that fact is you, Triss Mackey. Where is Edgar Ortiz?"

"You feds think you know exactly what's good or bad for everyone," I replied. "But you're making everybody in OrlanDome relocate just to save a little money? People have lives here. Who are you to say what's sustainable or not?"

Somer chewed on this. "I believe that I belong to the only society that has figured out how to live on this planet without killing it. We make hard choices, but the alternatives are worse. Where do you belong, Triss?"

"You said you knew everything about me already."

"Indeed." He cleared his throat. "Triss Mackey, raised by nomadic terrorists and IP thieves. But you got out. Signed up for the Second Civilian Conservation Corps to serve your country. Good for you. But then you weaseled out of it, right when they needed you most."

"Right when they started forcing people into domes."

"Cut to the present, and you're still living in a dome. Ostensibly anyway. You take advantage of a rather obscure environmental cleanup loophole where we teach you how to dive for old air conditioners and you get to defer your service. You escape to Florida, two years still owed, and you help yourself to our very generous subsidized housing, food, healthcare, the whole buffet, while contributing the absolute bare minimum. Instead, you use those skills we taught you to pull up unregulated salvage in the yoreshore in an unlicensed semi-sentient vehicle."

"So write me a ticket."

"You're sucking on the federal teat, Triss, and you're running out of loopholes to squeeze through. You've had challenges. We know all about them. What happened to you in Wyoming... well, Agent Gomer tells me that I should take it easy on you. I was hoping maybe you'd like to give a little something back. We'd really like to be friends. But we could also forward your case along to somebody in a little office in Atlanta who can find a way to get you back to active duty."

There it was.

"Or," Gomer piped in. "We can send it somewhere no one will ever find it."

"Just depends on how helpful I can be, I'm sure," I said.

"The Corps has a new jurisdiction." said Somer. "Maybe you've heard. Shackleton Crater is now a national park. They need fresh meat for the lunar divisions, but the debris field's been heavy lately. I think we're only at an eighty percent success rate in getting troops through the atmosphere. It's a bad time to get called up."

"Andy, stop," said Gomer. "She gets it."

Somer glared at Gomer.

"Agent Somer," he said, sternly. "In here, it's Agent Somer."

Gomer looked back down at his feet.

"Triss," said Myra, weakly. She was trying to prop herself up on her elbows. She looked very pale. "Just give them something. It's too loud in here."

I squeezed the handles of my Knuckles. I tried to think.

"Someone..." I began. "Lots of someones. The swarm of drones on the beach."

"The Church of the Invisible Hand," said Somer.

"You know who they are?"

"Sure. They worship the invisible hand of the market. A crypto-cult obsessed with orchestrating the conditions for maximum profitability. They're very dangerous. I was surprised they didn't kill you."

"They were about to, but they stopped. They started fighting with each other, and then they flew off, back toward the party."

"Did you hear what they were fighting about?" asked Somer.

"No. But there was a deal happening, and they were a part of it, but they were frustrated that Edgar Ortiz wasn't there."

"He wasn't?"

"According to them." I tried to move away from the topic of Edgar Ortiz. "They mentioned another name, too . . . Maurice something."

"Maurice Thibodeux?"

"Maybe."

"Ortiz's business partner," said Gomer, in an attempt to be helpful.

"Also I met a woman named Maria. She seemed important."

Somer nodded. "Feinstein-Reyes. Second-most important Mourner after Ortiz."

"Not Maurice?"

"He's not a Mourner," said Gomer. "Just a money guy. We're not really sure where he came from, but he's been associated with Edgar since the Astro America."

"Feinstein-Reyes tanked the deal," I said. That's what Deena had said. "Maurice sent someone to secure Riley. That must have been why the Church flew off, too."

"So it's the Church and Maurice and Edgar on one side," said Gomer. "And Feinstein-Reyes on the other?"

"Possibly," said Somer. "But why are there different sides to begin with? And how does the son fit in? As far as we know he's just a pilot, and a reckless one at that."

"No idea," I admitted. This time I wasn't lying.

"I'd love to talk to him," said Somer. "If he didn't just blow himself up."

A boat sped out from a long dock on the shore. It was moving too far out to sea to join the herd of Mourner boats in the bight around the other side. It seemed like it was looking for us.

I gestured to the boat. "May I be excused? If they're trying to find me, they might not be able to see me back here."

Somer nodded, slightly. "You didn't really give us anything useful. But I acknowledge that when pressured you did try. Your reward is stay of execution."

They allowed me to hurry them onto the deck. The barge had disappeared, the only sign of where it had been six trails of breaker smoke disappearing into the sky. I told the *Ghost* to go again and she pulled out of the man-made cove and into the open water. Their speedboat arrived to meet us, manned by someone wearing ill-fitting clothes in the approximate Mourner colors.

Gomer took my hand and held it for a little too long.

"Sorry for ratting you out," he said. "I saw your outstanding 2C3 service in your profile." He nodded to Somer, who was inside still, courteously filling up Myra's ice pack again. "He's my partner, you know."

"Really? I thought you just shopped at the same badge outlet."

"No, like my partner partner. We have a third. We're expecting. It's not a good time to move."

"Oh. Congratulations. He's cute. I like how the little barcodes in his eyes light up when he gets excited."

Gomer laughed nervously. "The only department that's expanding right now is the IXS. Andy says that whenever the feds pull out of somewhere they need the IXS to keep an eye on things, to see who fills the vacuum. So I took the reassignment. It's . . . I think it's hard on him. He thinks he has to look out for me. He's been in the department for years now."

"He drank the Kool-Aid."

"Yeah well. He's from Boston. 'Consolidation' isn't a dirty word up there. And he never served. He doesn't know what it's like."

"You do?"

"Oregon Reunification Division."

"Then you know I won't go back."

"Well, I just wanted you to know that we're more than just suits. And we'd love to be friends."

"I'm sure."

Somer left the lounge. "We'll be in touch," he said, curtly.

They stepped onto their little boat and sped off.

The medic arrived shortly after. He had steady hands and bad balance. He took hits from a vape that smelled like bananas and sunscreen and clutched the railing. He was desperate to assure me of his competence, and with great effort he mostly succeeded.

"Collisions are my specialty," he said, putting up a hand to stop me when I started to tell him about Myra. "If she'd been poisoned I couldn't help you. But out here people mostly smash each other up."

He sprayed my nose with some miracle numbing spray, that reduced the swelling and opened my sinuses to the oppressive odor of his vape.

We went into the lounge and I showed him the patient, then I went down to the master stateroom and looked at myself in the mirror, and thought about a shower. But then I saw my wearable on the bed, right where I had left it. I had several missed calls from Charlie, who owned the *Ghost*.

I don't wear implants, and I don't like gogs. My wearable is an old-fashioned flexible screen that snaps around my wrist and can send messages, make calls, and play videos and that's about it. Its greatest feature is that I can take it off and leave it places and forget it exists. When Myra tried it she equated it to a form of medieval torture, but only because she couldn't play "Plamingo."

I grabbed my wearable and went back upstairs. The medic had launched a bunch of drones to spin around Myra's head and was shining a bright light in her eye. She was making a face.

I stepped onto the deck and called Charlie.

He picked up on the first ring.

"You stopped," he said. He sounded a little paranoid. I was glad of it, actually, because when he was paranoid he got to the point. He was a diver, like me, at least before the bends had crippled him, so when we talked he'd sometimes find a way to tangent. "Then you started. Then you stopped again."

"We'll be on our way soon," I said.

He grunted. "You get anything worth the trouble?" Charlie wanted me to buy the *Ghost* almost as much as I wanted to buy her. He knew all about my loophole. A requirement of my deferred service was that I had to remain in federal housing. Once the feds pulled out, OrlanDome would close, and there wouldn't be any federal housing left, and my loophole would close.

But Charlie informed me that due to an obscure tax scheme set up in the early days of Consolidation, when the feds outsourced a lot of housing to various corporations, all CabanaBoats were technically federal housing.

That was why I needed her.

"No," I said.

He sighed. "Damn shame."

"I need more time."

"Sorry, Triss. We're out of time. That's why I'm calling. The feds are pulling out soon. Plan B is locked and loaded."

"You found another buyer?"

"Sorta."

His tone made me nervous.

"Sorta what?"

"I don't wanna say over the phone." He paused, though. I thought that maybe he did, and after a couple of seconds of waiting, sure enough, he said: "But it's sorta brilliant."

"Tell me." I tried to keep my voice even.

"I know a guy. Says he can build a reef in twenty minutes. Uses drones or something to move things around down there. Says during mean season it's impossible to map all the reefs all the time, and everyone knows it. Happens all the time. Easy claim."

I realized what he was saying.

"That won't work," I stammered. "She's too smart for that." And she was. But she was also an addict.

"Reefer says it will."

"What are Reefer's credentials?"

"Well," he said. "His name's Reefer."

I said nothing.

"Sorry, Triss. I don't like this any more than you do. She's a good boat. But it's gotta happen while the feds are still here. Once they leave, the insurance company will try to get out of it. I'm getting out now."

"Sure. Smart."

"Anyway. Reefer's almost booked up. This is happening day after tomorrow. If she's not back by then I'll call her back."

He hung up.

Something caught my attention in the night sky, a quick movement, but when I looked up all I could see was one particularly bright speck, too slow to be a shooting star or a satellite. It quickly faded away. A cry came up from the dregs of the party on the shore. A strange sound. Mourners in mourning, I supposed. Perhaps they had all just heard of Edgar's death at once.

The medic stepped back onto the deck. "I'm supposed to ask if you're coming back with me," he said.

"Can I leave her?"

He shrugged. "She's got a grade 2 concussion."

"That sounds high."

"She just needs to rest. Nothing you can do for her. I'll keep the drones spinning. I can send the data to that thing on your arm."

The events of the night washed over me like wakes, rocking me from all sides. I had lost the prize and Myra had been damaged. The feds had found me and the *Ghost* would die. My only chance to save her was a job that could only be too good to be true.

It made me weary.

There were only two ways to live in America. On one side, the Conditional Hand of Plenty that was the government, and on the other the Great Glittering Pyramid Scheme that was everything else. I was weary of them both, and all the artificial structures, too big for anyone to hold in their mind completely, too big for anyone to gauge just how top-heavy they were until they came crashing down on top of them.

There was no Third Way, at least for me. Gamma's camp and Wyoming had taught me that, and Kohl reminded me. I could not commit to either IXS or Mourners and expect to escape them unscathed, or at all.

I looked in the lounge. Myra opened her eyes and gave me a weak smile. The *Ghost* purred her outboards softly, to nothing in particular.

"Let me take a shower," I said. I was slightly offended when the medic wrinkled his nose and nodded.

I'd go to Riley's boat and hear him out. If I couldn't save myself, then maybe I could save some things.

I worked in salvage, after all.

There's a conspiracy theory that I actually believe.

Fifteen years ago a satellite exploded. Like, really exploded, so spectacularly that some people think it was sabotaged, which is a different conspiracy that I don't believe, mostly because it doesn't matter.

It exploded into so many pieces that those pieces blew up a bunch of other satellites, which hit others, and so on and so on, creating a chain reaction that made a debris field so thick and fast and deadly that it shredded through the International Space Elevator like it was a wet noodle and made space travel unpalatable to mostly everyone, except the lunar miners and the atmo-breakers.

The American military-industrial complex invested lots of money in space habitation. No space colonies meant no market.

So far all of this is the facts, not the conspiracy.

The conspiracy is that to fill that market, the military got the politicians to start proselytizing the idea of space habitation on

Earth—treating the planet like one big wildlife sanctuary and humans like alien colonists, whose carbon footprints should no longer soil the actual soil.

The feds built solar-powered domes with taxpayer money, made out of metals from the lunar mines. They subsidized all the food, water, and housing to entice people to move in, which was nice of them I suppose, but the domes are so efficient that it doesn't cost very much to grow, recycle, or extraterrestrially import all the basic human necessities.

Once they were done enticing, they started forcing.

I was briefly one of the forcers.

That's Consolidation in a nutshell.

I must admit, it's not a terrible way to live, if you can get over the fact that you must go where you're assigned. Everything's a little sterile, a little bland, like living on a mid-priced cruise ship, forever. I have a feeling that most Americans are perfectly content with living on a cruise ship.

But I can't help but see the proof of the conspiracy in the designs of the domes, their thick walls and hermetic sealing, which clearly look like they were meant for asteroid or lunar colonies. I feel it in the claustrophobic hallways, the lack of windows, the filtration systems that make each room feel like an ancient tomb, like if the outside air could ever get in it would whoosh over it all and decay it to dust in a matter of seconds and then suck you out into the black.

Myra has no particular love for feds, is after her Third Way, but still, she doesn't believe in the conspiracy. Or, at least, she thinks Consolidation did more good than bad. But she's from Philadelphia. Different places Consolidated differently. Weighing the scales of the success of rapid Consolidation against its horrors is one of Myra's and my great debates, that last late into the night.

I spared her one last look before I boarded the medic's boat. She was asleep on the couch. I didn't know when we'd get the chance to debate again.

The doctor took us through the yoreshore and around Key West Cemetery. The fading lights from the party helped me keep my bearings. We went the long way, past the dock that Deena had told Riley to go for and then around it, a side of the island I hadn't seen from sea or shore. I ate the banana I'd brought and tossed the peel overboard.

We were closer to the shore than the *Ghost* could go, weaving around the hazards of the old world. Occasionally he'd swerve too hard and almost topple himself over the side. I kept glancing back. I was afraid that the *Ghost* would start following me again. Chasing Kohl, I'd left in distress. This time I had tried very hard to make it seem like I was off to a party, so she wouldn't worry. I took a shower and dressed in a black tank top and wide-legged, breezy pink pants. There were pockets, but they were deep and loose, so I worked my one intact Knuckle back onto my left hand. Never get into a strange boat unprepared.

We wrapped around the island and she disappeared from my line of view. She hadn't moved, as far as I could see. I prayed that she would stay there, while I worked to save her.

I faced front again and was confronted by a gigantic bright red balloon, careening toward us from out of the sky. I gripped my seat. The medic was not fazed at all.

"Breaker coming in for a landing," he said. "The race must be over."

The balloon shot over us, missing us by a couple hundred feet, and splashing into open yoreshore. I scanned the sky and spotted three other colorful spheres in rapid descent.

We reached the yacht modules soon after.

They were a fancy fleet of four boats that came together to form a single megayacht. Three of them were coming together now, twin sleek single-hulls that filled out each side of the catamaran mother module. Its name, *Marino*, was painted on the side in teal and orange lettering. The fourth and smallest module was painted brown, and much farther off. It wasn't moving at all.

The doctor hummed. The fleet was guarded—half a dozen speedboats with armed Mourners peppered around the modules in various defensive positions. They acknowledged us, but made no move to stop us from speeding through them. I felt exposed. I smiled and gave a little beauty pageant half-wave.

We arrived at the aft deck of the small brown yacht. Its name was the *Pure Passer*. The tender docked itself in its own little modular slot. Russian nesting boats, within boats within boats.

I stepped aboard. The doctor stayed.

"Reentry shakes those pilots up," he said. "Sometimes they get a little carbonated."

I thanked him for the ride and he sped off.

The yacht was well over a hundred feet, with room enough for staff. No one came to greet me. I heard noises above me; little pops, like a tiny firecracker exploding very slowly, and a tinkling, like breaking glass. I followed the sounds up a flight of stairs. The sundeck was a custom job, with all the expected luxury bachelor fixtures—a 3-DJ booth, a drum set, a knocked-over chair with a screen facing the sky, which I deduced was a flight simulator, and a kitchenette with the latest Meehan's AutoBar.

A person with a short, tight ponytail in a blue jumpsuit like Riley's sat hunched over the bar, facing the giant screen attached to the AutoBar. They saw me and their preferred pronouns flashed on the lens of their hexagon gogs. I heard that popping noise again, like ice in a glass but precise, rhythmic.

The AutoBar offered to make me a drink. I'd heard the Bartender's Choice was pretty special in this model. I approached the kitchenette. Whatever was on the screen played on a loop. It was about five seconds of close-up footage of an atmo-breaker blasting through space, and then, at the last second, exploding. The volume was turned low, so the explosion was reduced to a pop.

"Calysta Chen," said the figure, and I thought they might be intruding themself, but then they gestured at the screen with a small object, maybe a straw. "She flew for ToyARC. The crowd lost it when she blew. A lot of people must have bet the Antifecta on her."

"Oh," I replied.

I hadn't heard of an Antifecta before, but I knew that the sports book for atmo-breaking was one of the reasons why it was so popular. On further consideration I figured that what I had mistaken for a collective keen from the Mourners might instead have been a reaction to what this person was describing. It had had too many different harmonies to have been purely grief for Edgar—I'd heard cheers and maybe even laughter among the cries. The whole cacophony sounded like a wave, crashing against a crop of sharp rocks.

"Were you there?" they asked me, suddenly. It felt like a loaded question, an interrogation. I wondered if they were drunk, and what they'd do to me if I said I had been.

"I was on my boat." I said.

"If you'd won you wouldn't be here. So I guess you lost."

"I didn't play."

They grunted, not with approval exactly but without disdain. They looked me over again.

"I'm Nepheli," they said. "You're the diver."

"Triss."

"Chen was young. ToyARC only called her up to the Astro last year. You know the worst part? The race tonight wasn't even regulation. She wasn't supposed to pass the Karman line, even though she did. All those Antifecta bets, and the race was supposed to end before the debris field. They *wanted* her to blow. They want everyone to blow. The only thing they care about more than money is blood."

"So how did it happen?" I asked. "If she wasn't supposed to be there."

"Riley fucking Ortiz," they said, and I thought perhaps the taps rang harder, lined up with *Riley* and *Ortiz*. "He crossed the Karman. She followed. She died."

"Is Riley okay?" I asked, trying not to sound too interested. He'd helped me get back to the *Ghost*, but really I was just after the money.

They frowned, and pointed up at the sky with the screwdriver. The moon was bright enough that I could see one last big sphere diving toward the water. "He's fine," they said. "Better than fine. It takes a little longer to come back down when you have to go through the field."

The AutoBar pinged out my drink. I took it and glanced at Nepheli's profile and saw that they weren't drinking anything at all. In front of them was a circuit board. The footage played again and Chen's breaker exploded again and, in response to the pop, Nepheli turned a screw on the board and tapped it twice, *ping ping*.

They caught me staring.

"Sorry," they said. "It's just something I do when I'm pissed."

"I knew someone who used to do that," I replied, softly, remembering Eli tinkering with his prosthetic arm.

Tighten the screws one by one, tap the tops twice in rhythm, repeat. He was very proud of his arm. Early on, in the salad days of the Corps I hopped through a slot canyon and tripped and sliced my head open on a rock. He sewed me up and wrapped the bandage. *Tap tap.* He'd do a stitch and touch the suture with the scissors and make me wince. *Sorry, force of habit.*

"It calmed him down," I said.

Nepheli looked at me again, then switched the screen off and put the screwdriver down.

"Yeah. Sorry for interrogating you. Riley told me you're unaffiliated."

"When did you talk to him? He left me to get into his rocket ship."

They tapped their gogs. "Pilot's only a part of the team. I'm most of the rest. I should be helping him land right now, but I hung up on him. Doesn't listen to me anyway."

I sipped my drink, which was cold and dry and left a lingering taste of peach.

"Did you know her well?" I asked. "Calysta?"

"No," they replied, picking up the screwdriver again. "Didn't know her at all."


We sat in silence and watched Riley's balloon hit the water a couple hundred feet away, bob briefly beneath the surface, then deflate. The rocket inside the bubble emerged. It was close enough that I could see its name painted on the side: *Bulls on Parade.*

A couple of boats of armed Mourners sped over to Riley to pick him up, but he kicked his cockpit window out with a "yeehaw" and told them all to fuck off and threw his helmet at them. Then he dove into the water and swam to us.

I finished my drink and told the AutoBar to make me something sweet, with a low ABV and extra garnishes. The adrenaline from my own eventful night was long gone, and one banana could only sustain me so much. I hoped Riley would get to the point quickly. The AutoBar churned and spit out something like a Shirley Temple with whipped cream and at least a dozen cherries, then started making something called the "R-Club Special."

We heard Riley grunting, pulling himself aboard. When he got up to the sundeck he had a towel wrapped around his neck. He'd unzipped his flight suit halfway. I saw that it was padded. It had hid his true figure: he was thinner than I'd thought, and long-limbed. I remembered how deftly he'd moved over the strange black sand of the beach, how he'd sprinted through knee-high water. His nearly hairless chest glowed with one of those blue UV-absorbing grafted tan tattoos, popular among the party class here, that reflected the day's rays back under rave lights. The *Pure Passer*'s sundeck was obviously equipped with rave lights.

"The Ortiz Orbitals are back," he said and grabbed his drink at the AutoBar. "And tonight everybody saw it."

Nepheli tucked their screwdriver and circuit board into their own flight suit. They were much shorter than Riley, but when they stood up Riley briefly quieted down. His drink hovered halfway to his lips.

The authority of stillness again.

They looked Riley over. They were not smiling.

"You should have gone to the medic," they concluded, quietly.

"I'm fine, Neph," he replied, and gave me a wink. "Had to swim. Had to cool off. I'm hot, baby. You see that time? Pas Adena ain't gonna beat it. We're in second position for the Canaveral for sure. At second I can win it. If it was Dad—"

"But it's not," said Neph. "It's you."

"Well don't sound so excited," Riley replied.

"I told you to take it easy tonight," said Neph.

"I tried. But it ain't just me, you know that. She *wants* to go fast. You built her to go fast. You think I could stop her? She's gotta trust me. If I stop her then she doesn't trust her own instincts, and it's those instincts that are going to get us through the Karman, and that's the whole fucking point! Neph, listen, there was one part where I really opened her up, and I could tell it was getting heavy. I thought I was fried, but she—"

"Somebody actually was."

"That wasn't my fault! What was Chen doing?"

"Following you."

"Listen, you're the one who said we need data in the debris field. I was doing this for you."

"Don't blame me, or the *Bull*," they said. "You went too fast because you wanted the better time, and you couldn't slow down so you went through the field too. The old man would've been happy being safe with a worse time."

"If he was happy being safe, he would still be alive."

"Don't start that again."

"You started it. You let him go out there."

"Last time I checked, you thought someone killed him. Are you saying I killed him?"

"Someone did," Riley said, glancing at me. "You can't just tear your breathing line in open water, can you?"

A torn breathing line. An interesting cause of death. When I'd found him he didn't have any equipment on at all, no tank or rebreather or mask. And I'd found him in the yoreshore, not open water. So he'd drowned in a different place and was moved.

"But no," Riley continued. "What I'm saying is that you were the last person that could have stopped him from going in the first place."

"I could never stop him from doing anything," Nepheli replied, coldly. They reached into their pocket. I could imagine them gripping the handle of their screwdriver the way I gripped my Knuckles. "Maybe you could have if you'd been around more, instead of here at the 'R-Club.'"

"I *was* there!" He slammed his drink on the bar. "Remember? I was the *first one* there."

They stared at each other. So much for hoping he'd get to the point quickly. I popped a cherry into my mouth.

"What's the Canaveral?" I asked, in an effort to get him back on track.

Riley and Nepheli looked at me as if they'd forgotten I was there. Then they looked back at each other. Riley wiped spilled drink off the counter with his towel. Nepheli sat back down. There was a feeling of retrenching, returning to battle lines previously drawn.

"The Canaveral Cup," said Nepheli. "Day after tomorrow. Biggest race of the year at the Astro."

Same day that Charlie would kill the *Ghost*.

"Usually it's my dad's race, but he's . . ." Riley waved his hands.

"Dead," said Nepheli.

"So I'm in it this year."

"You sure about that?" asked Nepheli.

Riley laughed. "There is no one else. What, you mean you?"

"Why not?"

Nepheli looked serious. Riley's laughter petered out. I wondered if this was a new line they were crossing. Riley squared up. "Neph, you hate flying."

"I do. But if it'll stop you from vaporizing the *Bull* and yourself I'll think about it."

"The *Bull* doesn't like you. Nobody likes you, 'cuz you're a fucking genius. Nobody likes geniuses."

Nepheli got up. Riley half-stood too. They waved him off and pointed behind him. A small, barnacled tugboat approached the *Pure Passer*. The deflated *Bulls on Parade* was tied up along the starboard side like a harpooned whale.

"My ride's here," said Nepheli.

"Ew. You're taking the circuit barge?" said Riley. "Why?"

"I want to get back to the Astro tonight."

"I'll just give you a ride in the morning," he said.

"No," they said. "I'm going now."

"Don't be dramatic. I'm sorry, okay? No matter what happens you know you'll always be the one I want building it."

"I need some peace and quiet, so I can figure out how to make her more idiot-proof."

Riley shrugged. "Fine. Get going then."

The *Pure Passer* shuddered to life, rocking us all off-balance. It pulled its anchor up and started moving away from the barge.

"Shit," Riley said

"What's happening?" I asked.

"I think Maurice is calling us in to the *Marino*," he said. "Deena wanted me to come straight there."

Riley gestured toward the bigger megayacht in the distance. All of its modules had come together except for the boat we were currently on. The space between its twin hulls was just big enough for the *Pure Passer* to squeeze into. "She called me after Nepheli hung up on me. Told me some bullshit about safety. I told her I was entertaining. Hold on."

He went to the little mini-cockpit and pressed some buttons and pulled some plugs. The whole ship shuddered off. The engines died and the AutoBar sputtered to a halt, right in the middle of shaking another R-Club Special. We kept floating a little bit.

"There we go," Riley said.

The person operating the circuit barge looked at us with confusion. Nepheli gestured for them to pull back up alongside.

"Why is Maurice on the *Marino* in the first place?" asked Nepheli.

"I'm letting him use it for a while. What? I don't need a whole megayacht."

"Riley," said Nepheli, very serious now, almost pleading. "Did you tell him about the *Bull*?"

"C'mon Neph, I'm not stupid."

"Did you?"

"Not yet," said Riley, but Nepheli kept staring at him. "He could help us, though. Everyone my dad knew, he knows. He wants me to fill in for my dad on the Mourner front, get everybody in line again. It's bullshit, I know, but maybe if I say I will . . ."

Nepheli had been at the foot of the stairs. The circuit barge was pulled up alongside the aft deck. But they strode all the way back to Riley and got very close to him.

"Listen to me, Riley. I'm willing to admit that you're a pretty good pilot, maybe as good as the old man. But he was also good at lots of other stuff, like this Machiavellian Mourner shit. You're not. You're a stupid little baby. Stay out of it."

"What do you know? You spend all your time in the hangar."

"I spent enough time with the old man to know to stay away from Maurice Thibodeux."

They got back to the stairs before Riley called after them.

"I love you, Neph, and it's real nice that you put in all that time with the old man. But don't forget who's the Ortiz and who ain't. At the end of the day you're just a stray he took in."

"A stupid little baby," they muttered, but their voice broke a little and they had their hand in their pocket again.

And Riley seemed to sense that perhaps he had gone too far. "C'mon, Neph. I just mean don't presume to know what he was thinking. I sure as shit didn't."

Nepheli ignored him and turned to me. "Nice to meet you, Triss. Don't forget: Calysta Chen followed him and now she's dust."

Riley put on an orange silk robe the color of his eyes. He pried the shaker out of the dead AutoBar's claws and sipped his half-made cocktail. Then he sat down on the nice couch and spread his long arms out, showing off his bare chest and the UV tattoo, which I saw now was shaped like his atmo-breaker, *Bulls on Parade*, taking off, a plume of smoke billowing out around his navel.

"Sorry," Riley said, with a wave of his hands. "Just a little sibling rivalry."

"I thought you were the only Ortiz," I replied.

"I am, but Nepheli's been on the Orbitals just as long as I have. We grew up together. My dad let them live in the family suite at the Astro."

"What happened to their parents?"

"Inter-lunar transport haulers, got shredded bringing up colonists. That's why they want to . . . well, it's not important."

Inter-lunar. That's the flight I'd be taking if Somer sent me back to the 2C3.

"That was a shitty thing to say then." I surprised myself with the coldness of my tone.

But as someone who does not belong anywhere, I am highly tuned to sense those dog whistles of belonging: the membership cards, clubhouses, and secret handshakes. Mourners have their little uniforms, Consolidators have their domes, and families have names, like Ortiz, to open doors and close them behind you.

Gamma's camp had various stages of orphans—children of dead revolutionaries, migrant workers, those displaced from the wildlife corridors. To not belong is to fight for scraps, to jostle for position on a curve approaching a limit, never passing into actual belonging. At Gamma's camp I was at the very top of the outsiders: I had a relative and shared her name and lived in her van. But she cared about keeping the camp together more than she cared about me. Eli was a true orphan. He floated near the middle-bottom, and sank when the threshing machine took his arm.

To the kids of the intact camp families, our scraps didn't matter. We were all equally on the other side of the line.

"Yeah," Riley replied. "Shit. We've been fighting like this ever since, well. Ever since we pulled the old man up from that dive. Dark shit. Neph just ain't listening to me, and we gotta be on the same page by tomorrow. I haven't even told them what I want you to find."

Riley's attention was on me, so I noticed something he didn't: Nepheli got into the cockpit of the circuit barge and a few moments later the operator left the boat entirely and transferred to another one. When the circuit barge took off, heading up the yoreshore in the direction of the mainland, as far as I could tell, Nepheli was sailing it alone.

I decided not to mention it to Riley. I wasn't sure what it meant anyway.

"You probably have a lot of questions," Riley was saying. "Let me start from the beginning."

"Start by telling me what you want me to find," I replied. "So I can decide if it's worth finding."

"Oh. Sure. It's a trading card. An UltiMon card, Series 1. Kappacop."

I choked a little bit on my drink. I hadn't expected him to say that. Most of the Series 1 UltiMon cards were lost when the convention center in Seattle collapsed in the Great Cascades Earthquake. Kappacop was the rarest of all. It had a picture of a kind of anthropomorphic turtle wearing a bobby cap.

"Salvagia?"

"Sort of," he said. "It was underwater, and it's got a good story. You know how much one of those is worth?"

I did. "You said sixty-five for half? That's wrong."

"I just said a number high enough to get you to come out. I was hoping the Church of the Invisible Hand could give me a ballpark, but well, you know how that went. What's it really?"

"The last one I saw went for . . . about one-eighty," I said. "And it was damaged."

It felt like such a small number when I said it like that. One hundred and eighty thousand kiloDollars, one hundred and eighty million dollar dollars. Enough cash to buy a fleet of *Ghost*s, probably enough in old paper currency to weigh them all down and sink them.

Riley leaned back, with a grin on his face. "Well, shit. That should be plenty."

"Plenty for what?"

"I'm going to buy the Ortiz Orbitals from Maurice. And don't worry, I don't mind splitting it right down the middle."

"Aren't you rich?" I said.

"Maurice is the executor of my dad's estate. He says all that money's tied up in the deal. Whether or not he's telling the truth... well, I dunno. I'm sure he's not telling me everything. But I don't have time to wait for all that, not when I know that card is out there. Besides, you saw how Nepheli felt about Maurice. They might go along with this better if it's with money that he doesn't know about."

"So Nepheli doesn't know what I'm looking for?"

"If they stuck around I might have told them. Doesn't matter. I'll tell them when we find it."

"So where is it?"

The grin disappeared. "Well, see, that's the thing. I don't know, exactly. That'd be, like, part of your job. I know where it *was*. My dad wore it on a silver chain around his neck."

I pictured Edgar's floating corpse. I hadn't seen anything of value on him. He was wearing a wetsuit, but his neck was exposed. I would have noticed. And if I'd noticed, I'd have taken it, and solved all my problems without having to get mixed up with hive mind drones, mechanical gators, and party boy sons.

"I was the first one to reach his body," said Riley. "No chain, no card."

"If you found his body then I'm guessing he didn't drown tonight," I said, remembering how unsurprised he had been when Deena had broken the news of his death to him.

Riley shook his head. "No. Two days ago. Up the yoreshore, off the coast of Little Lauderdale."

"How did he end up chained beneath Maria's boat then?"

"I have no idea. Wait, chained up? What makes you say that?"

I opened my mouth before I could think of a lie. Riley's gogs flashed over with an incoming call. He grunted and silenced it.

"Doesn't matter. I don't want to get into all that. What happened to him after I found him ain't important right now. He lost the card between when he went in and when he came out. So let's focus on that. I want you to find out where he was diving and poke around."

"You don't know where he was diving? I thought you said you were there."

"He said he'd be diving around the boat, but it was his DPV that brought his body back. DPV's an underwater speeder, got a range of at least twenty miles."

"I know what a DPV is," I said.

"So first step's finding out where he was diving. Then you go down and dive it yourself. With any luck the card's still down there. But I think it's likely that it ain't, and we're going to have to go to Plan B."

"Which is?" It was the same label Charlie had given to his insurance scheme to execute the *Ghost*, and I didn't like the sound of it here either.

"You look for clues. 'Cuz if it ain't there then I think chances are that whoever killed my dad took it."

"Why are you so sure he was killed? Nepheli didn't sound convinced. Maybe it was an accident."

"Nepheli didn't see him. I was the first one out there. I kept his equipment. You can look at it yourself. His breathing line was cut, torn by something sharp. He was in the middle of the open ocean. You think a jellyfish did that?"

"You just said you didn't know where he was diving."

Riley frowned. "He was a good diver. If it was an accident he would have just surfaced. No, somebody must have killed him. It was probably another atmo-breaker, maybe someone from Pas Adena Circuits. They're always eating the old man's exhaust and talking shit. Whoever it is, I want you to find them. Find the killer, prolly find the card."

"I'm a salvagia diver, not a detective."

"Girl, I ain't ever even seen you dive. I'm sure you're pretty good. I'm hiring you because I've seen you fight. I just saw you take down a mechanical gator. You zapped Deena with those sticks of yours. You can do some damage."

I was surprised at how much I appreciated the compliment. I was tall, and since I'd arrived in Florida I'd accumulated the lithe curves of an underwater laborer. But out of the water I still felt awkward, gangly, mostly elbows. I had been damaged, robbed, and rattled that night. It was nice to hear that I myself was capable of rattling.

"But the first problem is that we don't have any idea where he was diving," continued Riley. "I figured that's the kind of problem that's in your wheelhouse. Got any bright ideas?"

I thought about it, and realized that I did: Edgar's diving mask. Riley just said he'd kept Edgar's equipment.

Even if I hadn't recognized Edgar, I would have known he was rich, because of the wetsuit brand he was wearing. It was the kind of wetsuit you wanted to be seen in, with a distinctive orange stripe along the sides, like a racing stripe. But it also had a lot of fancy features that most people didn't realize they were paying for.

Including a subscription package with logged location data. The storage and the console were built into the mask.

I sent Riley to fetch all of Edgar's equipment, then spent a few minutes looking at the data on Myra's condition on my wearable without understanding any of it. I drained my drink. I felt a slight shudder, which I guessed was the activation of some sort of auxiliary power. The engines remained off, but the lights and AutoBar came back to life.

Riley still hadn't come back when I spotted another tender swing around the *Marino*. It sped toward us. I thought it might be the medic again, but then I picked out three separate figures, one standing facing us, two sitting, facing away.

The stander had peroxide blonde hair.

The tender docked in its slot at the aft deck of the *Pure Passer* and Deena leapt aboard. She spotted me peering down at her from the sundeck. She leapt back to the tender.

Riley appeared shortly after from the main cabin. He had a duffel bag of equipment slung over his shoulder. A woman stepped off the boat then, the older Mourner, Maria. And then a man, a stranger. He looked around Maria's age, or possibly younger but much worse kept. Maria wavered before getting off the tender, and Deena slunk over and pulled her onto the *Pure Passer*. Maria wasn't visibly restrained, but it seemed clear to me from her stifled movement that she didn't want to be here.

The man glanced up at me, then went to Riley and put his hand on his shoulder and spoke to him. I couldn't hear what they were saying, but I saw Riley's shoulders sag, then heard him shout something back, and the man spoke in a low voice to him again, and then he disappeared belowdecks. Then the three of them walked up the stairs to the sundeck. I braced myself, and fingered my Knuckle.

The AutoBar offered to make them all drinks. Maria ordered a vodka martini. Deena looked at me, and tried to get the man's attention, presumably to find out what should be done about me. She called him "Maurice." He ignored her. He was muttering to himself, like he was on the phone, but he wasn't wearing gogs. He stood still for a second, against the moon, and I saw that he was surrounded by a cloud of flies.

He was talking to them.

"As you can see," he said. "We have reasserted control."

He was broad-shouldered and muscular, with fleshy jowls and sunken eyes. He looked exhausted, but like exhaustion was his natural state. He wore a white linen suit and he kept fidgeting with it, like he had evaded sleep for so long that he was afraid that if he stood still and closed his eyes he might have to pay the full debt in one installment.

"Wave," Maurice said to Maria, and gestured to Deena. Deena nodded and pushed the small of her back toward the railing. She gazed out at the boats of armed Mourners. They had us entirely surrounded, and all of them were watching us. She waved to them all in a way that strangely reminded me of my own self-conscious beauty pageant wave to them earlier, except I saw a couple of her fingers flutter very specifically, at one boat in particular.

Secret handshakes.

Deena pulled her away from the railing and she sat on the couch, where Riley had been.

"We control the Astro America," Maurice went on, speaking to the flies again. "We control the heir apparent. Of the six families that run the six major revenue lines of Mourning in Miami, three are still in favor of the deal. Two are in active pursuit. And Maria Feinstein-Reyes is, well, there she is."

"The majorest of the major revenue lines," she said, grabbing her martini and sitting next to me. She was different here than she had been on the shore. She was acting like she was at a party. "Shipping, mostly. It's a shame your night got spoiled, Maurice. I just got a case of those PR Republic fireworks everybody's raving about, and the little pills that go with them. The flash bangs." She turned to me. "The fireworks are so bright they white out your vision and then the pills kick in and they sketch the face of God on your retinas. Or maybe the fireworks do that. I don't really remember. I did it last year in San Juan. I was going to give you a little show."

"I prefer the show you just gave now," said Maurice. "We are standing on Edgar Ortiz's yacht, we have Riley Ortiz secured, we are projecting an image of unification and stability, and I am confident that soon everyone else will return to the table and we will be back on track."

"You're twitching, Maurice," said Maria, sipping her drink. "Do you always twitch that much?"

"You're just upset that your little coup didn't work. It must have taken months of planning."

"You know what your problem is? You think everyone's like you, making these meticulous plans. Acting like the Church of the Invisible Hand. Most of us just play the hand we're dealt. It's called improvisation."

"Hmph," he said. "Killing Edgar Ortiz and attempting to kill his son with a mechanical gator on the night he was about to close the greatest deal of his career is hardly improvisation."

"That's the story, huh?"

"It's the truth. And look." He chuckled. "We even have the gator killer to prove it."

The flies spoke, all at once, using the same inflection I had heard on the beach. "You say you have control. But you don't yet have access to the required funds."

"I have contingencies. Plan B? Don't talk to me about Plan B. Talk to me about C through double Z."

"All of them half-baked," said Maria. "I won't let Miami be rebuilt on half-baked pyramid schemes."

Maurice shrugged. "That's how it was built in the first place."

The *Pure Passer*'s engines shuddered to life, and the boat started moving toward the *Marino* again. Riley slunk back onto the deck. He looked furious. He walked past me and I grabbed his arm.

"What's happening?"

"Maurice says Nepheli's flying in the Canaveral tomorrow, not me. Nepheli set me up. They acted like they were trying to warn me, but they just didn't want me to talk to him. I knew he owned the team now, I just didn't think he cared enough to do something like this."

"I meant what's happening to *me*."

"Oh. You're coming with us, I guess."

"I need to get back to my boat."

"Well I gotta get back to the Astro and talk him into letting me get back in that race. I told him I was the only one who can get the *Bull* to go that fast, if he doesn't listen to that . . ."

"What about the UltiMon card?"

But he shrugged me off and went back to the AutoBar.

I looked over my shoulder; the tender was still in its little slot in the aft deck. I thought about making a break for it, but Deena stood at the top of the staircase, blocking my way. And we were surrounded by guns.

"What neither of us have," Maurice continued, speaking again to the flies, "is time. The feds are experienced evacuators, they could be out of OrlanDome by the end of the week. And every hour that titan sits out there unused is kiloDollars down the drain. I can't spare the firepower to protect it. We should press forward with the plan. Tonight, we broke ground on our flagship property, the Conch Republican. You saw for yourself how quickly we can build and how unstoppable the titan is when it's in action. Give me back authorization and let me continue construction. The money will come."

"We were promised payment tonight," said the flies.

"Well obviously there were circumstances beyond our control."

Riley stood near the AutoBar, making another drink. He looked sick. He glanced over at Maria and me on the couch, then at Maurice. Time was running out for all of us. Maria seemed calmest. Maybe her time was already up.

The flies flew in that lightly unfocused way that indicated to me that they were discussing matters with each other.

Maria leaned over to me. "How's your friend? Did you find the medic?" She was noticeably more bubbly than she had been on the shore. She'd been on her guard out there, but in control. Here she was an actual prisoner.

"Eventually," I replied. "Did you really send that gator after Riley?"

"What do you think?"

"I think I wish I'd let it drown him."

"He's not so bad. Sure, he's a New Daytona brat who doesn't even speak Spanish. And he's stubborn, just like his dad, but to break you need to be up your own ass most of the time. Just don't date him. Don't date atmo-breakers in general. Short shelf life."

"They have a short shelf life or the relationship does?"

"If this then that."

The flies announced their decision to Maurice. "We acquired an item of considerable value tonight, quite unexpectedly. You were not involved, Thibodeux, but as a gesture of our goodwill in this partnership we will consider it a deposit, and return authorization of the titan to you. For one day."

"Two days would be better," Maurice said. "Contingencies, like I said." I noticed he glanced at Riley.

The flies conferred again briefly. "As you wish. But we expect full payment by sundown. Further extensions will not be considered, and consequences for nonpayment will be extreme."

"You won't regret it," said Maurice.

"I have to get off this boat," I said to Maria. When the flies mentioned the Ked I'd almost triggered my baton.

Maria's smile was thin. She leaned close again. "Close your eyes," she whispered.

I spotted a single Mourner boat peel off from the circle and slowly putter between us and the *Marino*.

Maria stood up, and sauntered toward the prow. She tossed the remains of her martini into Riley's eyes. He screeched "Shit!" and covered his face with his towel.

Then she broke into a bolting run. I noticed for the first time that she was wearing heels. Deena sprinted after her. Maurice turned to her in surprise. The flies dispersed.

She reached the end of the sundeck and pointed toward the lone boat. All the surrounding Mourners looked at it, just as the operator of the boat fired something into the air with what looked like a modified flare gun.

I closed my eyes.

I heard a bang, and then a light crackle, like a hundred Calysta Chens blowing on the AutoBar screen. And then screams, a much louder roar, and random staccato bursts of gunfire. I felt heat on my face, and then a tap on my shoulder.

I opened my eyes again. The sundeck and surrounding boats were all lit by the flames emanating from the *Marino* and everyone groped about, rubbing their eyes.

Except for Maria, who walked past me, quickly but calmly. The lens of her Chanel gogs were dark. I stumbled after her, saw her walk down the stairs and get into the tender that brought her and speed away, weaving through the boats of blinded Mourners with a deft luxury.

The black duffel bag lay where Riley had dumped it, next to the empty tender slot.

A burst of gunfire from one of the boats forced me to take cover behind the sundeck furniture. I accidentally kicked over Maria's martini glass and Deena heard the sound and started moving in my direction. Her gun was out, and she waved it around wildly, as if to compensate for her blindness.

I peered over the railing and saw chaos. The Mourners were shooting at each other. The flash bangs must have blinded them too, unless some of them were loyal to Maria and were picking off the other ones. Some were shooting at us, but whether or not they were doing so on purpose was unclear. Fast dark objects zipped out of the air, the size of basketballs and bigger. They moved diagonally down, in sharp straight lines. They burst on impact, hitting some of the attacking boats. Drones of the Church, I guessed.

And we were still backing into the *Marino*, into the little slot between the hulls which was now an inferno. A drone struck the deck of the boat that had shot at us, and I used the opportunity to sprint down the stairs and grab the duffel bag.

There was a DPV inside, just like Riley had promised. It was sleek and tiny, exactly the sort of quality product I was hoping Edgar had. It could be operated with one hand and it still had some charge, hopefully enough to get me back to the *Ghost*. It had been powerful enough to tow a dead Edgar Ortiz back from wherever he'd come from. I also found the mask, and a rebreather and a small orange oxygen tank about half full.

"Hey!" Riley appeared on the sundeck, still blinking vodka out of his eyes. "Wait!"

Deena was behind him, still blind, still waving her gun. A stray bullet hit the deck less than five feet away from me. It might have come from her. I had to get out of the open.

I took out the DPV and shouldered the duffel and jumped into the water. I left my shoes on the deck. The salt water would stain my nice breezy pants, too. I begrudged Riley for ruining them, and for keeping me there, but I had everything I needed now to find the card without him. I could use his half to buy new pants. I fiddled with the DPV and watched the *Pure Passer* back into the flaming *Marino*.

Another stray bullet hit one of the Church drones. It slammed into the sundeck, bursting the AutoBar. A piece of it smacked someone in the head with a wet slap that I heard from twenty feet away, and they careened over the side. They missed the deck by inches and hit the water. It was either Deena or Riley. I thought it was probably Riley.

The DPV buzzed to life, and pulled me away, through the line of Mourners just barely beginning to get their bearings.

I held on. It pulled me forward. Riley was important. He was a necessary part of Maurice's plan; he was the heir to Mourning in Miami. They wouldn't let him just drown.

But they were all still blind, including Deena, and it was possible that nobody had noticed.

When I glanced back I couldn't see him, or anyone, breaking the flame-tinted reflection of the water.

A few hundred feet down there was another line of boats. I thought they might be the Mourners loyal to Maria. They kept their distance, and I spotted what could have been the tender that she'd taken from the *Pure Passer*. They appeared neither blind nor confused.

She'd helped me, but I thought it best to try to pass them unnoticed.

I fished the rest of Edgar's equipment out of the bag and put it all together. I found the rebreather with the cut line that had killed him still attached. The tear wasn't clean, didn't even go all the way through. It could have been the result of an accident, Edgar catching it on a sharp piece of coral or yoreshore debris. But it could also have been caused by a knife, a good-enough assassination attempt against someone who was putting up a struggle. All to say, it didn't reveal much.

I found a spare line in the duffel, along with a spare tank. I fitted Edgar's expensive mask over my face, adjusted it and switched it on.

I dove down. I fiddled with the mask.

To my immense frustration, I realized that I needed Riley after all.

So I sighed out bubbles and took the DPV back, underwater this time. It was a little more serene this way, except for a couple bullets whizzing through the water. The glow of the flaming yacht did not provide much illumination, but I spotted the silhouette floating face down just beneath the surface.

There was perhaps some irony to saving Edgar's son with his own equipment, returning Riley to the surface the way I had returned his father, or at least I might have thought so if I wasn't still pissed off and worried about stray gunfire.

We surfaced just outside the circle of Mourners and flaming wreckage, and I pulled off Edgar's mask. The DPV had a handy flotation feature that I activated and put under Riley's head, stretching out his neck. Riley's face was covered with some sort of sticky green goo from the AutoBar. I put my mouth on his and tasted iron and appletini. He coughed water and blood in my face. I put the mask on him and made sure he could breathe. He flailed a bit, and reached out toward the *Pure Passer*, but then it screeched against the flaming hull of its mother ship and he took my hand instead.

It was awkward for both of us to ride the DPV, especially when we had to trade off the rebreather. And the air from Edgar's orange tank tasted funny, strangely sweet. It made my head swim, and I kept losing my grip.

The *Ghost* came to meet us at the break of dawn. We had gone most of the way back to her, so it seemed she had stayed put while I had gone, but when she scanned me in the water, she pulled her anchor and sped toward us.

I pulled myself aboard for the second time that night, then helped Riley with the duffel bag. He'd shed his flight suit in the water, and I'd shed my wide-legged pants. They were dragging us down. He only had briefs underneath. The *Ghost* started whirring her outboards as soon as Riley stepped aboard.

"Something's wrong with your boat," Riley said in a rough voice. He lay on the deck and pinched the bridge of his nose. I looked at him. Beneath the green gunk he was covered in blood.

"She's fine," I replied.

"Nose twins," he grinned at me. His teeth also had some blood on them.

"Mine was worse. Stay there. I'll get you a towel."

I slid into the lounge as quietly as I could. I dropped the wet duffel bag of Edgar's equipment in the galley. I went to the cockpit and quickly told the *Ghost* to pull anchor and go, so she would move up the yoreshore and away from the firefight. I grabbed my towel from the bathroom and dried myself off, put on shorts, and then grabbed a fresh towel and went back through the lounge.

I yelped when I felt a hand close around my wrist.

Myra pulled me toward her, but one of the med drones whizzed through my hair. She let me go and it resumed its cranial orbit.

"Ow," I said.

"Sorry," she muttered. "Forgot about those."

"How are you feeling?"

"Nauseous."

"You should be asleep."

"It's mostly from that disgusting vape. Who's the fleeceless flotsam? I don't mind a bit, but I'm afraid his indecency is scaring our girl."

"Riley Ortiz."

"Ortiz? As in . . ."

"Yes," I said. I opened the glass door and tossed Riley the towel and shorts, then shut it again. He could clean himself up.

"Well. Let's hope our agent friends don't catch you with him," Myra said. "Agent Somer looked mad enough to audit you."

"Worse. He wants to send me to the moon."

"Maybe he'll take Ortiz in your stead."

"Unfortunately I need Ortiz. But I'd rather toss him overboard."

"Then he'd be jetsam."

"What's the difference?"

"Flotsam you find, like salvagia. Jetsam you toss. Like Kohl."

"I didn't toss him, he got away."

"With the prize?"

"No. I stopped him from that at least. But I lost it, too."

She sighed. "He promised to show me panthers."

Myra had been sent to Florida in the first place on behalf of a Consolidated NGO, to collect data on native species. There weren't very many of those left in Florida, so she had lots of free time for her hobbies, collecting characters and pursuing her Third Way. When Kohl swore to her that he'd seen panthers on an island somewhere, she was filled with hope and wonder. It must have made his betrayal sting a little harder.

"I made him pay for what he did," I said.

"Good job."

"Not quite yet."

"What do you mean?"

"Charlie's going to scuttle the *Ghost*, day after tomorrow. No, wait. Tomorrow's today now. Tomorrow tomorrow."

"That made my head hurt."

"I need a score, and Ortiz says he has one. But I don't like it, or him."

"Scuttle her, you said? Why? The whole night's a blur. Catch me up."

Riley was still lying on the deck. I sat on the floor next to the couch and gave Myra a summary of the night's events, everything she had missed bookending the visit from the IXS. I even told her, in a low voice, about my releasing Edgar's body. I thought it might hurt her head to follow all the twists and turns, but when I reached the end she was, as usual, miles ahead.

"So Mourning in Miami is building high-rises in the yoreshore," she said, contemplatively.

"They're definitely building something. How do you know it's high-rises?"

"The construction titan, for one. And for another, it makes sense, because Maurice is in a hurry."

"Why would he be in a hurry?" I asked.

"Because once the feds leave, everyone's going to jump in and build in the yoreshore. You should hear some of the calls I'm on at Nativitee. Everyone up north has Florida fever."

"They do?" I said. I was surprised, remembering Somer's sweaty hands and his disdain for living down here.

"Not the feds, obviously. But speculators, developers, construction... I know you have your own problems with Consolidation, but the biggest problem right now is that it worked too well. We've got a mint-condition emerging middle class in America again, and a lot of them are itching to get out of the domes. There's something to be said for giving people access to cheap housing, food, water, power, education, and healthcare. Economically, I mean. And if you know your history then you know Myra's Law."

"Which is?"

"Every generation or two, an American demographic in search of paradise will 'discover' Florida—in particular its resistance to regulation."

"Discover, huh?" I said. "It's not exactly virgin coast. And Somer said that nothing as big as a high-rise could last very long down here."

"It doesn't have to be *good* housing," she said. "He's right, high-rises are a terrible design for the yoreshore, with storms the way they are now. Domes are pretty wind resistant, actually, but these people are *leaving* the domes, they don't want to move to another one. And without the feds to enforce much of anything, whatever does get built only has to last as long as it sells."

"But if high-rises are so flimsy, why would anybody buy them?"

Myra swatted her med drones away and propped herself up on the couch. "Maximum waterfront views. Sure, the beaches are gone, and the hurricanes are much worse, and you can't count the hundred-degree days on just your fingers anymore, but you can still get a few months a year of lovely, breezy weather, especially on the coast. That's more than enough footage to put into a virtual tour. Remember, these are people who are tired of domes but are used to dome living. They still want climate-controlled buildings with amenities, but now they're hungry for pink sunsets."

"Like living at the Astro America."

Myra nodded. "Nobody's talking about living on CabanaBoats. Did you know the Astro America is the third most visited tourist attraction in the *country*? It beat out Niagara Falls last year."

"Niagara Falls has that weird smell now."

"It's why I got so weak in the knees when Kohl started talking about the panthers at Coral Castle."

"Florida panthers are extinct."

Myra nodded. "Probably. But if we *did* find one . . . from a promotional point of view, a Florida panther is basically a sexy unicorn. Lots of important people will give us money to protect it. Nativitee can get me real funding to buy up the land. Land that we can keep from being developed."

"Where you can attract your Third Way."

"It could be your Third Way, too. Living on the *Ghost* off the coast of our very own panther preserve. Better than the lunar colonies, that's for sure. Or nightmares in the domes."

"Panthers are a pipe dream. They're never coming back."

"You better hope they do," she replied. "If the developers come in, that means no more yoreshore. No more salvagia. Your loophole will be gone. They'll build up the whole coastline within months of the feds leaving and price you out. It makes sense that the Mourners want to start now, if they can get away with it. My guess is that your man Maurice is trying to jump the gun and build while the feds are too busy pulling out to do anything. And maybe he could, when he had someone like Edgar Ortiz on his side. Now it might be harder."

I looked back through wraparound glass windows to the cloud of black smoke, all that I could see of the burning megayacht. Had it sunk? Had Maria escaped?

"Now he might be dead," I said. "But if he's not, I guess he'll be coming after Riley."

"Speaking of," said Myra, pointing at the spots of blood on the deck where Riley used to be. "I hope you hid your nice shirts."

I found him on the *Ghost*'s sundeck, which was not as nice as his. Its primary function was to be the top of the boat, but it had a railing and a little collapsible canopy and some deck chairs and random bottle caps that I hadn't picked up.

He was examining the *Ghost*'s outboards from up above. I cleared my throat and he turned to me. Little white fluffs of towel stuck to his face.

"Where are we going?" he asked.

"Back up the yoreshore."

"Yeah, but we're heading north. Like we're going up the gulfside yoreshore. I gotta get to the Astro America. That's oceanside."

"I know where the Astro America is. We're not going to the Astro America. We're going to get the card."

"The card can wait. I can buy the team anytime. The Canaveral's tomorrow."

"Too bad. It's my boat."

He glanced at the outboards again. "Funny thing about this boat. Doesn't look like anybody's sailing it. And I don't know where the card is exactly, but I know it's gotta be south of Boca Raton. That's oceanside too."

"I know."

"I know you know. So you should change your bearing."

"Noted."

"But see, I got this feeling you won't. Or you can't. Just like I got this feeling that the only reason you rescued me is because you realized you need me to unlock my dad's mask."

It was true. I'd put on his mask and it had prompted Edgar to blink five times. Diving gear didn't have the most sophisticated biometrics, but I couldn't spoof it. A son with the same genetically modified eyes as the father, on the other hand, probably could.

"You ditched me first," I replied.

"What could I do? Maurice controlled the *Marino*, there was no way I could get my boat out of there. And besides, he pulled me from the Canaveral! I gotta be in that race. The Orbitals were almost a joke even when my dad was alive. If Neph flies it we'll lose and be one for sure. If a breaker killed my dad then they probably did it so they could win that race. I'm the only one that can beat them."

"I don't care."

"Ah, but you should. I can win it because I can sweet-talk a semi-sent better than anyone. Better than Nepheli, and they built the *Bull* basically from scratch."

"Your breaker's semi-sentient?" I hadn't expected that. I didn't think they still made semi-sents. The feds discouraged it.

"You bet," Riley replied. "That's top-secret info, by the way." This he said hurriedly. I remembered how worried Nepheli had been that he had blabbed about the *Bull* to Maurice.

"It's a brand-new class of breaker," Riley continued. "It's gonna put the Orbitals right back on top. And I'm the only one that can maximize her potential, because I got that magic touch. Which means I can sweet-talk this semi-sent here into going wherever we want to go. She is a semi-sent, right? That's why she's sailing all on her own? Bet I can talk to her better than you can at least, which seems to be not at all."

"She's heading back to her owner," I said. There didn't seem to be any point in denying it. "He can program a route back around for us." It wasn't the best plan, but maybe if I brought Riley Ortiz, Charlie would take me seriously enough to call off Reefer, and I would have more time. "And Myra needs to get back to dry land so she can recover."

"Where's he live?" asked Riley.

"Lakeland."

Riley groaned. "That'll take at least all day! I heard you talking to your friend. You need the money by tomorrow. Boca Raton's on the way to the Astro. Come on, I'll unlock the mask, I'll sail the ship, we'll get to Lauderdale by lunch and dive for the card and get back in time for the Canaveral. I'll even throw in a spa day for your friend."

It made some sense. But I remembered what Nepheli said about Calysta Chen: *The last person who followed him is dust.*

"I can't let you sail the *Ghost*," I said.

Riley's mouth twitched, and twisted into a cruel smile. "Why? You jealous? You want to buy her, right? That's what all of this is for? Must be pretty embarrassing to not even be able to sail her."

I primed the stunner of my Knuckle and triggered the baton, then turned my palm to him and showed it sparking. "Call it whatever you want. But if you touch her controls, I'll make sure your hands aren't in a state to use them."

To my surprise, Riley put his hands up. He looked guilty. Maybe even a little afraid.

"Shit," he said. "Sorry. I'll behave."

"Good," I said. I'd been frustrated all night. I was running out of patience, and with my Knuckles I could break, instead of being broken. But I wasn't sure where to take it from here, with Riley. I wasn't used to winning a fight or an argument so completely. Unless I threw him overboard, we were stuck together until we got to Charlie's.

Fortunately, he spoke first.

"You saved my life you know," he said. "Twice."

"Only because I wanted something," I said.

"I know, but . . . I am grateful, really. It's just sometimes when I think I got a good idea I go scorched earth with it. Like with this Kappacop card. I know you can beat my ass, even without those sticks of yours. I'll get off in Lakeland, catch a ride to the Astro somehow. I'll come find you after the Canaveral."

I relaxed a little, but he had gotten to me. It really was embarrassing to not be able to sail the *Ghost*. I needed her more than she needed me.

Except without me, she would die. And without Riley, I would fail.

"Sorry," I muttered. I switched off the stunner. "It's been a long night. Sometimes I don't play nicely with others."

"You and me both," Riley said. "I think I've pissed exactly everybody off. Nepheli, Deena, Maurice, now you. The only one who likes me is *Bulls on Parade*, and I treat her rough too. I guess I just forget sometimes that people ain't breakers."

"Myra's about the only one that can stand me for long periods of time," I said. "She'll probably like you too. She liked you better with those shorts off."

He grinned. "Well, who wouldn't?"

He put his hands down and leaned on the railing and looked at me in a funny way. I realized that I was also grinning. I half-expected him to step a little closer, but he didn't. Probably because I threatened him. Probably because I was still armed. That was another, less common reason why my Knuckles were best kept hidden. They were a deterrent in those rare moments when a little intimacy might actually be welcome.

I dismissed a ridiculous urge to slip my Knuckle off in front of him. I believed he'd submitted, but I didn't quite believe he agreed.

He cleared his throat. "Uh, listen. Do you mind if I grab a shower?" I was blocking his way off the sundeck. "I'm attracting flies. Real ones, not drones."

The trip back to Charlie's would take most of the day, and it was shaping up to be a hot one. A long braise, as Myra called it, relentlessly bright and humid, without a cloud in the sky or much breeze at all. It was barely dawn and the *Ghost* had already tinted her windows against the sunlight, but that might have just been for Myra's sake. I was having trouble keeping my eyes open, having gotten no sleep and spent much adrenaline. But there was still work to do, and plans to make. While Riley took his shower I made iced coffee and huevos rancheros for three and changed Myra's bandage.

"I just can't believe you actually touched a dead body," said Myra, taking a quick bite of her food before the med drone clipped her hand. We realized quickly that huevos rancheros were a difficult dish for someone to eat on the couch with projectiles whirling around their head, so I remade hers into more of a burrito.

"I don't think I did," I said. "Just the chain it was tied to."

"So do we think he did it?" she asked, in a particularly loud whisper.

"Did what?"

"Killed his dad, obviously."

"Riley?"

"Sure. Didn't he say his dad always raced this race he wants to get to so badly? And you said Edgar's body disappeared for two days and he didn't even care?"

"He thinks another atmo-breaker did it. And if he killed Edgar then he'd already have the Kappacop card."

"If there even is one. Maybe this is just a big setup to get you to dive for something else. Something Edgar hid from him."

"I don't think he's that clever."

"I'm definitely not," said Riley, stepping out of the bathroom. The goo was gone but his face was pink from a hard loofa scrub, and he'd stuck wads of toilet paper in his nose. I'd lent him one of my old T-shirts from the Corps. He was tall enough that it exposed his midriff a little. "Is this plate for me?"

"It is."

"That's very kind, thank you." Since our conversation he had been on noticeably better behavior. But I was also trying to be more considerate.

"You said you thought another atmo-breaker killed him."

"That's right," he nodded. "But if they killed him to get him out of the race, then it wouldn't explain why the card's missing. So who knows. Any other suspects? I guess I'm one of them, but I didn't do it. We couldn't stand to be in the same room together long enough for me to kill him."

"The nice thing about killing someone underwater is that you don't have to talk to them," observed Myra. "I'm not saying you did it, but if you did it . . . I'm sure you had your reasons. We're not here to judge you."

"I'm sure I did, too," said Riley. "But I didn't do it. Maurice said Maria did it, and that she sent the gator, too. But Maurice is the one who lost his body, so I'd say both of them are suspects. And the Church of the Invisible Hand. But all three of those folks are too rich to kill the old man just for an UltiMon card, even Kappacop."

Except I had learned firsthand that the Church had an interest in collectibles. "The Church told you they were upset that Edgar wasn't there for the deal," I remembered. "But they could have been lying to you."

"Why would they bother? They don't care what I think. I'm not involved in the deal, or anything at all when it comes to Mourning in Miami. That's my dad's thing."

"You said Maurice lost the body? How? What does that mean?"

"Well Maurice was with us on the *Marino* when his body came back. I swam out to him first. But then he sent some people out and I swam back to the *Pure Passer* to dump his equipment. He told me later that the current swept the old man's body away before they could grab it. Which, yeah, I never quite bought, since I was out there myself and it wasn't so strong."

"So Maurice could have done it. Sent Deena or someone to do it."

Riley chewed, thoughtfully. "I guess so. But Maurice needed my dad. You saw how quickly that deal fell apart without him. None of the Mourners really trust Maurice. But him losing the body and Maria finding it again tonight . . . I dunno. Obviously that's weird."

"So maybe Maria did do it. Or it really was just an accident."

"Yeah, but an accident's weird too," he said, talking with his mouth full. "We were in the yoreshore. Shallow water. Like I said, if it was an accident he had plenty of time to get to the surface before he drowned."

"But drown he did," said Myra.

"He might have gotten caught in something and it trapped him and tore his line," I speculated.

"Then how'd he get back to his DPV to come back to us?" Riley asked.

"Maybe he got free but was too deep to surface without getting the bends."

"Or maybe someone put him there," said Myra. "After they killed him."

Riley did the dishes and then, as promised, he put on Edgar's mask and blinked when prompted.

"I'm in," he said, then meekly asked for permission to take a nap. I gave it. Myra was already dozing on the couch.

"You look like you could use one too," he said.

He was right. The food and coffee were already wearing off.

"I'm going to get his location," I said. "Then I might close my eyes. You can use the master. The room below."

"You don't want it?"

"I don't sleep down there."

He went down the spiral staircase, then popped his head back up.

"Hey, it's got a window!" he said, with excitement. The master stateroom had a wraparound window below the surface. The water was usually too murky and the yoreshore was nearly devoid of life anyway. During the day it gave the room a nice mossy glow. But at night it was as dark as any other lightless place.

I set my Knuckles to charge on the little power pad next to the recliner, then sat down and put on Edgar's mask, spent some time fiddling around with the UI. Then I blinked around for the location data. I saw where it should be. Then I checked again to be sure.

"Shit," I said, loud enough to make Myra twitch and frown in her sleep.

It was scrubbed.

I looked through every menu and settings configuration. It was set to save location data, which meant Edgar must have deleted it intentionally. Wherever he'd been diving, he hadn't wanted anyone to know about it.

Which was interesting, but not helpful.

I went back through the menu, desperately scrolling through every setting. I combed through all the data that was saved, putting some particular hope in the cache of incident videos, which he hadn't deleted, possibly because they were tucked in an obscure subsection.

The mask was set to record everything, but only to preserve "incidents," moments when Edgar's heart rate spiked or the mask sensed sudden motion or trauma, presumably for insurance purposes. There were three such incidents saved with a timestamp that lined up with his last dive.

I stifled a yawn. The work was tedious and I was already exhausted. But there was no time to waste, so I cued up the first video.

The display on the mask came to life and immersed me in Edgar's point of view.

The stream began with Edgar already in the water, below the surface, his DPV in his hands. He swam calmly, facing the seabed below him, upon which was littered the remains of a playground: jungle gym reduced to rusty rebar, something that could have been a slide. So he was in the yoreshore, and he was just floating. A serene scene, which made it especially soporific.

The only action, which briefly jolted me awake, came when he swam back up, breaking the surface right in the path of a small boat that had to swerve to avoid him.

Riley and Nepheli were on that boat. The *Marino* was anchored close by. Riley yelled something at Edgar and kept going, toward the *Pure Passer* in the distance. Edgar's hand came out of the water, a goodbye wave, maybe. Only Nepheli waved back.

I fell asleep soon after.

Later, when I woke up, it was difficult to recall exactly what had been on the feed, and what had merely mingled with my own nightmares. It was an uneasy sleep, like drifting off drunk or furious.

I remember staring into the guts of an underwater shipwreck, a barge-type houseboat. It could have been the *Ghost*, except it looked much older and it was lying on its side. I held the railing, stared into a split amidship, a jagged opening just big enough for me to squeeze in.

I floated there, staring into that cruel mouth. I got right up to the edge and then pulled back again, in a sort of hypnotizing undulation, and my own anxiety began to ebb and flow with it. It was less than dim in there, a total blackness that recalled the entrance to the boat that held the prize yesterday (only yesterday?) and that initial dreaded darkness, way back in Wyoming.

I was diving alone, and I knew that soon I was going to die.

I wondered, later, how I had slept through so much of this, when a simple jolting action in the first video had been enough to temporarily startle me awake. My guess, from piecing together what I recalled, was that there was no sudden action on these later videos, but that made me wonder why the mask had captured all of this in the first place. Edgar pulling himself up to and away from the edge a dark place was not objectively traumatic, but if I had read the settings correctly, then his heart rate must have been elevated for that sustained amount of time. Why? What could have caused that? Was he as afraid of deep dark places as I was? That was surprising. He was an atmo-breaker. Space was one big dark place.

At some point he must have pulled himself through, because I remember that everything went black and his breathing became intense, labored. I heard sounds in it, the screech of metal, a glimpse of Eli's face the moment before the lights went out, Eli looking at his hand, realizing that he'd lost control of it.

Eli's hand. It was an old fed prosthetic, modified to accommodate his three remaining flesh fingers. Eight fingers, plus five on the other hand. Thirteen beautiful fingers in all. His hands were small, graceful, and delicate. He took Gamma's Knuckles with us to the 2C3, and the left one only fit over the prosthetic fingers.

I saw my own hands—veiny now, pruned. Jet black. They floated, lifeless, in green-brown yoreshore water.

The darkness fled and I saw fingers (not my own, not Eli's) wrapping around my neck. Not thirteen, just ten, colored an uncanny purple, like a tarantula in a cartoon.

They belonged to someone named Flaco.

The fingers burrowed into the neckline of my wetsuit and pulled the thread of a silver chain, a turtle with a tall black hat. I tried to stop it, but, like in all the worst nightmares, I couldn't move. Eli couldn't stop moving, his fingers were eight wriggling tendrils, none of which belonged to him at the end.

Eli screamed, from the shock and the pain. The turtle slipped out of my grasp, sank to the bottom.

They split. All four hands, mine and Flaco's, they split the same way—index and pinkies bent back until they cracked, the wet twig snap of breaking bones. They peeled away from the palm like strips of bark. Blood should have billowed the water. There was so much blood I'd slipped in it backing away from Eli. I looked later in the mirror in my hab, and it was all over my hands, my face, my gun.

The last thing I remember before my head hit the wall behind the recliner in the lounge and I startled awake was the word "FLACO," glinting gold like the stitching of Riley's flight suit.

Then blackness. I ripped off the mask.

Myra wasn't on the couch anymore. I thought the swerve must have thrown her, but I couldn't see her on the floor, either, just her med drones, sputtering, face up like turtles on their backs. I looked out the window. We were still in the ocean, but the water was brown and silty. I could tell we were in shallow water, but it wasn't yoreshore. It was almost entirely flat. No ruins poked above the water at all, just a few massive black piles. In the far distance were mangroves, and that was the direction we were heading now, full speed.

Riley stood at the cockpit, his fingers frantically tapping at the console. He saw me stand up, pull my way toward him.

"Shit," he said.

# 6

Riley put one hand up to stop me but kept tapping at the console with the other.

"What did you do?" I growled.

"Sorry," he said, talking rapidly. "That little bump was my fault. I asked her to look for a way in, she was just so excited when she found one. Maybe I got a little overeager with the praise routine. She's got really good hazard charting. I didn't think she'd be so interested in the—"

"Where's Myra?"

"Huh?"

"Here," came her voice, and there she was, in a chair behind Riley, next to the cockpit. She didn't look hurt, as far as I could see.

"Move," I said.

"Triss," said Riley. "Wait. It's not what you think."

"Now!"

Obediently, his hands hovered above the console. And immediately, the *Ghost* swerved again and threw me back into the galley.

Myra fell into Riley. The *Ghost* turned all the way around and headed back the way she came. Riley grabbed on to the console and kept his balance, like he had expected this to happen.

"Ow," said Myra.

"Sorry," said Riley. "Just following orders."

"What's happening?" I growled.

"I told you!" he shouted. "I praised her too much. She's going back for seconds. She's saying . . . wait, that's weird. She thinks we're over a road."

"A road?" said Myra. "Interesting. Maybe she thinks we're still in the yoreshore."

"Her hazard charting's been killer so far. So if she says it I believe her. Anyway, listen, Triss, can I just fix it, please?"

I didn't answer, but he realized I wouldn't be able to get to him in time, so he put his hands back on the console and did something again and she stopped. Turned back around, and gently continued the way she was going. Toward the shore.

"See?" Riley said, gesturing to the console. "I got it all under control. Just like I said."

I pulled myself up again, and looked at Myra. "You let him do this?"

She shrugged. "I'm an invalid. But he made some good points."

"Can't believe the smell didn't wake you up," said Riley. "We must be over what used to be the Everglades. River of Grass? More like River of Smells Like—"

"You lied to me," I said.

"You were asleep," he retorted. "You're lucky I woke up, she would have run right into one of these peat mounds. And before you bash me in the head just take a look out there."

He pointed to a small speck in the distance, in the open water. It was almost at the mangrove tree line that marked the shore.

Another boat, towing something submerged in the water behind it, like a whale.

"It's Nepheli," he said.

It was difficult to tell for sure.

"The *Ghost* saw them and started following them all on her own," he said. "I just got here in time to help her along."

I was incredulous. "Why would she do that? She's on her way back to Charlie."

He shrugged, but he wouldn't meet my eyes. "Who knows? She's your boat. If I hadn't been there to guide her she might have missed this canal entirely."

"You know she doesn't always do what she's told," Myra piped in.

I ignored her. "What would Nepheli even be doing out here? Didn't they say they were going back to the Astro America?"

"Exactly!" exclaimed Riley. "We're on the other side of the state. You ever heard of anybody using the Everglades as a shortcut to anything?"

"Think about it, Triss," said Myra. "Why would there be a human-made canal, all the way out here? Especially a canal deep enough for a barge to tow a rocket ship? There are people out here! It could be our panthers, Triss! Our Third Way."

"If this canal cuts all the way through to Miami," said Riley. "We'll get to Boca much faster. And it's heading in that direction."

"Miami?" I exclaimed. "We're not going to Miami. Absolutely not. The *Ghost* would scuttle herself."

Myra and Riley looked at each other.

"Listen," he said. "We'll catch up to Nepheli soon anyway, way before Miami. We'll find out what the deal is. I can hitch a ride with them and get out of your hair. They can tell Myra where they're headed, and if there are people out there. And in return, I'll tell the *Ghost* to go on to the dive spot, and you don't have to go all the way back to Charlie to do it, and you'll get there twice as fast even if you have to go back the way you came. Deal? Where is the dive spot, by the way?"

"I don't know," I admitted. "Edgar erased his location."

"What do you mean?" he said. "Like on purpose?"

"Looks like it."

He blinked. "Well you must have found something. You had that mask on for hours. Or were you just asleep the whole time?"

I thought about peeling that smug smile off his face, but he had Myra on his side now. I stormed out onto the deck instead.

"Wait, Triss. Come back!"

The sun had just barely cleared the mangrove line that Nepheli, if that was even Nepheli, was heading for. It must still be morning, but the long braise was well underway. The heat washed over me, fueled my temper. I sweated and fumed. And there was a smell, just like Riley had said. Like rotting seaweed, an entire forest of it, dark and wet and putrid. Organic. The smell of that which had once been alive. The yoreshore never smelled like much of anything at all.

I thought that Riley was lying. It was too much of a coincidence that out of all the boats moving up and down the gulfside coast, the *Ghost* would choose to chase what he thought was Nepheli's. And while I knew the *Ghost* could get distracted (she'd followed me almost all the way to the shore last night, after all), I had never once seen her do it for another boat. Only for shores or sandbars. Her specialty was hazard charting. Boats weren't hazards, unless they were wrecks. I was sure that he had snuck up here, spotted Nepheli, or whoever it was, and told the *Ghost* to go after them.

But it didn't matter, because he really could talk to her.

Not just talk; he could command her. She'd responded instantaneously. It had been so easy for him. I'd caught a glimpse of the console once it was clear she was listening to him. I saw pictures and videos, no text at all. It made no sense to me.

What did make sense was his plan. It would save time. We all had deadlines. He'd already convinced Myra, who wanted proof of her Third Way. I owed her for putting her in danger.

The only contribution missing was mine. But I had come up empty so far.

I watched the two of them confer with each other through the wraparound windows. Riley seemed upset. They were trying very hard not to look at me, but occasionally Myra would glance out. Then she went downstairs to the master and Riley came out onto the deck.

"What's your problem?" he exclaimed. "Can't you see that I'm trying to help you?"

"You're helping yourself," I replied.

"We're helping each other. We're partners, aren't we?"

"If we were partners you wouldn't be stealing my ship."

He laughed. "Stealing? Even if I wanted to, I don't think I could. She's crazy about you. Do you even notice all the little things she does for you? Tinting the windows when you walk by so the sun doesn't hit you in the eyes? She wouldn't even let me change the height of the cockpit seat. The only way I could get her to follow Nepheli in the first place is by saying you wanted her to."

"So you lied to her. And you lied to me, when you said she started following Nepheli on her own."

Riley winced. He'd been caught. "I wasn't planning it, you know. I was planning on taking a nap. I couldn't sleep because she wouldn't let me pull the blinds down in the bedroom down there. You must really like that underwater window."

"I just hate dark, tight spaces."

He looked at me. "Yeah. So did the old man. Certified claustrophobe."

"Really?"

"Sure."

I remembered him floating, just outside that dark space, pulling himself right to the edge and backing out again, so many times that it lulled me to sleep.

"Then why was he diving a shipwreck?" I asked.

He blinked. "What shipwreck?"

I pushed myself up from the railing so fast that Riley flinched. I went back into the lounge and grabbed the mask and watched the video again.

"Do you recognize it, where he is?" Riley asked.

"No," I replied. "There are probably dozens of shipwrecks around there. This looks like a houseboat of some kind, an old one. But it's on its side. I can't see the name or anything."

"What's he doing?"

"He's just floating there," I said. But now I could believe that he was doing something else. Psyching himself up, gathering courage to go inside the wreck. I hadn't just been projecting my own fears onto him, he actually did seem anxious. He'd pull himself all the way to the mouth, even stick his head in, and then jolt back, like the blackness was boiling. It was still hypnotizing, but Riley standing next to me made me anxious enough to stay awake. "Wait," I said, freezing on a particular moment.

"What?"

"He's changing tanks."

I hadn't noticed it before, he must have done it after I dozed off. But he pulled out a little orange tank. I recognized it. It was the same one I'd shared with Riley when we escaped on the DPV.

The air had tasted funny, almost sweet. It had made my head hurt. It wasn't just oxygen.

"It's a mix," I said.

"A mix? A mix of what?"

"A diving mix. Divers use it sometimes at depth, to stay lucid and to reduce their decomp time. It doesn't make sense to use it in the yoreshore, though, it's too shallow. So he must be diving somewhere deep."

"Okay. Like how deep?"

I'd used mix before, but I usually couldn't afford it. I had never tasted anything like what was in that orange tank. It was probably expensive. "I don't know. But if I knew what was in his mix I might be able to guess. Different proportions of different gases work best at different depths."

"Would that help us?"

"Maybe. The *Ghost* keeps a depth record of everywhere she's been. And she charts wrecks. She found one for me just the other day." And Charlie had almost definitely let her wander around Lauderdale on a walkabout.

"Hmm," Riley bit his lower lip. "So if we knew how deep he was diving we could ask the *Ghost* if she knew any shipwrecks at that depth?"

I nodded. "Exactly."

"So how do we find out what's in his mix?"

"We need an expensive mix machine. Or we need to ask someone who knows his equipment. Is it too much to hope that you do?"

"It is," he said. "But . . . Nepheli stayed in his suite at the Astro the night before he went on that dive. He kept all his equipment there. And I know they helped him with it, fixed it for him and stuff. If anyone knows, it'd be them."

"So I guess we're catching up to Nepheli."

"I guess so."

We were grinning again.

"Come on, then," he said. "We have some time. Let's do this, if we're doing it."

"What are we doing?"

"Proving that we're partners."

He invited me to sit at my own cockpit. He hovered close behind. I swiveled the chair around and plopped down.

"Okay," he said. "I'm not really sure how good a teacher I'm gonna be. Nepheli taught me, and they're a shitty teacher."

"So how did you learn?"

"Because I'm a great student. So. Nepheli says to talk to a semi-sent you gotta understand two things. The first is that they're naturally curious. Your job is to use that curiosity to get the *Ghost* interested."

"Interested in what?"

"Well, see, all semi-sents have a preprogrammed purpose. That's why they're only semi-sentient, I think. They don't get to decide what their purpose is, but they *do* have enough intelligence and free will to choose how they achieve that purpose.

"For example, during a race, *Bulls on Parade*'s purpose is to be on the other side of the debris field. She decides *how* she does that, so my objective is to get her excited about my particular how. Like, if I want her to go faster, I might ask her what she thinks the moon looks like right now with no debris in the way, and it'll make her want to get there ASAP and see it for herself. But if I want her to go *safer*, I'd ask her something else."

"Why not just ask her to do both?"

He shrugged. "Conflicting agendas. To go safe might mean to go slow. Try to do both at once and that's how you blow. And besides, that's a broad example. The basic idea. Things change a lot over the course of a race and if I change my queries too much she might get confused. She has a million sensors and takes in a lot of data, and can process it faster than I can, but she needs to be focused. That takes race experience, and I got more of that than her. More than anybody, really, except the old man. I can take a pretty good guess by how much she drags in the troposphere how heavy the debris field's gonna be when we hit it. And the *Bull* knows that I know more than her. She trusts me. That's the second important thing you gotta know, and it's why it was so hard for me to stop her from crossing the Karman last night. It'd betray that trust. But I'll get to that later."

"So what's the *Ghost*'s purpose?" I asked.

"Not sure," Riley said. "Myra told me she's a, what? A CabanaBoat? I had to look that up. What do you know about them?"

"They were resort hotel rooms," I replied. I had done what little research there was to do long ago. "The company that built them used various shady business practices that took advantage of multiple tax schemes. They shut down suddenly and didn't leave any instruction manuals. I found some of their old marketing materials, though."

"You still have them?" Riley asked.

"Think so."

"Put them up on the console."

I found them on my wearable and flicked them to the cockpit console. The first one was an aerial shot of a tropical shore, with a herd of CabanaBoats, all in a circle. Families sat on their sundecks and waved to each other. A couple of them were docked together, making a little floating patio for a party.

"Perfect," he said. "This is something. Now here's how you talk semi-sent..."

Talking semi-sent consisted mostly of making a sort of pictographic idea of what we wanted the *Ghost* to do out of images and videos. Riley said that any kind of data that the *Ghost* had a sensor for would work, but that visual images were the easiest and least prone to confusion, since the way semi-sents processed that data was somewhat similar to how humans did.

We passed the thick mangrove line and sailed up a little delta. At the point where that delta started to narrow out, we saw a big towering island, almost like a trash heap, rising out of the sea. I thought it looked a little like Charlie's head.

So I sent the *Ghost* a picture of Charlie and a close-up of the marketing shot with the CabanaBoat taking a family to an island. And to my delight she scooted over to the island and started sniffing it. Then Riley sent her whatever message had sent her toward Nepheli in the first place and she resumed her previous route.

She followed Nepheli through the maze of waterways and little islands that made up the yoreshore south of Miami. It quickly became crowded, labyrinthine, not flat and open like the Everglades, and the circuit barge disappeared from view. I had never been here before, and I had never heard of people living out here. They clearly had once: some of the waterways were straight, organized on grids, like canals. I thought that maybe these were the ruins of old suburbs, the way that some of the canals ended in cul-de-sacs.

I wondered if the *Ghost* could track Nepheli by following the path in the water that was dredged, that showed signs of human life. I realized that I was excited to sail her for the first time, trying to think of ways to communicate that to her. Riley helped me choose the images, we sent them to her, and, sure enough, we caught a glimpse of the circuit barge on the next bend down the canal she chose.

Riley stayed close, hovered over me. I didn't mind so much. He had lied and made promises that were likely unkeepable. The UltiMon card felt closer to a shared delusion than a solution.

But to talk to her was real, a gift he'd given freely. And I was grateful.

The *Ghost* and I stayed on the same page right up until we came upon the little harbor.

It wasn't so much a harbor as it was the terminus of the dredged canal. I counted three total seacraft tied up to stakes driven into the dirt along the bank. One of them was Nepheli's circuit barge. The nose of *Bulls on Parade* bobbed up and down in the water. A trail cut through the mangrove line and into the interior, blazed wide enough to fit an atmo-breaker. I couldn't see where it went.

There were two other boats in the harbor and one of them, a black one with a thin stiletto prow, was floating around the circuit barge. As soon as it came into view, the *Ghost* charged toward it, full speed.

"What's happening?" I asked Riley, panicked.

"I don't know," he replied. He sounded calm, but he was gripping the lip of the console more tightly than he had been.

I remembered last night, the sound of her hull screeching against concrete, so I ran the emergency stop routine that Charlie had given me. She listened but jolted to a halt so quickly that I heard a thump, followed by Myra yelling "Ow" from the couch.

The black boat stayed where it was. I expected whoever was sailing it to come out onto the deck and tell us to back the hell up. But nobody did. And it didn't back out, either.

It just floated there.

I thought maybe it had just come loose. But I could have sworn I saw it move.

I tried to back her out of the harbor. "She won't move."

"Hmm," said Riley. "Remember that second important thing?"

"What's that?"

"Trust. Trust is very important."

"You think she doesn't trust me?"

"No, *you* don't trust *her*."

"What was I supposed to do? She was going to ram right into that boat."

"Maybe. Maybe not. Listen, I know it's hard. And it's something that Nepheli doesn't get either. It's the thing that only I get, and why you should only listen to me when you're learning how to live with a semi-sent. When I break with the *Bull*, and we get past the Karman, sometimes I just let go of the controls entirely."

"Are you even piloting her if you don't have your hands on the controls?"

"If I kept telling her to stop and start and getting in her way, that'd confuse her, and we'd be much more likely to blow. You gotta think of yourself like a cool boss. In charge, but chilled out."

"So I should think of a cool, chill way to get her to back up out of this harbor?"

"No," Riley said. "You should keep Neph boxed in, just like this. Just 'til we get answers."

"You don't really think they got Maurice to pull you from the Canaveral, do you?"

"I don't think anything," he said. "But why would they bring the *Bull* all the way out here? What even is this place?"

"I know," said Myra.

We looked at her. She pointed above the mangrove line. Rising above the treetops were a crop of towering limestone slabs. Some were crumbling, some were taller than others. Some were topped with sculptures: a stone moon at the top, a ring of giant stone chairs.

"This is Coral Castle."

It was a short but slippery jump from the prow of the *Ghost* to the butt of the *Bull*. Riley did a couple test runs to the end of the *Ghost* to psych himself up, and it reminded me of Edgar, pulling himself endlessly into darkness.

"Watch out for gators," I said. "Your Triss Mackey gator rescue policy only covers the first incident."

Riley made a face and took a leap, missed, and hit the water, but quickly clambered up the fuselage. He gave his breaker a little pat on the cockpit and climbed onto the barge and disappeared into the cabin.

"They're not here," he called out soon after. He looked into the black boat, but the windows were tinted. The other boat was a big fishing trawler with all its fishing equipment removed, and it seemed abandoned too. Its aft deck was facing us and the name on the back read *Instant Pot*.

Riley disembarked and marched down the path through the tree line. I called after him to wait, but he didn't listen.

"Let him go," said Myra. "Let's go panther hunting."

"Can you even stand?"

"Sure," she said, and shakily got to her feet. "But I might need you to throw me to shore."

I grabbed my Knuckles from the power pad and checked the primers to make sure the stunners were charged. Then I put them both on. Neither of them would be much good against panthers, or even against more than a couple people, but I felt safer with them on.

The black boat hadn't moved, and still nobody had come out on deck, so it must have been empty. But the windows were tinted, and I couldn't shake the feeling that somebody *was* on board, watching us. Just to be safe, I made sure not to turn my back on it.

I sent the *Ghost* a message to stay put. I tried to seem like a cool boss, which was difficult to do with images. Then I pulled out her little mobile gangplank and attached it to the aft deck. I helped Myra over.

"How do you even know what Coral Castle looks like?" I asked her when we were safely on the other side.

"Kohl described it to me," she said. "He said it was just like this. Stone sculptures in a ring, out in the yoreshore. Panthers stalking around it at night."

"He said he was living out here? By himself?"

"No, I don't think so. He made it sound like a community of some kind. Self-sufficient."

"He said what you wanted to hear."

"Maybe, but he was really specific. And look."

We'd followed Riley down the path, which ended at a printed gate that was now open. The limestone sculptures were encircled by shorter limestone walls. On the inside were a half dozen printed shacks. Only these were neatly kept, organized by a rough street grid that led to a big shack in the very center.

It was all relatively new. The overgrowth had been cut back to the other side of the limestone walls. We passed Riley, rummaging around in the nearest shack.

"Where is everybody?" he exclaimed. He didn't wait around for an answer. He was going door to door, looking for Nepheli. I stuck to Myra, who was looking around, fascinated.

"It's a little town," she said, in awe.

"But why here?"

She didn't answer. She just took it all in.

Myra walked through the printed gate on the other side, which opened up onto a beach. She saw something and kept walking toward it.

"Where are you going?" I exclaimed, following her onto the sand. It was black. Myra's foot sank into it. With some effort she pulled it out and continued. I bent down and touched it with my finger. It was the same color and consistency as the sand on Key West.

And then, with dreadful premonition, I looked up. The beach was facing water that led to the oceanside yoreshore. The mangrove line was thinner, the coast was closer. Myra peered up at a crumbled limestone sculpture and I saw, beyond her, at an uncertain distance, Maurice's construction titan.

I watched it long enough to confirm that it was heading right for us.

"Myra . . ." I said, my mouth dry. She wasn't paying attention to me. On her outstretched hand was a purple bird.

"Triss," she squealed. "Look at this! It's a parakeet of some kind. Look at the color. It's beautiful."

"We have to go," I said, moving toward her quickly.

Startled, the bird took flight, circled around us once and shat directly on Myra's head.

She glared at me. I was about to apologize, to show her the titan, when out of the corner of my eye I saw something leap up from the undergrowth and sprint toward us.

For a second I was afraid that it really was Myra's mythical panther. But it was just a woman, medium-sized, running at us with a knife in her hand.

Running for Myra, I realized. The knife was long and cruel, made for gutting big things.

I pivoted and tackled, got her around the ankles just in time and brought her down. The knife flew to the ground. She kicked at me fiercely and I grappled at her with one hand and primed a stunner with the other. She was barefoot and covered so thickly in the viscous black sand that it was tough to get a grip. She looked more frightened than fierce, but I brought my stunner up anyway.

Myra backed up to the shoreline.

I heard a click behind me. The woman froze and went limp. Lunar titanium has a particular twang when it strikes itself. A hammer being cocked on a lunar metal gun is sustained and high-pitched, like a tuning fork.

"Gotcha," said a voice, painfully familiar. Soft and gritty, like wet sand.

# 7

Kohl marched us back through the little makeshift town. I helped Myra along. The other woman put her hands on her head and walked in front of us. Myra stared at her, and I recognized the look, since she still gives it to me sometimes. It was utter fascination, attraction. This woman who just tried to kill her had passed the audition and if we lived she would soon be added to Myra's menagerie of Florida tall tales, if not her conquests.

The woman looked up. Above us were thousands of those same purple birds, nesting in the crevices of the limestone sculptures.

I glanced back at the shore. The titan was definitely getting closer.

"Why did you attack us?" Myra whispered to the woman. She didn't even sound angry, just curious. It broke the woman's trance for a moment.

"I saw him sneak up on you," she said. "I knew he'd take you."

"So why didn't you go for him?" I hissed.

"Needed your hair," she said. "Tried to cut and run." She smirked, absurdly.

Myra laughed. If she wasn't marching, she might have swooned. She touched her own hair and saw that there was bird shit on her fingers. The woman flinched. "Don't," she began, but then Kohl pushed her along.

He seemed to have recovered from his night at Key West. He was wearing tinted gogs again, but a cheaper pair than he'd had yesterday. If he was surprised to find us here, he didn't show it.

He took us back to the harbor, to the *Instant Pot*, the fishing trawler that didn't have any fishing equipment. He marched us aboard and brought us belowdecks. I was a little proud to see that the *Ghost* hadn't moved and was handily blocking all the boats in, though for once it would have been helpful for her to lose herself a bit and charge the boat, just long enough to startle Kohl so I could reach him with my stunner.

But she didn't. She floated peacefully. Perhaps she didn't realize that I was in danger.

We descended into the belly of the fishing boat and found a workshop, the walls lined with tools and printers and parts, all neatly organized and tied down.

In the very center of the workshop was a metal cage, with an elevated bench that rocked back and forth randomly. There were four people already crammed into that tight space. Riley and Nepheli were two of them, and Riley swore when he saw us. It made me a little seasick to look at the cage, until I realized that it was attached to stabilizers, and that it was really the boat that was rocking around it. It was like solving a brain teaser. Once I saw it that way I couldn't unsee that they were actually the ones who were still and I was unmoored.

I recognized one of the other two from the party on Key West: Félix, who had given me a boost onto a gravestone and a pitch. He banged on the bars and shouted at Kohl, who ignored him.

The last one was an older man with wild white dreadlocks that went past his shoulders. A stranger, but something about him was oddly familiar. His body was covered with spectacular neon tattoos—silver outlines of wrench sizes, metric conversions, rulers, and other measurements.

The something that was familiar was the tattoo on the side of his neck: a red fist holding the yellow wrench. It was the symbol of Void Warrant, that radical faction of the right-to-repair movement. I'd seen it spray-painted around Gamma's nomad camp. The man glanced at me briefly and went back to staring at the floor.

Kohl unlocked the cage and motioned the three of us in. We just barely fit. The woman climbed on top of the bench and sat cross-legged.

"Got you too, huh, Sof?" said Félix. "Figured you were hiding in the brush somewhere."

The woman grunted back.

Kohl halfway closed the cage again. "Forgot one thing," he said to me, and stretched his hand within striking range. "Give me your . . . what'd you call them? Your Knuckles? Your sticks."

I jabbed the primed stunner of my right-hand Knuckle at him. He was quick. He clawed his hand and grabbed the end of the Knuckle. His fingertips took the full shock, but I could see now there was something wrong with them—they were too smooth, too pale. The Church drones had burrowed up his fingernails, splitting them and spewing blood. These were replacements.

The stun sizzled and dissipated on them.

"You know," he said, conversationally. "My grandpa used to do security at a biotech lab in Arizona. People snuck in, stole the IP, burned it all down. He said they had these funny hidden weapons—sticks that shot out from nowhere and zappers and a bunch of other little nasty tricks." I tried to catch his arm with the other stunner. He grabbed my wrist and held it. "They're not so nasty when you can see them coming."

His fingertips dug into my flesh, hard enough to leave a mark. I winced.

"Take them off," he said again, and loosened his grip enough for me to comply. He took them and locked the door to the cage and tossed them onto a bench.

I squeezed into a spot next to Myra and saw that the older man was staring at the Knuckles.

Kohl grinned at the older man. "These new fingertips work a treat, Ermie. Grip like a trap."

The older man's name was Ermie, and he was a Void Warrant tech who built prosthetics. Gamma had brought Eli, whimpering, clutching his mangled arm, to a van. I thought I remembered the red fist and yellow wrench spray-painted on the rocks behind it.

"So what happens to us now?" asked Félix.

"Not sure," said Kohl. "That titan's on its way. I don't really know what the blast radius is when it nails those pylons down. Do you, Fey? At Key West it looked like it really blew things apart."

"You brought that thing here?" said Félix, distressed. "It'll destroy everything we built."

"Nothing personal," Kohl replied. "Just a job."

"See?" Riley said to Nepheli. "I had nothing to do with that thing showing up."

"You're still an idiot," Nepheli replied.

"Why? Because I trust you? Because I didn't go behind your back and get Maurice to kick you off the team?"

"I didn't *do* that. And if you trust me why did you follow me?"

"Quiet," said Kohl, and tapped the bars of the cage with his gun.

"Just sail us back out the canal," said Félix. "You don't even have to let us go."

"Maybe I would," said Kohl. "But I already wasted too much time. Triss here boxed me in, so now I have to figure that out." He turned toward the exit.

"Wait!" cried Félix. "What if . . . what if I told you where the money was?"

Ermie and Sofia glanced at him.

Kohl stopped and grinned and leaned on the cage bar. "What money?"

Félix swallowed. "I see how interested you get whenever I mention that we're fully funded. You're always slinking around. I never really believed that you were a believer."

"You just weren't tough enough to run me off," smirked Kohl. "Sorry. I'm calling your bluff. I don't think you got any. I've been out here for weeks and we're still living like hermit crabs. Poor Sofia over there is scraping up bird shit with her fingernails and storing it in cans. If you had it you'd have used it by now."

"We do have it," said Félix. "Really! It's just . . . it's complicated. What we're trying to do down here has never been done."

"Yeah, yeah; I know. Co-operative kumbaya living. Well now you can all sing kumbaya in here."

Myra looked green. The heat in the workshop was stifling, we were packed together like sardines and the boat was rocking around us. She closed her eyes and rested her head on my shoulder. I took her hand. While Félix and Kohl argued, I looked at the workbench, then at Ermie, who was staring at the floor.

He pulled a screwdriver out of his wild white hair and began to tap it on the bars at his feet. *Ping ping.* Just like I had seen Nepheli do earlier, while they were processing the death of Calysta Chen. Just like Eli had done, out of habit.

Eli was the son of Void Warranters, I remembered now. They had died in the crackdown that followed the John Deere riots, which had started with farmers stealing IP so they could repair their own equipment and ended with the near-total automation of American agriculture.

Ermie's tapping was a hypnotic rhythm, and I found that it was easy to focus on it, despite the bickering and the heat.

And I began to have the makings of a plan.

"Now I just gotta move Triss's damn boat out of the way," said Kohl "Or maybe I'll just take it."

He was staring at me. I was so lost in thought I almost missed my cue.

"No, please," I said, after a beat that I hoped wasn't too long. I tried to sound as convincingly distressed as possible. I wanted him to leave. I didn't believe that Kohl could take the *Ghost*. In fact, I felt fairly confident that the *Ghost* wouldn't even let him on board. Maybe this was what Riley had meant by trusting her.

Kohl took the bait. He smiled cruelly and walked out.

We were left alone.

"Does anyone have water?" I asked. Sofia nodded and pulled a small canteen from her cargo shorts and handed it to Myra.

"I'm fine," said Myra, but she took a couple grateful sips. "Nice to meet you all. Would love to hear more about this co-operative kumbaya living."

"And I'd love to tell you," said Félix. "But it looks like we won't get the chance. I'm Félix."

"Myra."

"Nice to meet you." He looked at Riley. "And you must be the famous Ortiz junior."

"Riley," said Riley.

"I knew your dad," he said. "And of course I know Nepheli. I actually helped design part of the Astro America."

"Ask him which part," muttered Sofia.

"All right you caught me," said Félix putting up his hands. "The boring part. The foundation. Sometimes if I don't say it people think I built the Waxing Moon Lounge. And I know everybody else here except you . . . Triss, you said?"

"We met last night," I replied. "You gave me a boost."

Recognition dawned on him. "That's right! CabanaBoat! You brought it here? I'd love to see it. I dragged Kohl back from the party last night and Ermie nursed him back to health. He said he got ambushed by a crazy woman who nearly clawed his eyes out. Was that you?"

"Wish it was. I just hit him in the face."

"Would like to have seen that. Sorry for the sorry welcome. Coral Castle was really something. Too bad he got you in the end. And us."

"It's not the end yet," I said. "He's not leaving. He'll be back soon. He won't be able to move my boat, so he'll try to make me do it."

"So we need a plan!" said Félix, and jumped into action. "Anybody got any ideas? Ermie, can you open the cage?"

Ermie shook his head. "It's locked both ways. Remember, you asked me to build you a brig? This is it."

Félix made a face. "What about weapons?"

Ermie nodded over at my Knuckles. "Just those. This is a workshop, not an armory."

"But you are a Void Warrant tech, aren't you?" I said. "I thought you guys built bombs out of shit and wristwatches."

"And I thought an echidna fighter would be able to disarm a leech like him," he replied. "You've forgotten your training."

"A what?" asked Félix. "Sorry. Do you guys know each other?"

"I don't have any training," I replied.

"June Mackey's grandkid, not trained?" Ermie looked incredulous. "She's the only person I ever met who called her echidnas her Knuckles. And those are hers, aren't they?"

I nodded.

"Thought she passed those on to that other kid."

"Eli," I said. "He's dead now. Thanks to you."

"Me?" His voice rose, in that old man tone where they don't know whether to be surprised or offended or surprised that someone would dare to offend them.

"You," I said firmly. "But I know how you can make it up to me."

And then, against the background noise of Nepheli and Riley bickering and Sofia pulling out all of the workshop drawers, I told him what happened to Eli in Wyoming.

Eli and I joined the Corps when we were seventeen, the same day that Gamma's camp got raided by the feds that final time. We'd missed the raid by pure chance; he and I were in a nearby town getting supplies.

I had been ready to leave for a while, actually. The van I shared with Gamma was cramped and tense. I just needed that extra push, and seeing a federal convoy speeding down the dirt road that led to our camp ended up being enough. Eli wasn't as ready, but when I walked into the local Second Civilian Conservation Corps recruitment center, he followed. We gave them three years each, and they promised Eli that they would try and keep us together, which is a promise I'm still surprised they kept.

From the beginning of our service Eli's arm gave him trouble, made him different. It was an outdated prosthetic that had been extensively tampered with. The recruiters offered him a brand-new arm after signing up but he refused it, because he wouldn't get to keep his extra flesh fingers. But Void Warrant had gone underground, Gamma had been arrested, so Eli couldn't find anyone who would even attempt to maintain it.

For the rest of that year, our duties in the Corps amounted to blazing trails and restoring ecosystems, rock climbing, and hiking, and just generally enjoying the rewilded part of the country. The debris field had shredded the Space Elevator by then, but it wasn't until the following summer that the 2C3 was militarized to assist with Consolidation.

The feds assigned us to stalk the southeast corner of Wyoming, which the vast expansion of Yellowstone Park didn't quite touch so Consolidation was technically voluntary. But it was another exceptionally dry High Plains summer, so all we had to do was park near the most vulnerable towns and wait for the prairie grass to smolder and the wildfires to do our work for us. Once a town was obliterated we would swoop in, get all the shell-shocked and newly homeless to sign some paperwork, and then cart them off to DenverDome for processing. It was a good summer for wildfires, and by August we had made almost double our quota.

It's a strange sort of plausible deniability, the Consolidator's delusion that they are there to help. It's hard to make the case that we overtly destroyed these communities: we did not bring the fires, whose path was merely predicted by our algorithms and whose intensity was reliably apocalyptic. We had no part in the quintupling of insurance premiums the previous summer when those foreseeable fires consumed two adjacent neighborhoods (the free market had taken care of that for us). We did not believe that these inferno fires could be fought in any meaningful sense—they were consistently rated above Rank 4, "past all resources" in fire-fighting parlance—but we never stood in the way of local crews in their attempts to save their homes and families, even gave them access to our predictive data though this was mostly to encourage them to leave.

But the towns blamed us, hated us, invented conspiracy theories about us, claimed that we started the fires, that we even controlled the wind. We could have had a better PR campaign, to be sure. We arrived in their towns like bad omens, often setting up camp at the highest point the same day that clouds of black smoke appeared in the distance. It was the first time most of them had ever seen anyone from the government, and so the fire was their only association. The feds had never given them anything.

They weren't quite wrong about the conspiracy theories, either. We usually targeted mining and processing towns, whose products were the rare earth metals that directly competed with the lunar mines. That wasn't a coincidence.

But I wouldn't think too much about that until I was safely through my loophole.

We came to these towns with our machines, great extractors of carbon and people. Toward the fire we launched huge open-mouthed zeppelins that rode the thermals created by the fire itself, sucking up the smoke before it could disperse too far into the atmosphere, compressing it into acrid black bricks that would often crash into people's backyards like brimstone.

Toward the town we deployed beetle domes—mobile halfway houses—that would scuttle up and down their main streets. Eli and I accompanied the beetles, knocking on doors, giving tours of dome life to whoever wanted one, though not many did.

The 2C3 had given me a gun, which at first I'd found bewildering, but the longer I spent in these hostile towns the more often my awareness, and even my hand, would stretch down toward my waist. One day a crowd met us in the street, loud enough and close enough that the beetle dome shuddered to a halt. I gripped the handle.

Eli saw my hand and stepped in front of me. He went out to meet them, while I stayed behind. He was wearing Gamma's Knuckles, which were weapons some of them recognized, and they softened when he held his clearly bootleg hand out and spoke to them, like them, nodding and squinting like Gamma used to do.

They dispersed, slowly, warily. He came back to me.

"What did they want?" I asked.

"They asked me if we were the same people that came through last summer, when the town across the river burned."

"What did you say?"

"I said we were different."

He left that night to go for a walk and didn't come back.

Before, when we were just camp orphans, I'd thought of him as the follower, the complacent one. But in the Corps I was the one who assimilated. Eli had kept his true arm, after all, and not the Corps upgrade. He was a nomad to the core, Void Warrant. He clung to me because I was the last he had of his community, and community was important to him.

It's what broke him, in the end.

We were short on time in the cage, so I blew through a lot of that history to get to the hard part. By the time I did, everyone was listening. Nepheli and Riley weren't bickering anymore. Myra had only heard some bits and pieces. I didn't want to tell it, but for the plan to work I knew Ermie needed the details. As bad as it was in there, hot and cramped and humid and spinning, the telling would have been worse in the dark. Kohl had been considerate enough to leave the lights on.

When I finished, Ermie nodded, cleared Sofia off his workbench, and built what I asked him to.

We waited. Sofia found a pair of scissors in a drawer and took her canteen back from Myra.

"May I?" she said, gesturing to the lock of shit-covered hair.

"I suppose," said Myra. "But why do you need it?"

"Studying it."

"Those purple birds, you mean? I've never seen anything like them."

"You see a lot of birds?"

"I work for Nativitee. We're always looking for native species."

"Well, hate to disappoint your Consolidated overlords, but these birds are definitely not native. They're a kind of parakeet, I think, but the color is GMO. Probably they descended from someone's escaped pets. Typical Florida story. But that doesn't mean they're not special." Sofia grinned and held up Myra's smelly lock of hair.

"Their . . . excrement?" Myra said, wrinkling their nose. "Is special?"

"Notice anything strange about this place?"

"The sculptures?"

Sofia nodded. "The sculptures are part of it. Seems like they're the perfect nesting ground for them. But no. What's special is that I've been here six months and I haven't seen a single python."

Myra's eyes got wide and she gave a low whistle. I couldn't help myself. "What's so strange about that?" I asked.

Myra answered me. "This area below Miami, where the rock ridge is low but still forms a sort of barrier is probably the closest we're ever going to get to getting something like the Everglades back. And a lot of native Florida species were only native to the Everglades. The problem is, any ecosystem Nativitee tries to rewild around here gets immediately dominated by pythons."

"And pythons aren't native?" I asked.

"They've been here at least a century," said Myra. "So maybe they qualify. But no, technically not."

"I don't really give a shit if they're native or not," said Sofia. "They eat almost everything. Without a bigger predator to take care of them they can decimate a system and throw it out of balance."

"Like a panther," I said.

"Yes!" squealed Myra, as the mother does to the toddler who does something cute but stupid. "Like a panther! Exactly, Triss! That's why Nativitee wants one so badly."

"No panthers here," said Sofia "But there's something about these birds the pythons don't like. I think it's their shit. Whatever it is, it could be a real breakthrough."

"To what?" I asked.

Sofia smiled, wistfully. "To something new."

"Something new," echoed Myra. "That's what I want to build too! I call it the Third Way."

"Sure," said Sofia. "We've been calling it a co-op. Félix here organizes it. Ermie builds it. I'm one of the ones finding out what we can do with it."

"One of? Who else is there?"

"Well there was Kohl, I guess. But I have a feeling he's not renewing his membership."

"He told me there were panthers here," said Myra.

Sofia laughed. "I told him that to scare him off, one night when he followed me into the brush and got too close. I've been here six months and haven't seen a whisker."

"Oh," said Myra, sadly. And it was another tone I was familiar with, that came with the dashing of yet another potential Third Way. Sofia held up the lock of hair again.

"Birds, babe. Trust me. Birds are better."

We waited long enough that I did begin to worry that I had been wrong, that Kohl had been able to take the *Ghost* after all, that any second now the construction titan would blow us away. But then we heard agitated footsteps on the deck. He appeared soon after. He was soaking wet. I smirked.

"Did she throw you overboard?"

He frowned. "Wouldn't even let me get close to her."

"Then why are you all wet?"

"None of your business. Now I need you to come out of there and move her for me."

I blinked, and froze, acted like I wasn't desperate to end this.

"Now," he said. "Or I'll finish what I started yesterday."

Myra whimpered, convincingly.

"Fine," I said, and stood up. "Just don't hurt anybody."

He unlocked the cage and let me out. We walked past the bench where my Knuckles had been tossed. He was distracted enough that maybe I could have grabbed them.

But for this, I didn't need them.

He brought me on deck, then on shore. The little gangplank to the *Ghost* had been thrown into the water, and she was nestled even closer to Nepheli's circuit barge.

The titan was much, much closer. There was an entire island between it and us, but it loomed tall enough to block out the sun. And it rumbled, a low, steady mechanical keen that sent waves of Sofia's purple birds bursting from the sculptures and over our heads. I hadn't been close enough to hear it, even on Key West.

"I should have been gone by now," muttered Kohl, looking at the titan. "Just move it for me and let me go, and you can go back and let the others out."

"I don't believe you," I said. "If you didn't need me you would have left us."

"I didn't kill you last night, or Myra. I could have."

"Maybe. But you won't do us any favors."

"You were just waiting for the chance to do the same to me," he argued. "You wouldn't let me near that Ked. We were supposed to be partners."

"That's not true," I replied. "I would have split it with you."

"Then I guess I'm smarter than you after all."

"But still stupid enough to work for the Church of the Invisible Hand after they cut your fingers off. They're the ones operating that titan, you know."

"You think they gave me a choice?" he hissed. "Months ago I agreed to do one job for them, and I did it. I pulled up those barrels of black stuff from a cache over there and hid them in the brush, but they never paid me, and they didn't leave me alone. Last night they followed me back here and told me to open those barrels and spread what I found out on the beach. Tomorrow I bet they'll make me do something else, unless I get far, far away."

"You'll have to get pretty far. Looks like they're taking over the yoreshore. And you're helping them."

"You're right," he said. "Maybe there's no such thing as far enough. I thought if I brought them something big, like the Ked, they'd forget about me." He stared at me, and through his tinted gogs I could see the outlines of something where his tear ducts had been, something silver. "But they don't forget."

"The black stuff," I said. "What is it?"

"Ask the mastermind inside. Félix. He might be all kumbaya living now, but he designed that goo. For your fancy friend's dad, or so I hear."

"Edgar?"

Kohl nodded. "Dive down to the base of the Astro America sometime, you'll see it there. It's some sort of next-level concrete, protects against storm surges. Terrible for the environment. Pisses off the feds. If they caught me with it they'd lock me up, or at least kick me out of OrlanDome. Good thing I don't want to be there anyway. Too many people in too many domes across this great country of ours that won't be very happy to see me."

"But you're such a charmer."

"Just wade out there and move your boat."

I turned instead and ran toward the mangrove line, toward destruction.

Kohl caught up with me, easily. I struggled, until I felt the fingertips digging into my arm again. He pulled me close to him, tried to force me around. He smelled the same as he had on the *Ghost*, body odor and seawater, plus something else—something strangely familiar, sickly sweet. Just like the air from Edgar's orange tank.

I pulled out the tiny bit of solder on which Ermie had imprinted what I'd asked, and I put my hand over his and found the tiny diagnostic port on the tip of his silicon pinkie, and slid the metal in.

And the fingers jolted away.

It was one thing to describe it, but another to see it again. Kohl looked so much like Eli did, when he realized what was happening *to* him was being done *by* him. There had been a sick determination to it, a look disturbing enough to haunt me all these years, and it was just as chilling now, even on the face of someone who I thought deserved it.

But no, nobody deserved this.

The night after we met the crowd in the street, Eli left camp to go for a walk. He went in the direction of town. While he was gone, the wind made a sudden change, and the fire sped toward us. It stopped at the little muddy river that formed the border of the town, and I saw the line of fifty-foot trees ignite like Roman candles, bursting embers that our data predicted would blow across the banks within the hour, at which point the town would be lost. We had strict orders to stay in camp and only help the people who came to us. The klaxons went off all across the town but Eli didn't come back. I went after him.

I brought my gun.

The smoke crossed the river first, a thick blanket that blotted out the setting sun. It wasn't yet late enough for the streetlights to come on, so partway down the hill I found that I was walking in almost total darkness. I followed the street from our camp to the little downtown, where we had been just that afternoon.

The beetle dome was right where we had left it, in the middle of the street. The few vehicles that were still evacuating had to drive on the sidewalk to get around it. The beetles were built to withstand temperatures in the thousands of degrees, and we left them so they could be used as an emergency shelter. Of course, this only applied to anyone that was willing to sign the Consolidation contract. As a result, they typically stayed empty until the fire passed through, since anyone too stubborn to stay when the fire was at their literal doorstep wasn't the type to Consolidate under any circumstances anyway.

But when I jogged past it I saw that the door was wide open.

The persistent campfire stench that had enveloped the town since our arrival dispersed once I stepped inside, it had no chance against an HVAC strong enough to sustain life in a vacuum.

But Eli still smelled like smoke, and so it was easy enough to find him, hunched over the guts of a security terminal, a cable pulled from his arm like a loose vein.

"What are you doing?" My voice wavered. I was startled to see him like that.

He looked up. He'd triggered his baton. I'd startled him too.

"It's here," he said. "Just like they said."

"What is?"

"Last summer, before they recruited us, the feds came and picked off another little town across the river. Close to here. They had friends and family there. The feds wouldn't tell them where they went. They said they'd have to Consolidate to get that information. But it's right here, they have it. They're just keeping it from them. It's leverage."

"I'm sure they have a good reason. Security, or compatibility, or . . ."

"They didn't keep them together at all, they split everyone up. We've been sending these people all over the country, and they can't even stay in touch."

"So what are you doing?"

"I'm going to take this data and give it to them."

"It's too late. The town's burning already. We have to get back."

"Triss," he said. "They just want to see each other again. That can't be too much to ask, can it?"

He stuck the cable from his arm into an open port on the terminal.

"They won't let you take that," I said, though I did not quite know how I knew that. An instinct, perhaps, ingrained in me by Gamma, that it was more difficult to operate unnoticed by the feds than it seemed.

And, sure enough, they didn't.

Instead of just rejecting Eli's prosthetic, the beetle tried to force it into its system, just like we were forcing the town to Consolidate. But Eli's prosthetic wasn't compatible with the federal design. It wasn't compatible with any design, it had been jailbroken and integrated with his own biology.

It wiped his arm, installed its own operating system, did a reboot, and then a full diagnostic.

He couldn't control himself. He took the flesh fingers on his prosthetic hand and bent them all the way back, snapping them to touch the silicon. He screamed. I dove for the cable jack.

And then the lights went out.

The fires had come. We couldn't smell them, but the intense heat had triggered the beetle's lockdown. I fumbled around in the dark until he struck me. I heard a metal clang as my gun clattered to the ground. Terrified, I scrambled for a corner of the room and spent the night listening to the last of my community tear himself apart. The inferno raged around us.

By contrast, I watched Kohl writhing on the ground and wondered if I could just let him die. One of his pinkies had already popped out of its socket and was oozing in the grass. I'd told Ermie to put in a kill routine on the other end of the solder, but if Kohl lost the other pinkie I didn't know how I would run it.

And that would be a way to kill him where I wouldn't have to take much blame. Like how he had planned on killing us just by leaving us in the cage.

In the end I put a foot on Kohl's chest and grabbed his other arm and popped the pinkie all the way back in and then the solder. He shuddered several times and was still. He appeared to be breathing and I decided I'd made the right decision, though he was now my responsibility.

I took the cage key from him and tossed his gun in the water and left him on the shore. I released everyone. As soon as we left the *Instant Pot* we felt a great shudder in the earth when the titan made landfall. We quickened our pace.

Riley helped me drag Kohl aboard the *Ghost,* who obediently inched back up to shore when she saw me. Sofia helped Myra aboard as well. Nepheli got back to the circuit barge, Ermie took charge of the *Instant Pot*, and Félix manned the black boat that Kohl had meant to steal, and we got out of there, back the way we came, down the dredged canal.

Félix led us to a little inlet and motioned for us all to get behind the shell of an old concrete structure that was there, just like the *Ghost* had done last night to protect us from the noise of the race. He pulled his boat alongside the *Ghost* and hopped on board.

And we watched the titan destroy Coral Castle.

Its spidery limbs chewed up the mangroves and cypress that separated the black beach from the square of sculptures, Sofia and Félix and Ermie's little town. Flocks of purple birds burst from the sculptures like smoke from chimneys. They flew as a single cloud at us, and then past us. Sofia cried out, and swore, and reached out her arms as if to catch them. They turned inland and were soon gone, quick enough to miss the titan rise up on all its limbs and bring the entirety of its weight down on the black beach and the limestone sculptures, pounding them in several dozen seismic, pylon-deploying strokes.

In the end there was nothing. Nothing of any substance at all, except a grid of massive concrete pylons sunk into a swamp of black sand, amid a radius of rocky pulp. You would never believe that anyone had ever lived there.

"This," said Myra. "Is what the yoreshore will be, once the feds go. This, everywhere."

Félix nodded in solemn agreement.

As if in reply, the titan rose on its half-dozen haunches, deposited some amount of sludgy material out of its exhaust, and lumbered off, not quite the way it had come. Northbound, back toward the oceanside yoreshore, tearing up a fresh path of mangroves.

"Where's it going now?" Riley asked.

"The Church gave it to Maurice for two days," I said. "He's probably making use of that time."

"Are we safe back here?"

Félix nodded. "It will only build where the black composite is. Everywhere else in the yoreshore the ground is too soft for it."

"Kohl said you invented that black stuff," I said. "Is that true?"

Félix hesitated. "For the Astro America, to protect it. Not for this."

I noticed that he was wearing work gloves, bright purple ones. I thought that was important, but I couldn't exactly remember why.

"The Flaco's gone now," said Sofia.

"The what?" I asked.

"No," said Félix. "We never let it begin. Maybe Kohl was right about one thing. Maybe we spent too much time spinning our wheels. Maybe this is the kick we need to make it reality." He turned to me.

"You've saved our lives already. I hate to ask more of you, but, will you help us?"

He put his hands on my shoulders. That name, "FLACO," was stitched on the back of each glove in gold lettering. I remembered where I'd seen those hands before—they were wrapped around my neck while I was drifting in and out of sleep, they pulled a silver chain over my head in the final incident video on Edgar's mask.

"I'd be glad to," I replied, and invited him into the lounge.

# 8

"'FLACO' actually stands for Florida Aquatic Co-op," said Félix. "A floating community, dedicated to maximizing the power of the individual to benefit the collective. Got a nice ring to it, don't you think?"

"Sure does," I replied, with a false cheer that I hoped obscured my nefarious intentions. I led him to the couch because it was in the corner and Riley and I could block both of the exits to the deck. Myra was comforting Sofia on Félix's boat. Ermie had retreated back to his workshop, and Nepheli was on shore working on *Bulls on Parade*. Riley had tied Kohl to the deck.

"Excuse me a second," I said. "There's a pretty nice rum collection in that cabinet over there. Help yourself."

I grabbed Edgar's mask and pulled Riley over to the prow of the ship, out of view of the lounge but in sight of the deck, in case Félix tried to leave. I showed Riley the last video on the mask. We watched it, one after the other.

The incident began and Edgar was already dead. His hands floated limply above his mask, undulating back and forth. They looked black, decayed already, but it might have just been a trick of the light. Another diver shook him by the shoulders. He had his mask on, but even so I was sure it was Félix. The general build was the same, and he wore the same purple gloves with "FLACO" stitched on the back. He reached around out of the camera's view and pulled something off of Edgar's neck. We caught a quick glimpse of a strand of silver and blue, and then a rectangle that glinted holographic colors, an upright turtle wearing a bobby cap.

Kappacop.

Then the video cut out.

Riley pulled off the mask. "So Félix did it. He killed him."

"We don't know that," I said. "Maybe he just found him."

"You heard him. He blames my dad for spreading that black stuff around."

"The Church hired Kohl to spread it around."

"My dad was working with the Church, wasn't he?"

"He was planning to, I guess. But the timing doesn't really add up. And if Félix killed him because he was angry at him, then why did he take the card? How did he even know about it? You saw the video, it was completely hidden. He had to pull it out from under your dad's wetsuit."

"I told you," said Riley. "My dad wore it all the time. He probably saw it some other time."

"And why did Edgar erase his location? What was he diving for in the first place?"

"I don't know!" he cried. "He never told me anything!"

"Well, what did Nepheli tell you?"

"That the old man brought them to Coral Castle," he said, glumly. "And that I just fucked it all up. For all of us."

I peered around the corner to look into the lounge. Félix was still sitting on the couch, drinking rum. He was maybe two-thirds Edgar's size, and didn't seem capable of overpowering him, even underwater.

Kohl stirred against the railing. Félix had promised him money as a last-ditch effort to convince him to let us go. He must have meant the card.

"It doesn't matter," I said, though I thought about what I might have to do to get that money myself, and I found that part of me wished he actually *had* killed Edgar. "He has the card and we need it."

Through the windows, I thought Kohl was grinning at me. I'd let him keep his tinted gogs. I was scared of what his eyes looked like.

"Watch Félix for a second," I said to Riley. "Make sure he doesn't leave."

I hopped over to the *Instant Pot* before he could answer.

I found Ermie back in his workshop. I'd noticed he hadn't come on deck to watch the titan destroy Coral Castle with us. He was dismantling something on his bench in the cage where we had so recently all been trapped. It was cool down there now. He had the fans going, and the bench smelled like rubbing alcohol, though underneath it I could still detect a whiff of mass sweat. I heard the double-ping again, that Void Warrant rhythm, and I saw that he was taking apart my broken Knuckle.

My Knuckles were what I'd come for. I didn't think I'd need them to overpower Félix, but if I was about to turn on the people of Coral Castle this was my only chance to get them back. And maybe they'd intimidate him into just giving us the card.

Ermie looked up. He didn't seem surprised to see me. I came right up to the bars of the cage. I would have grabbed them off the table if he didn't already have one of them in pieces. I didn't like him touching them, even if he might have built them originally. He spoke first.

"I've been thinking on what you said to me." *Ping ping.* He spoke slowly, in a measured tone. "That I killed that boy. Eli."

The splintered remains of the baton were laid out on his work mat like a shattered black mosaic.

"You built his arm," I said. "His arm killed him."

*Ping ping.*

"I remember him," he said. "Remember you too, a little bit. You were just kids."

"We grew up fast. Didn't have anyone to raise us."

"He died free. He didn't Consolidate."

"He would have been better off if he had," I said.

"If you really thought that, you'd be in a dome now, letting the feds take care of you. Not out here with your grandmother's echidnas. What are you doing out here, anyway? That's what I'm trying to figure out."

"I'm a salvagia diver."

"Salvagia. Nostalgic salvage. Dangerous work. Got a nice boat, must do well."

"Beats getting shot or torn apart for stealing tech from feds and corps."

"You think we free IP for the money?" he said, disbelieving. "Didn't your Gamma teach you anything?"

"She was too busy trying to hold the camp together."

Ermie grunted, frustrated. "She was a real echidna fighter. Fearsome. Echidna herself, reincarnated. Do you even know why we call them echidnas?"

I shook my head. I'd heard the term before around the camp. There had been something too reverential about it. I preferred the term Knuckles, since it made them feel more like a part of me.

"Echidna was a monster, with a pack of monster children, all with special powers—Hydra, Chimera, Cerberus, bunch of others. Echidnas are modular weapons. You pack them with all sorts of things and conceal them until you need to be your own special kind of monster."

"Concealing them is mostly what I do with them," I said. "I don't go looking for fights."

"But here you are," he replied. "Nobody ever sees an echidna fighter coming, because nobody knows exactly what an echidna fighter is carrying. Your Gamma liked to use sticks and taser. Unusual combination, but she liked to work up close. She's the only person I met who snuck into a federal reserve."

"So she stole money as well as tech."

"She'd be dead if she'd stolen anything. She just wanted to prove she could do it. That rocket ship out there? There must be at least two dozen liberated patents stuffed inside of her. Pressure sensors, weather sensors, particle density scanners, pattern parsers . . ."

*Semi-sentience,* I thought.

"More than a few of those patents have your Gamma's block-chain on them," he said. "She always got the good stuff, the stuff that they really didn't want us to have. And if I do my job right it might just give us the power to float through that debris field up there."

"If you'd done your job right on Eli, then a reinstall wouldn't have split him open," I said, leaning on the cage bars, pulling him out of his glory days.

He sighed and put his screwdriver down.

"I suppose you're right," he said. He met my stare and held it 'til the fight in me dimmed a bit, and then he spoke again. "I'm just one guy, with one bench. There's less left of Void Warrant than the team it takes to build the pinkie finger on one fed prosthetic, but no matter. I'll carry his death, if you want me to. And I'll fix your echidnas—excuse me, your Knuckles—even though an echidna fighter should fix their own. Then I'll teach you how to fix them, and I'll teach you to fight with them. Proper fighting, echidna fighting. This I'm willing to do, for your Gamma and for your friend. This I'd swear to do, and swear to do better by you than I did by him."

I hadn't expected that. I leaned back from the cage. I'd been considering snatching as many pieces as I could and dashing out of there.

"That's . . . something," I said.

"I told you; I've been thinking on it."

I thought on it, too.

"And then what happens after?" I asked. "I join Void Warrant? Break into OrlanDome while the feds are pulling out and steal IP for you? For your Flaco?"

"Freeing IP is about moving the needle," he said. "Moving power away from those who have it to those who need it. Your Gamma was a woman who moved the needle. Her work gives us the chance to make our own way, to dream of something better. Your friend Eli died because he was trying to move the needle, too. Doesn't that mean anything to you?"

I thought of Eli then, and Myra, pursuing her Third Way, disappointed at every turn. I thought of Coral Castle, destroyed just minutes ago by a machine that a thousand Ermies couldn't build. As far as I had ever seen, the needle never moved far enough to make a difference.

"Keep the Knuckles," I said. "You're used to taking things that aren't yours anyway."

I left him then. Maybe I would find a way to take them later. Or maybe without them I could finally forget.

Kohl was awake when I hopped back onto the *Ghost*. It was afternoon now and past the hottest part of the day, but I could feel the heat of the deck through my shoes. It wasn't nearly as stifling as it had been in that cage, though. Riley had left a bottle of water for him and I gave him some. He still reeked of Edgar's breathing tank.

"Why do you smell like that?" I asked.

"Like what?" Kohl slurred his words a bit, like he had something caught in his throat.

*Like rotting flowers, like the peat of the Everglades covered in sugar, like a corpse in the water.* "Sweet and dead," I said.

He smirked. "I guess I've been spending too much time around these Flaco folks. Sweet and dead is all they'll be soon enough."

"The titan's come and gone."

"I meant you. What are you still doing here, if not waiting to fleece them?"

"Félix is pitching the Flaco to me."

"Sure he is. You save his life and your reward is a lecture. You and I are the same. Solo predators. If he's in there, why are you out here? Tell you what I think: you think he's got a score, and you're out here trying to work up the nerve to take it from him. I thought he was lying about the money, but maybe you know something I don't."

He pulled against his bonds. He tried to whisper, but it came out wet.

"How will you do it? You still got my gun?"

"I threw it in the water."

"Stupid. But you kept me around, and that was smart. Let me go and we'll split it."

"Just like the Ked."

"It's different this time. Now I know better than to cross you."

"What good are you to me with no fingers? You tried to kill everyone here with full fingers and couldn't even manage a single one."

"What I lack physically I make up for in no shits given. You don't want to handle them rough, fine. But I can."

He snickered at that, right up until I flicked the nub where his pinkie used to be and he screeched. Hurting him felt good. If I spoke again I was afraid I'd agree with him.

Because I did think the Coral Castle people were weak, too trusting. Félix had taken Kohl back from the party and Ermie had fixed him, without asking anything about what he was doing there. If they had, they might have figured out that he was working with the Church and saved Coral Castle. But more likely he would have just tried to kill them sooner, and if I hadn't been there he would have succeeded. Ermie was a nomad thief, and nobody protected them. I knew that from experience.

The truth was, if not Kohl, if not me, then someone, some wandering warlord, would come along and seize whatever they built, whatever they had. If I could use their money to save the *Floating Ghost*, something that really existed and that I could protect, wasn't that a better use of it than wasting it trying to build something that would fail, or flood, or be destroyed?

Besides, it was all an act. It was a lie. Félix had killed Edgar Ortiz. Probably, anyway. Even if he hadn't, he'd stolen the card in the first place, so what right did he have to keep it?

I was running out of time. The hottest part of the day had already passed. The *Ghost* would die tomorrow. If I could get the money myself I owed it to her to do so.

I snuck around to the aft deck and slipped in quietly and sat at the cockpit. I scrolled through the marketing materials I had uploaded and sent the *Ghost* a single image of a CabanaBoat, floating alone.

"Take me to a quiet place," I muttered to her. "Somewhere out of the way."

She whined her outboards, but didn't budge.

I tried again, a different image. I told her to go find the island that looked like Charlie's head. I told her to pull up her anchor and go. But she wouldn't.

"I'm trying to save you, you tub!" I hissed.

I heard Riley excuse himself in the lounge. He must have heard her outboards and identified it as semi-sent talk. He found me soon after.

"What are you doing?" he asked. "Did you sneak aboard your own boat?"

"She's not listening to me."

"Are you trying to tell her to leave?"

"Just to go somewhere where we can have a conversation."

He looked at me, sadly.

"I'm . . . sorry about your friend," he said, quietly. It shocked me enough to look at him.

I was surprised to find no fight in him anymore, but I realized that he'd been that way since we were in the cage together. Something had happened when he'd finally found Nepheli. The cocky atmo-breaker, the man who'd commandeered my boat, was gone, replaced by someone who looked at me now with something that seemed very much like pity, for me and for himself.

But I gripped the cockpit and gritted my teeth and tried to control my temper. No matter. I didn't need him anymore. I'd never done well with partners anyway.

"I'm not going to hurt him," I said. "I won't have to, anyway. We just have to scare him enough."

"She probably doesn't want to leave Myra," he replied. "Remember Myra?"

I hesitated. I was pretending that I was giving her some private time to get to know Sofia, but I didn't want her to watch me do this. She had seen Coral Castle destroyed, the Third Way wiped out, but she wouldn't approve of this, even if it was to save the *Ghost*.

"We're coming back for her," I said.

"Triss," he replied. He put his hand on mine. "Stop. You don't want to do this."

"This is what *you* wanted me to do, remember? You said when you had an idea, you went scorched earth with it. Well, this is scorched earth."

"I was wrong. I was wrong about everything."

"Félix—"

"Needs your help."

"What?"

"He told me everything, Triss. I believe him. And . . . and I think you should."

Félix made us all fresh drinks. Sofia and Myra returned to the *Ghost*, looking cozier than when they'd left. Sofia held one of those purple parrots in her hands by the wings, stroking its feathers. Her eyes were puffy like she'd been crying.

Through the window in the lounge I saw that Nepheli was using the crane on the circuit barge to set *Bulls on Parade* up on the shore. As far as I could tell they hadn't spoken to any of us since we'd left Coral Castle.

Everyone sat except for me. I stood, itching for Félix to get around to it.

"I met Edgar maybe five years ago," he began. "He hired me to work on the Astro America. I was barely out of school."

"Oh!" Myra perked up. "Where'd you go?" She loved asking people about their education, which was how you knew she'd come from the calmer Consolidated states in the Northeast. To her perpetual disappointment I had actually never stepped foot inside a physical classroom.

"UPR Río Piedras," said Félix. "Masters in Speculative Urban Planning specializing in Materials Science." Myra looked sufficiently impressed. "My thesis was on sea walls, and through my research I got connected to Edgar. He hired me to develop something to reinforce the foundation of the Astro America from getting pummeled during the Florida mean season. Nobody had ever built anything like it in the yoreshore before, and I thought it might be impossible; I thought it was too big. But I liked Edgar. He was a dreamer, and he was good at getting other folks to dream too. So I dreamed big and did my job."

"And created that black stuff," I said.

Félix nodded. "My research was an essential part of it, I hate to say. I wish I could take it back. I wouldn't have dared to develop that sealant without Edgar's encouragement, but I think it's important that you know that he decided that it was too destructive to use."

"What does this have to do with the card?" I demanded, losing my patience a little again.

"He's getting to it," said Riley. "Hold your horses."

Félix nodded. "You said I could pitch the Flaco to you, this is part of the pitch. It's all connected."

"I want to hear about the Flaco," said Myra. "Don't mind Triss's bad manners. Please, continue."

"Edgar and I had another thing in common," said Félix. "He fled Miami as a young boy, after Sweeps Week. That was when six hotels in South Beach all collapsed in the same week, including the Fontainebleau. My grandfather was from Miami, too; he was older than Edgar, but he stayed for another ten years, until SuperCane Kermit finally forced him to flee to PR."

"For ten years?" exclaimed Myra. "After Sweeps Week? How?"

"He lived offshore," said Félix. "On a houseboat, in a community of houseboats in a little rundown marina called Dinner Key. Didn't really think of himself as being from Miami, really. The night the Fontainebleau collapsed? He always said he slept through it.

"The community became entirely self-sufficient. They already mostly were. And they kept it going for a decade, with people coming and going whenever they pleased. A Ship of Theseus of ships. My grandfather told me the stories, and I ate them up. Edgar did, too. It was the perfect community for our transitional times, especially in Florida when the tide of people is about to come in again. Everyone in Dinner Key was there because they wanted to be there, they had the power to leave at any time, but as long as they *did* stay, things were set up so that they contributed to something that was better than the sum of their parts. An accidental floating community, that maximized the power of the individual for the overall benefit of the group. I pitched it to Edgar, told him I could improve on that idea, make it intentional. I called it an aquatic co-op. I thought as the head of Mourning in Miami he would be interested in it as a potential home for his people."

"And what did he do?" Riley said, setting him up.

"He fired me." Félix smiled. "It was the same day I'd asked Maurice Thibodeux to stop using the sealant I'd developed," said Félix. "Edgar called me in; I asked him for money and he fired me. Very awkward."

"But why would he just get rid of you?" asked Myra. "If he agreed with you?"

"I don't think he had a choice," said Félix. "The thing you have to understand about Edgar Ortiz is that he always dreamed big, and achieved many of his dreams, but by the time I met him he was already tied down. He was asking *me* to dream because he couldn't anymore. He was just one man, and he was the face of the new Florida, which was already attracting outside investment. It meant something to be associated with him. The Flaco is radical, almost certainly unprofitable . . . Ask Ermie why he calls his boat the *Instant Pot* . . . Edgar couldn't fund something like that openly." He gestured out the window, toward Nepheli and *Bulls on Parade*. "Just like he couldn't talk about making atmo-breaking safer when all people do is bet on them to blow, or admit that reinforcing the Astro America's foundation would be an ecological disaster. Even if he believed in all these things."

"But he tried to get you the money anyway," I said, guessing at where this was going.

"Not at first," said Félix, though he was nodding. "At first he just kept in touch. I would always get invited to his parties. The party last night, Edgar invited me weeks ago. He made opportunities for me where he could, bringing me to places where I could pitch my ideas. I met Sofia at one of those parties. She was here on a research grant back then. Edgar introduced me to Ermie, who wasn't very enthusiastic but needed a reason to get off the mainland.

"He strung us all along, for a long time." Félix said this with a strange admiration in his voice. "That was another one of his gifts, I think. Knowing just what to say to keep things going. He made us believe without promising anything that there would be money, and it kept us together."

"And attracted Kohl," I said.

We all glanced at Kohl, still tied to the railing. He was looking out at the water, but I knew he could hear us. Myra kept stealing looks at him, when she wasn't whispering to Sofia.

"And finally," said Félix. "Here we are. The last time I saw Edgar was at a party. I didn't know anyone. But somehow I got stuck in a corner with him and a bunch of bigwigs, big Mourners and others. He showed us this trading card that he was wearing around his neck on a silver chain. An UltiMon card, the one with the turtle. Holographic. Looked special. Said he always wore it for good luck. I thought it was strange that he was showing it to me. But then he did something stranger. He made kind of a joke."

"A joke?"

"He said if he died while he was wearing it, it would probably be worth ten times as much the next day."

"Funny," I said.

"Yeah. It got a laugh. But it felt, I don't know, staged. Or like he had told it before. And he was looking at me."

"Why would he say something like that?"

"He was talking about it like it was an investment."

"Or like salvagia," said Riley.

"Yes, exactly!" said Félix. "He did compare it to salvagia. They were talking about ways of holding on to salvagia, what they could do to it. You know, the way rich people talk about property in

Alaska." Félix looked at me. "Riley said that you're a salvagia diver," he said. He sounded hopeful.

I nodded. "I don't usually keep it," I said.

"But you know what to do with it?" he asked, hopefully.

"I'm not sure what Edgar meant, if that's what you mean."

He looked crestfallen.

"Tell her the rest," said Riley. Félix nodded.

"So a couple of days ago, I got a text from Edgar, out of the blue. Edgar doesn't text. And the text was just coordinates. And every five seconds, I got the same text, on a loop. I looked up the coordinates and they were about an hour away, in the yoreshore. So I went up there, alone. There was nothing there. I had a bad feeling, I can't explain it, that it was *in* the yoreshore. I'd maybe scuba-dived twice in my life, but Kohl had left a spare suit on the *Oystercatcher*, so I put it on and dove down and . . ."

"And there was Edgar?"

"There was Edgar . . . just floating there. Already dead."

"And the card?" I asked.

"The card was just floating there, too, around his neck."

I made a face. "You're telling me he texted you *while he was drowning*, a set of coordinates so you could, what? Come take the card from around his neck?"

"I don't know," said Félix. "I'm just telling you what happened."

I looked at Riley. "You believe this?"

Riley shrugged. "Why not? Nepheli told me they've been coming out here for months. That the old man *brought* them out here. I'm out of the loop. If Nepheli trusts these folks, then I guess I do too. All I know for sure is that whatever it was, the old man didn't think I should know about it. But I don't think they're murderers, Triss."

"Definitely not," said Félix, nodding at Kohl. "We're not like him."

"And I think they might have at least as much of a claim to the card as we do," Riley said.

"So if you took the card," I said. "What do you need me for?"

Félix shook his head. He suddenly looked uncomfortable. He drained the rest of his drink. "I . . . I had to touch him to pull it off, and I couldn't . . . my hands were shaking. And I got tangled up in his equipment and I panicked, so I . . . I dropped it."

"You dropped it?"

"By the time I got untangled I couldn't see it. I searched the seabed but I couldn't find it, and then I had to surface. I think I saw it fall . . . into one of the wrecks."

I hesitated. I had seen the video, watched Edgar pull himself into the narrow, jagged opening. Did he drown right above it? The thought of diving any wreck gave me pause, but watching Edgar pull himself into that one in particular had made me gasp, had brought up the old anxieties.

"So it's still down there?" I asked. "And you know where it is?"

"I do," said Félix.

"Why don't you get it yourself?"

"Because that wreck . . . that wreck is a horror."

Félix agreed to take us to the place where he found Edgar, and I agreed to search the wreck for the card in exchange for whatever percentage it would take to buy the *Ghost*. Riley did not ask for a cut, which annoyed me, but he did confirm that the spot Félix pointed out was close to where he had last seen Edgar alive, in the northern part of the Miami area yoreshore, about twenty miles below Boca Raton.

We were south of Miami now, and the time it took to get there would depend entirely on how long it took us to get to the ocean from Coral Castle. Félix told me the canal we'd followed also cut all the way east, but the destruction of the construction titan on that side looked like the fallout of a hyper-targeted hurricane—flattened mangroves and other flora floated in thick clumps, damming the water in the exact direction we needed to go.

The alternative was to go back the way we came, which would let us out gulfside, and we'd have to wrap back around the Everglades.

It would take all day. Neither Félix nor I were thrilled about the idea of diving Edgar's gravesite at night.

Félix and Ermie went out in the *Oystercatcher* to assess if escape that way was even possible. I stepped onto the deck and waited for them to get back. I was restless, just like I had been when Kohl convinced us to drop anchor at Key West.

Standing on the opposite side of the deck from Kohl, I wondered what to do with him. I thought he could be a prize for the IXS, maybe enough to get them to forget about me again. It probably depended on how much he knew about the inner workings of the Church, or the high-rise scheme. Even if he wasn't valuable to them, I hoped they'd take him off my hands. I would have to wait to call them until after we had the card, maybe until after we sold it. Which meant holding on to him until then.

Maybe I could get Ermie to throw him in his cage. But then I would have to talk to Ermie again, and I didn't think I could stand another lecture on echidna fighters. There was some mysticism involved, I knew, enough so that Gamma justified spending all of her time sparring, strutting around our campsite, herding the nomads like cats, and none of it taking care of me. In the end she lost it all. Two sticks and a bad attitude can only protect so much for so long.

I worried that by diving for the card I was giving Ermie the wrong idea. I wanted to make it clear that I was only doing it for profit. I'd even pay him to fix my Knuckles, so long as he did it quietly.

I heard footsteps, and soon Riley stood next to me on the deck.

If Ermie *did* have the wrong idea it was because Riley was helping them for free, because Myra was wandering the beach with Sofia, giving out advice, squealing with excitement and energy despite her concussion. Ermie and Félix both probably thought they had three new recruits.

I was the only one who had asked for a cut. I was the only one who needed it, the only one doing any actual work, the work that Félix didn't have the guts to do, that I might not even have the guts to do, since it was diving another wreck. Of course it was another wreck, and of course I would have to actually go into it this time. I should have known the Ked would be too good to be true when I'd pulled it out of the mud. I hadn't earned it.

So, yes, I was restless. I had come so far, accomplished so little. The clock was ticking, and soon the *Ghost* would march herself to her own execution, scuttle herself on Reefer's famous reef. What would Charlie say to get her to go? How do you get a semi-sent curious about suicide?

"We still don't know what happened," Riley said, interrupting my dark thoughts. "To the old man. We might have the card but we don't know the first thing about what he was doing out there, or who killed him."

"What does it matter?"

"You don't want to know?"

"If I have the card? No."

"I don't believe that. Myra told me you were the one that unchained him from . . . well, from where he was. When you were chasing Kohl. Why'd you do that?"

Because he wasn't supposed to be there. Because nobody belongs alone, in the dark. But just because I did him a favor didn't mean I was responsible for all his unfinished business. "He was in my way."

"Well," Riley said, looking me over. "Thanks anyway. For me, though, I need to know. I didn't, until . . . until I came here. But now I do."

We watched Nepheli on the shore, working on a section of *Bulls on Parade* near the exhaust. A long diagnostic cable snaked out of the middle of her fuselage. Propped up vertically like that, the *Bull* looked a little like an arm.

"The why doesn't matter as much as you think," I said. "Take my friend Eli. He died for lots of reasons. He died because someone built him a faulty prosthetic. He died because the feds who designed the security protocols of that beetle used military tactics to stop him from taking a list of civilian names and locations. He died because I fit in better with the other rangers in the 2C3 and he didn't, so when I really needed to talk him out of something I couldn't anymore, because he didn't trust me. He died because he just couldn't believe the feds could possibly care enough to stop him. I don't really think Ermie killed him. I just said that because I needed him to help me. The truth is that my list of things that killed him is long and I think about it all the time. But there is no one single 'why.' There never is. Collecting them all doesn't make it much better."

"But maybe I can still do something," Riley replied. "If I knew the whole story, if I knew why he was diving and who killed him, maybe I could . . . help."

"Help who? With what?"

"I don't know! But something's happening down here, and the old man was involved. Someone stole his body and chained him up! I'm the son of Edgar Ortiz, I should be able to do something."

"Not unless you're smarter than Edgar was. Are you?"

"Just at atmo-breaking."

"Then leave it. Go back to the Astro with Nepheli. Will they let you race in the Canaveral?"

"I didn't ask," said Riley. "I only wanted to race because I thought an atmo-breaker killed him. I thought atmo-breaking was what really mattered to him . . . but he did *this*. He died to do *this*, whatever it was. So it does matter. If you do find anything down there, promise you'll tell me. Can you promise me that? I'll make it worth your while."

I smiled a little bit. "With what?"

"What do you want?"

The way he asked, it sounded like he was genuinely curious. He leaned in a little bit.

"I just want the *Ghost*," I said.

"What about when you have her? Where will you go, Triss? What happens next?"

I shrugged. I hadn't ever thought that far ahead. Bad luck to start now.

"Anything's possible," I said. "Now that I can talk to her. That's something you did. Thank you for that."

He nodded. We were very close to each other now.

The *Bull* made a noise, like the atmo-breaker equivalent of the *Ghost* whining her outboards.

"You missed something," Riley called out to Nepheli. They ignored him. He grunted and walked down the little gangplank to shore. "Come on, Triss."

"Me?"

"I want you to see this. This is what I'm talking about, how you gotta listen to your semi-sent, take her seriously."

I shrugged and followed.

We got close to the *Bull*. I caught a whiff of that sickly sweet smell again. Maybe it was a certain kind of flower or plant that grew around here. Maybe Kohl had fallen into it when he was chasing us down.

Or maybe he'd been near the *Bull*.

"Leave us alone," said Nepheli. They saw us coming and quickly began to shut down everything they were working on and close up the *Bull*. "I don't need you looking over my shoulder."

"She doesn't make that noise unless something's wrong," Riley said, going over to an open valve labeled N2OFUEL in big red letters.

Nepheli slapped his hand away. "The logs say she's fine." They closed the valve almost on Riley's fingers. "She always acts like this when I add something new to her. You think you're a semi-sent whisperer? You have no idea how complex this is. After you fly her I have to find new ways to get her to be more careful."

"You shouldn't. It'll just confuse her."

"You just can't help yourself, can you?" they exclaimed. "You had to follow me all the way out here, you had to get involved. You told Maurice that the *Bull* was semi-sentient after I specifically told you not to."

"You did?" I said. I had been there when Nepheli told him not to. "When?"

He looked away. "On the *Marino*. I thought . . . I thought if I did, he'd put me back in the race. But I told you, I don't care about that anymore. I just want to help."

"Did you really think he'd be *excited* about a breaker that was safer?" said Nepheli. "He's the head of the circuit gambling commission. This is a sport where you can bet that every single ship in a race will explode. It's a named bet! People bet on it every race! You think he's interested in making atmo-breaking *safer*?"

"She's not just safer," he said, defiantly. "With me, she's faster."

"Your dad never told Maurice that we were racing with a semi-sent. Don't you think he had a reason?"

"If he did he didn't tell me," said Riley. "Neither did you. What was he even doing out there? And why didn't he want me to know?"

"I have no idea."

"You're lying," he said.

The smell was gone now, but it had reminded me of what we had wanted to ask Nepheli in the first place. "You handled his equipment," I said. "Didn't you?"

"That's right," said Riley. "He was always pulling you aside to talk about his tanks and stuff. He didn't tell you anything the night before that dive?"

"Maybe something about what kind of diving mix he would need?" I added.

"Diving mix?" Nepheli replied. "What does that have to do with anything?"

"I'd like to know what kind of situation I'm getting into," I said. "It would help to know what he was doing down there. If I knew his diving mix I could guess at how long he planned to be down there, the depth, if he was going to exert himself. Did he mention anything like that?"

"I showed him how to use his machine, the one that filled his tanks," said Nepheli, turning away. "That's all."

"The one in his room?" Riley asked.

"That's the only one I know about."

"So he didn't tell either of us what he was doing out there," said Riley. "And he didn't tell Félix. You're saying he didn't trust Maurice. So who did he tell?"

"I have no idea!" shouted Nepheli. "Don't you get it? He had at least two sides to his life and he kept them as separate as possible."

"I'm not trying to fight, Nepheli. I just want answers."

"You're just like him, you know. One second you talk about me like I'm family and the next you're making it clear that you're the only Ortiz. I was always on the hidden side of his life and you were the golden child. The atmo-breaker. You could run Mourning in Miami too, if you wanted to; you just didn't want to. But things weren't always so great over here on the dark side of the Edgar Ortiz moon. I bet Félix even apologized for him, didn't he? Talked about how he was the great man of Florida and he couldn't talk about us openly like we were some dirty secret? That's bullshit. He was Edgar Ortiz. If he really believed in the Flaco, in me, he could have gotten us the money. He could have sold the team, or his high-rises, or his precious Astro America. But that wasn't even considered. He wanted to keep being the big man in Florida, so he kept us all in the dark. We're just lucky he gave us the chance to rob his corpse."

"So you did know about the card," said Riley, accusingly, but with a little less wind in his sails.

"Félix told me," they shot back. "*After* it happened, so no, that's not another thing I was keeping from you."

The *Oystercatcher* pulled into our little cove then and Félix hailed us. Nepheli waved back, and left us to help him tie up to a nearby mangrove.

Félix had mixed news—it seemed like there was a way through but it was difficult to confirm it from the surface. Ermie clocked that the *Ghost* was a CabanaBoat and said he might have some leads on how to maximize the hazard charting initiatives in her semi-sentience. He wanted her to go ahead and scout, to make sure there was enough depth for all the Flaco's seacraft to leave. I was, understandably, hesitant to let him aboard to program her, and we had a small argument.

By the time we had figured it all out, Nepheli was gone.

They had packed up *Bulls on Parade* and set off on the circuit barge, back through the canal the long way, toward the gulfside yoreshore. They didn't say goodbye to any of us, and we didn't even notice until Myra pointed at them backing into the canal.

## SALVAGIA

With Riley at the helm, the *Ghost* negotiated her way through the debris, followed by the *Instant Pot* and the *Oystercatcher*. Sofia rode with Félix and Myra joined Riley and me.

We emerged, finally, into calm open water, clear of debris like the Everglades but much less stinky. Myra told us that this was the ghost of Biscayne Bay. The featureless landscape left a clear sightline to the ruined Miami skyline.

Once she was out in open water Riley took a break and I took over. He took Myra to the window of the lounge and pointed out all the skyscrapers and started naming them, one by one, like pointing out constellations in the sky, including the empty spaces where the melted ones should be.

"You really know them all?" I asked. "You're not just making some of them up?"

"I would never," he replied, with possibly false solemnity. "I am the son of Edgar Ortiz."

"One thing I never understood about Mourning in Miami," said Myra. "What's the endgame?"

"When do we stop mourning, you mean?"

"You stop when you rebuild Miami, don't you? That's what I always heard. But what does that mean? What is Miami? Is it the buildings, the beaches, the food? The attitude? Is it a city funded entirely by property taxes but built on sinking property?"

"I figured it was a 'next year in Jerusalem' kind of thing," I said.

Riley shrugged. "Depends on who you are. Like I said, what the old man cared about was atmo-breaking, building the circuit. Mourning in Miami was usually whatever he needed it to be to do what he needed to do."

"Syndicate, political movement, corporate mafia . . ." Myra counted off the possibilities with her fingers.

"But all the old fogeys are different," said Riley. "Ask Maria Feinstein-Reyes and she'd probably say yes, we're actually building Miami."

"She works in shipping," I remembered. "Being on the ground floor of reopening the port of Miami would be in her interest."

"That construction titan can build fast and it can build tall, but it can't build ports," said Myra. "And it can't rebuild South Beach."

"Maybe that's why this deal got her so upset," agreed Riley. "But it's not all business with them. Every year the annual Mourners meeting is out here, off the coast, and everyone comes in their yachts and brings their families, and they set up one of those disaster tourism holograms, where the way the city used to be gets projected over the way it is now, and you can see how great it all was, and the drones go out and use lasers to show you which celebrities lived in exactly which little windows in which condo buildings, and they gather around and tell us all about it, and then we party."

"'How is this night different from all other nights?'" said Myra, maybe to herself.

"I should have paid more attention to the business part of those meetings," said Riley, frustrated. "Maybe it could help us figure out what he was doing. But I was never interested. I wasn't born there; I don't see it the way that they did. All I ever wanted to do was race."

He thought for a while, staring off into the distance at the old ruined city, which I supposed was his birthright, whatever that meant.

"But there is something," he said, finally. "Some way that Miami keeps us together. Maybe 'mourning' is just the only word that gets close."

We sailed around Miami and past it, up the oceanside yoreshore in a little convoy. It was late afternoon and the long braise finally broke, with a stiff breeze coming in from the north and blowing some of the heat away. The *Oystercatcher* pulled ahead and guided us. The *Ghost* seemed to trust Félix's boat instinctively. I only had to tell her to follow once.

"Where are we?" asked Myra. "Is this still Miami?"

Riley shook his head. "Different city. Hollywood or Fort Lauderdale, maybe. My dad told me there were a bunch of cities, all built on the same ridge that's underwater now, all the way up the coast. And then there was a channel, and then a set of sandbars, and then the ocean. We're at the edge of the channel now, I think. That's why it's so clear. But look."

He pointed to a little slice of sandbar that stuck above the water. The remains of a building, six or seven intact stories of at least ten. At the top were the remaining letters of some kind of sign: A MAR

Black dots peppered the curves of those letters.

"What are those?" I asked.

"Birds," said Myra, looking out to the *Oystercatcher,* which had just dropped its anchor. Sofia was already on deck, shielding her eyes from the setting sun and looking at her.

I had left my diving gear at Key West Cemetery but I still had Edgar's mask and tank and a spare tank of my own. It was almost empty, but Edgar's orange tank with the funny-tasting mix was still mostly full, so I took it. I still had no idea what kind of gas it was, but I was about to dive the same wreck that Edgar had when he was using it.

Félix was not a particularly competent diver. I had to help him with his wetsuit, which, he reminded me, was actually Kohl's. He admitted that he had no wreck experience, had only started to learn because he had plans for the Flaco to start farming oysters. But I needed him. Just knowing that there was someone else in the water with me would put me at ease. I hoped so, anyway. If Edgar had needed a special mix to dive here, I was expecting a deep, dangerous, technical dive that required all my wits and skill.

So I was surprised when we jumped in and saw that it was, in fact, shallow and beautiful.

It was not standard yoreshore, murky and crowded. The water was clear, the bottom littered with shipwrecks protected on all sides by a steep incline of mud.

A flooded marina, turned into a ship graveyard.

It was deeper than standard yoreshore, but not nearly as deep as I expected. Typical yoreshore, at least the busy yoreshore that used to be street or surface, bottoms out at about ten feet. The ship graveyard couldn't have been much more than thirty. Not nearly deep enough for Edgar to require anything but plain air.

There were at least twelve different wrecks in the marina. They sketched out the layout of the old marina with their neat positioning, still adhering to a grid of long-rotted decks and slips. Beyond them, that grid was shattered—seven more wrecks lay haphazardly, probably shifted around during a particularly violent storm.

Félix took longer to orient himself than I did, but eventually he grabbed my shoulder and pointed at a wreck in the very center. I recognized it immediately from the stream as the ship that Edgar had bobbed back and forth in front of, putting me to sleep while he prepared to pull himself in.

It was exactly the same, down to the jagged opening in its side, except for one thing: The opening was leaking a thick squid-ink cloud that billowed and dissipated, obscuring the entire wreck in a haze that made me wonder if there was something on my mask. My heart sank, and I followed Félix to the bottom.

We spent a little time searching the seabed around the wreck, on the off-chance Félix had been wrong about what he'd seen. I felt around in the silt, remembering that moment, only yesterday, when I had stumbled on the Ked. Hoping I'd get lucky twice.

I didn't, and I used up most of my air delaying the inevitable.

The wreck was a barge-type houseboat, about fifty feet long, resting on its port side against a mound of rock and concrete. The opening that Edgar had pulled himself into was a jagged slit in the middle of the boat. I swam around it and found myself at the aft deck. I brushed around the outline of a name. Too eager. A cloud of grime billowed in my face. I froze. My heart raced, more out of instinct than danger. Avoiding silt-outs is the diver's equivalent of the floor-is-lava game. Inside the cramped confines of a wreck, a silt-out is very dangerous, even if you know the layout. You become disoriented, you forget which way is up. Getting in a wreck is hard, but getting out of it is harder. A silt-out makes it even worse. Every surface is covered in it, so once you cause one you're almost guaranteed to cause another trying to feel your way out.

My visibility was already going to be obscured by the black cloud coming out of the wreck. A silt-out would make that ship my tomb.

And Félix's look confirmed what I already suspected—this was the same black sealant that he had developed for the Astro America, that Kohl had spread around Coral Castle by order of the Church, that Félix said attracted the construction titan. What was that sealant doing in a shipwreck that was clearly from before the floods? And, more importantly, did that mean that the titan was on its way here? It had had a head start on us, and we hadn't passed it on our way. It might have passed us already, or maybe the water thinned the sealant out enough to no longer be effective.

Still, I shouldn't linger any longer than I had to.

I swam around to the starboard guardrail and found, to my relief, an orange diving flag tied to it, attached to a standard diving line, basically colored fishing wire. It led up into the jagged mouth.

Edgar's expensive mask had comms, but Kohl's didn't. I gestured to Félix to come over to the dive line, and I tried to communicate to him that he should keep his hands on the line, that I would pull on it every five minutes. And, most importantly, if I missed more than one check-in, he would have to come in after me.

His reaction was not encouraging.

I looked into the dark maw of the opening and began to hyperventilate. It was even worse than it had been on the stream, pitch-black and impossibly narrow. It would be difficult to pull my way in without scraping against something. The water was inky black. I stuck my hand in and watched it disappear, turn into nothing more than a ghostly version of itself almost as soon as it crossed into the ship.

Of course I couldn't see any sign of the UltiMon card. I swore, cursing the insanely bad luck it had taken for it to fall from Edgar's neck all the way back down into this wreck.

I hesitated there, just like Edgar had, staring into the mouth.

I reminded myself that without the money, the *Ghost* would die. If she died, I would be forced to leave, and if I left, the 2C3 would find me and ship me to the moon, and leave Myra all alone. I even told myself to do it for Félix, for his stupid Flaco, for Riley and his closure, for Gamma because she probably would have done it if she had been here.

But it didn't help. I couldn't do it.

I looked away, at Félix, who held the line in his hands like I had showed him and looked at me with useless sympathy.

I was breathing so fast and so hard from nerves that I depleted much of what remained in my tank. I switched over to Edgar's orange tank and tasted flowers left too long in the vase. I forced myself to take longer breaths, hold them, space them out.

Around my fifth breath, something clicked. I suddenly felt calm, then almost euphoric. I stared back at the maw.

Its blackness surrounded me now, and I did not look away again. It beckoned.

I turned on my mask light, useless as it was, and pulled myself into the dead ship very carefully. Everything was at an angle; I knew it would be easy to become disoriented. I was in a small stateroom. Any hope that the card would be right there (and it should have been!) was dashed by a quick survey of the room.

I pulled myself down the line and felt along the wall leading to the bottom of the wreck. It was warped and decayed, pocked with holes big enough for a card to fit through but too small for me. If I left the line, I could probably break through it, but I'd also probably cause a silt-out.

I pulled myself through, into the next room and then down, into a hallway. The air from the orange tank was starting to make my head swim, just like it had before, and I found my mind wandering, both hands in front of my mask, which meant that neither of them were on the line.

The dark, yawning port to the inner guts of the ship called me closer.

The line led into a room down the hall of the entrance. The inky blackness coming from that room was of a slightly different quality, to a point where I thought that something must be illuminating it. There must have been another hole on that side. I knew the card couldn't possibly have fallen that way, but I took a quick look anyway. Light could mean a hole, another exit.

It was the engine room. The hole to the outside was big enough for me to fit through, but rusted machinery blocked my access to it. I saw that it might be possible to get there from the next room, the one that might have the card.

In the back I saw smooth, curiously unrusted surfaces. But I couldn't see them very well, and the diving line ended right at the entrance. That meant that this was as far as Edgar had gone. Was he already drowning by the time he'd reached this room? I tried to move even more carefully, but I kept getting distracted, losing focus . . .

I saw that the wall between the engine room and the next room had decayed as well. Maybe it would give me a better angle.

I left the line. I inched down the hallway. There was no other way. I was aware that I was becoming disoriented, that I kept forgetting that the boat was on its side, but I was curiously unafraid. I reminded myself constantly to slow down, to inch at a snail's pace, counting "Mississippis," counting breaths, every trick I knew to pace myself.

I pulled myself into the next room, which was entirely clear of black ink. I scanned it with my light. It was a bathroom, the master bathroom by the size of it, the scant remains of tacky wallpaper floating in the water, the cracked porcelain of a gaudy jacuzzi-sized bathtub, with a pile of silt and . . .

A holographic glint, nestled right in the middle.

It took all my resolve not to lunge for it.

Instead, I grabbed the porous wall between the bathroom and the engine room. It was spongy in my hands, it crumbled. I couldn't grab it too hard.

I was maybe five feet away from it when I looked through the wall, back to the engine room. I had a better angle this time, and I could see behind the equipment. The clear water flowed in that way.

There were plastic barrels, four or five of them. One of them was open, oozing sealant. The others were closed, but I saw numbers on them, written in red.

Coordinates.

I was distracted by one of those numbers in particular, long enough that I forgot where my hand was and felt it disappear into a soft part of the wall. Mush gave way to something hard and slimy that slithered back at my touch.

The eel snapped at me and I jolted back in surprise, scratching the floor with my fin and pulverizing the wall behind me. Silt billowed up from the floor of the stateroom.

I caught the holographic glint again, just for a second, before the whole room was shrouded in a murky green-brown. I lunged for it. My head slammed into the porcelain of the tub. I grasped around desperately for the card, but I couldn't even see my own hand.

I swam around, blindly. Fear crept up on me from a distance, a black outline of terror. I couldn't tell which way was up, which direction I was going in. Whenever I thought I'd oriented myself I hit my head against the floor or the ceiling. I ran my hands along the walls, into the silt, over everything. My shoulder slammed hard into fiberglass more than once. The water got darker, black as ink, and I was hyperventilating again now, breathing that deathly sweet air, back in the beetle dome—only this time I was Eli; I was the one thrashing out, no escape.

Something touched my leg and I kicked it away, afraid it was the eel. Then it clamped down and pulled, hard.

Félix got me out through the engine room, the other exit. Then he grabbed my hand and took us up to our decomp depth and helped me switch back over to my other tank. One of us dropped Edgar's orange tank, and I watched it sink down to the bottom while I sucked in air.

Almost immediately I started feeling normal again. My head was pounding, from the air and from when I hit my head.

He pointed at my ankle.

I looked down and found a chain wrapped around it, silver with spots of blue. I held the chain in my hands—the blue was carved sapphire turtles. A thick plastic case hung off the end.

The light through the water hit the case and made the card glint psychedelic colors, in a way that made Kappacop seem to grin, to tilt his bobby cap in a rakish fashion. The case was scratched but the card inside looked like it was still in near mint condition.

The feeling was the same as when I had held the Ked—this was an object that could save me.

When Félix saw it he clapped me on the back, hard enough that I almost dropped it. I spent the rest of my decomp staring at it.

We were just about to surface, when Kohl came down to meet us.

He sank past us without a mask, without his trademark tinted gogs. His dead eyes were a dull gray, ringed with metal where Ermie had repaired them. Two wisps of blood billowed from his ears.

I looked up. The hull of the *Ghost* was gone. A different hull had taken her place, much larger. The dead body and the hull gave me déjà vu, but I didn't have time to think about it. My tank was almost out of air. I had to surface.

I signaled for Félix to stay and he nodded, looking fearful. After some hesitation I gave him the card.

And then I swam up.

The boat was another yacht, in the same style as the *Marino*, but not part of a module fleet. The deck was crowded with people in black fedoras. They spotted me immediately and called out. Riley ran to the railing but was quickly restrained. I saw his nose was bleeding again. It looked like he had put up a fight.

Deena peered down at me from the railing. A swarm of drones buzzed around her head.

# 10

Deena barked orders and pulled Riley away. The Mourners on deck argued about which of them was supposed to carry out these orders. Then they argued about how they would get to me. None of them wanted to get wet. They made rude gestures in Deena's direction.

The *Ghost* and the Flaco fleet were gone. If I had enough air I could probably have escaped and hid in one of the wrecks. But I didn't, so I made it easy for the Mourners and swam over.

One of them took charge and stuck out a hand and pulled me up. He was the biggest, and he wore his fedora slightly crooked on his head. He grabbed another Mourner, who wore black suspenders and no jacket, and they shoved me toward the stairs belowdecks.

I recognized this yacht. I had seen it from below and from the shore, but never up close. It belonged to Maria Feinstein-Reyes.

"Riley would want you to let me go," I said. My voice was raspy from Edgar's mix, and I coughed. "You should ask him. That's Riley *Ortiz*."

Crooked Hat considered this. "Seems like a nice guy," he said. "Sometimes I'll bet his breaker, and sometimes I win. But he don't write my paycheck."

"Who, the 'heir'?" Suspenders said, mockingly, and the first one snickered. I'd seen they didn't like Deena very much either. Maybe I could use that.

"So who does write your paycheck?" I asked. "This is Maria Feinstein-Reyes's yacht, isn't it? Do you work for her?"

Crooked Hat made a sour face. "Nah. That bitch attacked us."

"We work for Nestor Ortega," said Suspenders. "He said if we found you we'd get a spa weekend at the Astro. The good spa, the penthouse."

"Shut up," said Crooked Hat.

On the *Marino* Maurice had said there were five Mourner families, and that he was still aligned with three of them. Ortega must be one of those.

They took me down into the small, cramped section of the boat usually reserved for staff. Crooked Hat opened the door to what I thought might be a closet. It was a small windowless room with two bunks stacked on top of each other. Another Mourner was taking a nap, her fedora over her eyes. Crooked Hat kicked the bunk. The sleeper snorted awake and fixed her eyes on me. "You the bitch that wrecked the gator?"

I blinked. "Yes, actually."

"Thought you were supposed to be blonde."

"No, stupid," said Crooked Hat. "This is a prisoner. Now you're on guard duty."

"I never got my turn," Sleepyhead grumbled, but got out of the bunk. They shoved me inside and locked the door. It was too small to pace. I drummed my fingers on the fiberglass bunk. I missed my Knuckles, and wished I had told Ermie whatever he'd needed to hear to fix them for me.

I'd been so close. I'd held the card in my hands.

I felt the yacht lurch forward, hard enough that I braced myself against the bunk.

I needed to escape, but even if I did I had no idea where the *Ghost* had gone, or the Flaco. Was Myra with them, or had she been killed, along with Kohl, and I'd missed her body? Would they come back for Félix? Would he keep his word to me about the card? I figured he probably would. If Myra was still okay, then she could call Charlie and tell him I had the money.

And then maybe the *Ghost* would live, even if I didn't.

Trapped in this dark, bare room, my mind raced and I began to panic. Félix was right, that wreck had been a horror, and the brig I was in was the same shape and size of the one I'd silted out. I found myself there again, looking at the mealy walls, through them to the . . .

The engine room. Full of leaking barrels of Félix's black sealant. That must have been what Edgar had been looking for.

I clutched to the memory, pulled at it like thread from a sweater.

There was no black stuff leaking out of the boat on his stream when he went in, which meant that he must have opened the barrel while he was in there. Or he had put the barrels there himself. No, he hadn't been carrying anything on any of the streams that he could have secretly brought from the *Marino* to the wreck on his DPV.

Wouldn't have needed to, anyway. The Church had told Kohl that they had barrels hidden in caches up and down the yoreshore. Hiding the barrels in the first place would be Kohl-level minion work, not Edgar Ortiz work.

But why were they hidden at all? And why had Edgar gone looking for them? And why didn't he want anyone to know he was doing it?

Much of my memory of the dive was a haze, but one thing stuck, and I wasn't sure why: there had been two sets of numbers painted on the lids of those barrels.

I couldn't recall the whole sequence, but I remembered some of each: "25" on the top and "80" on the bottom. Why was that important? I must have seen a degree symbol or something, too, because I knew somehow that they were coordinates. The first set ended in "N" and the second set in "W." How was it possible that I could remember so much of it?

Then it hit me. I had seen those numbers before, or something close to them. Some part of me knew those numbers in that sequence by instinct.

They were on a list, taped above the *Ghost*'s cockpit, places that Charlie told me to never take her.

I was pretty sure they led to a point in Miami.

My breath caught. Outside the door my guard gave a loud yawn.

The Church was planning to build high-rises in Miami.

If Edgar had been looking for the barrels in secret, it stood to reason that he wasn't supposed to know that. And after what I had seen the titan do to Coral Castle, I thought I understood why.

The construction titan would level what was left of Miami, and the sealant would make the area around it a wasteland. Maybe Maurice and the Church were worried about what would happen if the Mourners actually knew what it took to build high-rises in the yoreshore.

Because I remembered what Riley had said, that the main thing that kept the Mourners together against their own agendas was Miami itself, the actual site of the old ruined city, the melted buildings beneath the disaster tour hologram. If they knew that Maurice and the Church would level all that, it could be enough to unite them, at least enough to derail the funding.

So Edgar had gone looking for proof, in secret. Maurice or the Church must have found out.

Now that was a reason to kill him.

Félix taking the card was unrelated. Edgar must have rigged something to the vitals in his fancy wetsuit so that if he happened to die underwater it would text Félix his coordinates, so he could fund his Flaco.

So who was it, then? Maurice or the Church, or both working together? I remembered that the Church had expected to see Edgar at Key West, was alarmed when it turned out he was dead.

That left Maurice, working alone.

And Maurice had told Riley that he'd lost Edgar's body, only for me to find it chained up under this very yacht two days later, a boat belonging to his main rival and someone who was against the high-rise deal. He must have seen the black stains on Edgar's hands and panicked, hid the body from Riley, from everyone, and then decided he could use the body to frame Maria, so he could take charge of the Mourners.

But then I'd come along, let Edgar free before his time and given Maria a heads-up. She'd fought back, and based on how the Mourners I'd met treated Deena, I figured Maurice's hold on them was still tenuous at best.

Was that what he needed Riley for? To strengthen his claim? These Mourners didn't seem to care much about Riley, either.

A soft, consistent buzzing in my ear disrupted my train of thought. I stopped pulling the thread.

"Where are we going?" I whispered to the Church of the Invisible Hand.

The buzzing stopped. I felt the prickle of legs bristling along my earlobe.

"The Astro America," it said. Its harsh voice made my eardrum tingle. I remembered the blood billowing from the side of Kohl's head. I recognized this voice—soft and reedy. It belonged to the drone that had goaded me after Kohl and warned me about the gator, not the voice that had led the rest of the hive.

"And what do you want with me?" I asked.

"Riley Ortiz exchanged himself for the departure of your CabanaBoat, as well as your own safety. We thought that was interesting."

That didn't really answer my question.

"I guess that safe departure didn't extend to Kohl," I said.

"He was not specifically named in Ortiz's terms. And he started talking. That did not work to his advantage."

"No, it usually didn't."

What would Kohl talk about? That was obvious: Coral Castle. If the Church had killed him to prevent him from talking about it in front of the Mourners, that would confirm my pulled thread. No matter the why, they'd killed him as easily as they could kill me now—with a drone through the ear to the brain.

The Church had seemed ready to kill me once, too, simply for no longer being useful. I figured I should find a way to be useful now.

"I'm glad you're here," I said. "I think we can help each other."

"Oh?" came the buzz.

"I found a piece you might be interested in. Salvagia."

"And you know us to be such reliable business partners," said the drone, their modulated voice distorted by sarcasm. "Especially to an independent operator like yourself."

"It belonged to Edgar Ortiz."

The buzzing stopped. I had its attention.

"Belonged to him?" it hissed. Its voice was different now. "Salvagia? Where did you find it? When?"

"Just now. Where you picked us up."

"It's an item that was in his literal possession when he drowned?"

"Yes."

"Can you prove it?"

"I have a video stream of him wearing it."

"Show us," the drone said hungrily.

"Of course," I said. "Just let me out of here."

It hissed and then crawled just inside my eardrum. I closed my fist instinctively, around a handle that wasn't there.

"Don't toy with us," it whispered. "We can kill you at any time. We can go anywhere, we can summon as many or as few of us as we need. There is no place on or in your body that we cannot access."

"Good thing I don't have it with me," I replied, with gritted teeth.

The drone hissed again and crawled back along my earlobe. I thought it might be muttering to itself. "Well, why didn't she just say so?" it asked, irritably. A few more hushed whispers, then finally, it spoke again.

"I apologize," it said. Its voice had returned to its original intonation. The soft and reedy personality had taken back control. "We are treating you like your deceased associate. We think you are more capable."

"Thanks."

"Do you know what makes salvagia so valuable? How one piece of sea trash might be worth tens of thousands of kiloDollars while another, lying right next to it, is barely worth the microbes that feast on it?"

I'd spent hours on the forums, memorizing the going rates of various items that might be found in the yoreshore—clothes, dinnerware, furniture, collectibles, appliances, pages and pages of junk. And I had to admit, it often did seem sort of arbitrary, but I assumed it was because I was a have-not and setting prices was the purview of haves.

"Beauty?" I guessed. As the diver, I was the only one who held the salvagia in its natural environment, underwater. To me, it looked special there. The way the Ked had decayed made it sparkle on one side, catch the light in a special kind of way. Kappacop, too. "Salvagia turns loss into beauty."

The drone made a sound that hurt my eardrum.

"A romantic," it said. "Beauty has its uses, I suppose. Take the piece you brought to us last night. Beauty certainly drove up the price, got ignorant people interested. But no. What sells it in the end is the story."

*What story?* "Who bought it?" I asked.

"Officially, we have no idea, of course. Discretion is one of our central services."

To help their clients hide from the IXS, I assumed. Among other things.

"But we can make certain inferences," the drone continued. "Salvagia from South Florida is in vogue right now, and concentrating around certain channels. There are signs that these channels are also preparing resources, aggressive legal action."

"Legal action? With salvagia?"

"The federal government is going out and the tide is coming in, and we, along with everyone who matters, are looking for the right way to ride the wave."

"I thought you were building high-rises," I said.

"That's one way. A crude one, as you've seen. And Thibodeux hasn't yet fulfilled his end of the bargain. We may need to diversify. Some of us think that salvagia is the answer."

I didn't understand it. I remembered that Félix had said that Edgar told a crowd that the card would be worth ten times the amount on his corpse than on his living body. Félix said he'd talked about it like an investment. And Edgar had set it up so that Félix could only take the card from his corpse. So he must have really believed it.

But why? How did Edgar's death make the card more valuable?

"So are you interested in my item or not?" I asked.

"Oh yes," said the drone. "I am, anyway. And some of the rest of us. But not most of us. Not yet. The only thing we all agree on is that we would prefer Riley Ortiz to be safely away from the Astro America, away from Thibodeux's control. So we came to see you."

"Why?"

"We don't believe Thibodeux has his best interests at heart."

"And you do?"

"We are the ones who helped you rescue him at Key West. Thibodeux was the one trying to kill him."

Sleepyhead yawned again and I remembered what she had said about me: *Thought you were supposed to be blonde.*

Deena. She had been the one to rig the gator to go after Riley.

"We also told your associate to let you all go at Coral Castle. You don't need to trust us," said the drone, echoing what it had told me on the beach when it had warned me of the gator in the first place. "But we don't want him dead. And the Mourners at the Astro America have orders not to let Ortiz leave."

"So what?" I replied. "You want to hire me to free him?"

"Hire you? No. We think you want to free him, all on your own."

"Did the Invisible Hand tell you that?"

"In a way I suppose," said the drone. It was quiet for a moment. "Your boat appeared to be semi-sentient. At least, when it left us, no one was operating it. Where do you think it would go, if you never went back to it? I mean if it were truly free? There are no wild CabanaBoat herds. It would die in a matter of days. It requires your supervision. Its meager portion of free will can only flourish under your maternal gaze. To us, that's what you're like. We are the Invisible Hand, Triss Mackey."

The bristle legs scurried up to the top of my ear.

"Now, let's loosen your collar and see what you do."

I tried the door a couple times. I had expected the drone to unlock it or something, Sleepyhead to be gone or dead at the door.

But it stayed locked. I pictured the drone hiss-laughing at me. Eventually the door opened and Crooked Hat pulled me up on deck, deposited me unceremoniously at Deena's feet.

"Where's the mechanic?" she demanded. "We know they were with you."

"No idea," I replied.

"For your sake I hope that's not true."

"Riley chased them off. Ask him. Listen, I could really use a shower. I've been in this wetsuit for hours."

Deena peered down at me. "What are you exactly? Mercenary? Spy? Fed? Did Feinstein-Reyes hire you? I don't think you're going to see a payday from her anytime soon."

I had leashed myself to every power that had come my way: the feds, Riley, the Church. At this point I had no idea what I was, though ironically the only person I wasn't at least implicitly working for was Maria Feinstein-Reyes.

"I'm just a diver," I said.

"A diver, huh? And you just happened to dredge up Riley Ortiz?"

"He hired me."

"To do what?"

This was dangerous. "I was looking for a piece of his atmobreaker that broke off after the race last night. He thought it hit the water around where you picked us up."

"Why did you stop in the swamp?"

"He thought it might be there, too."

She looked me over. I could tell she didn't believe me, and I couldn't blame her. If she had been the one to kill Edgar, then it was too much of a coincidence that we would be diving in exactly the same place for an unrelated reason. "I'll have to ask him about that," she said finally. "You're definitely a bottom-feeder. Just have to figure out what your scam is exactly. Ortiz is my cargo now. I won't let you damage him anymore."

"Hope you're insured," I said, before I could stop myself. "I recall him getting all wet and flipped over on your watch. And that was after you sent a gator to chew him up," I added, to see her reaction.

Deena didn't say anything, but she didn't deny it. She looked out onto the horizon, and I followed her gaze.

The Astro America rose in the distance.

# 11

The Astro America was comprised of two distinct parts: a glass dome in the front and a rectangular box overtaking it from behind. The walls of the box were painted in pastel pink with green highlights, with three giant window facades on the top floor that looked like eyes and a big one right below that looked like a mouth. It rose several stories above the yoreshore, mounted on massive pillars that made the construction titan's pylons look like toothpicks. The printed highway leading out the back to OrlanDome was a leash, restraining an enormous, sunburned, three-eyed golem with stick legs stuck in the sand.

We sailed right between those pillar legs and pulled up to a massive dock, with at least a dozen slips, each one three times the width of the *Ghost*, wide enough to accommodate a small battleship.

Deena marched me off the ship and up a massive ramp. The Mourners stayed behind.

The back half of the dock was a warehouse of equipment hanging from the rafters. Deena hurried me along, under a crane arm swinging a massive object: a rocket ship, sleek and simple, with a snub nose and a long tapered fuselage like a purple arrow. An atmo-breaker. We were in the hangar.

Deena found a nearby utility closet and filed me away like a spare part. She zip-tied my wrists together.

"Don't worry," she said. "I'm coming back for you. This is just a pit stop."

She bumped me in the shoulder on her way out, and something fell out of my hair and into my open hands.

Disgusting. I wished they had let me shower. My hair was always sort of a mess, but it had never trapped a physical object without my knowledge.

But then, upon closer inspection I saw it was the drone.

It was dead now, a delicate husk. It crinkled like paper between my fingers. Its wings had come together to form a single stubby blade with a surprisingly sharp point, and with some careful maneuvering I used this to file through my bonds.

I waited until it was quiet outside my door, and then I tried to use the wing knife to jimmy it open, but snapped the wings off. If this was what the Church had meant by freedom, then I was certainly getting what I'd paid for.

I picked up the drone pieces and saw that the legs had curled into a compact rectangular pattern, two rows of fine copper teeth that resembled the male end of a standard data port. More than resembled.

I felt beneath the smart lock on the door until I found the diagnostic input and stuck the legs in it. The drone twitched with a final breath of life, and the lock clicked open.

Collar lightly loosened.

## SALVAGIA

I opened the closet door and a breaker flew past me, attached to a mover running on tracks on the ceiling. The machinery of the hangar churned to life. Movers pulled breakers from their hanging berths and flew to a central point near the front of the hangar. I saw a gigantic version of the atmo-breaking barge that had been at Key West, saw the machinery stop just long enough for pilots to jump into the cockpits of their ships and then continue on, positioning the breakers on top of the barges. Through the whir of metal I could see an elevator, all the way at the other end, through a series of hallways whose floors were covered in yellow caution tape.

I took my chance and sprinted down the hallway, diving under a moving breaker and its surprised pilot and ducking into an elevator just before it closed.

The elevator opened in the least expected place: a circular dining room directly beneath the glass dome belly. The floor looked like it had been carved from a single giant piece of lunar rock. The room was packed. Two exquisite bars wrapped around the sides with real bartenders.

I was in the very center of the room, the center of attention, but the crowd was looking out the glass dome now, watching the barge putter out to sea. A sign above the bar read WAXING MOON LOUNGE. The Jumbotron above the window blared CANAVERAL CUP QUALIFYING RUNS in an explosive font.

I scanned the room for Riley, for an exit. Someone grabbed my arm.

It was Agent Gomer Afti of the IXS, in an Orlando Dolphins–themed Hawaiian T-shirt and sunhat.

He pulled me away, behind the elevator and toward a quiet corner of the lounge. "What are you doing here?"

"Trying to escape."

He looked incredulously at my outfit. "What, did you swim here?"

"I need to find Riley Ortiz," I said. "We need to get out of here."

"Riley Ortiz?" he said. "I saw him here a little while ago, at one of the big tables."

"Can you help me get him out? You wanted to talk to him, didn't you?"

"Will he talk to us?"

"Of course," I said, even though I had no idea.

Gomer looked pained. "Come with me."

He pulled me down the main concourse, through the lobby.

The entrance was guarded by Mourners, standing there like armed mascots.

"It won't be easy," said Gomer. "There's extra security everywhere. I thought it was because of the Canaveral Cup, but maybe there's another reason. Checkpoints at the entrances. There's only one road by land, that printed highway that goes all the way to the OrlanDome Airport. That's how everybody comes and goes."

He knew a surprising amount about the hotel's defenses. "What are *you* doing here, Gomer?" I asked.

He hesitated. "We have a package coming in tomorrow."

"A package?"

"Early morning," he said. "Right before the race starts. If . . . if you can both meet us outside I think we can get you out."

I blinked. "How do we get outside?"

"It has to be tomorrow because we can only do this when nobody will be watching the fire doors. We have an hour window starting at six a.m. All the alarms will be disabled. All the fire exits lead to a central exit with a service dock. It's a real bottleneck, a fire hazard if you ask me, but no one did. We'll be at the dock."

"For how long?"

"An hour, exactly. How are you going to get to Riley?"

"I don't know yet."

Gomer looked at me and pulled me into the nearest storefront.

"You need clothes," he said. We walked into the cheapest-looking boutique. He sized me up and grabbed a few items on the sales rack.

"Go change," he said. "I'll pay and stand guard."

"I can buy my own clothes—" I began, but then looked at the prices and changed my mind.

I slid the curtain on the changing room and peeled off my wetsuit. I looked at myself in the mirror and winced. I looked like an exhausted swamp thing, like you could make a nest out of my hair. And I was using the mirror filter that made you look good.

I checked my hair for more drones, pulled out a couple rat-tails and tried on the clothes Gomer had chosen for me—either a wildcat-pattern jumpsuit or a white tank with high-rise jeans.

Both were exactly my size. Agent Gomer had a secret superpower.

I chose the tank top and the jeans and put on the brown leather sneakers Gomer slid under the curtain (he guessed my shoe size, too?) and then I came back out.

"I talked to Andy," said Gomer, looking nervous. "He says when you get Ortiz you should come to our hotel room right away. Room number three-two-five."

"All right."

"Oh, and Triss? If he asks, I didn't tell you about the package. Okay?"

"Okay. I need you to do one more thing for me."

"What's that?"

"I need to get a message to Myra. My wearable is still on the *Floating Ghost*."

One of the many downsides of federal implants is that you can't share them. But Gomer could make the call for me. I gave him her number. "Tell her to call Charlie and tell him I have the money. Gomer, it's very important. She needs to convince him to call it off until I'm free, until I can get it to him. Can you tell her that?"

"Sure, I'll do my best."

"Thank you, Agent Afti."

"Be careful, Triss."

I returned to the Waxing Moon Lounge and looked for Riley, but I only saw Deena sitting at a table by the window. She turned in my direction and I veered to the only empty seat, all the way at the end of the bar. It was the dingiest corner of an elegant room, backed up against the door to the kitchen. The bartender couldn't even see me behind a big machine whose purpose I could not discern except I knew it wasn't an AutoBar.

"Know how to use one of these things?" the woman next to me asked. I jumped a little bit. She had a small, sharp nose and a round face, like an owl, and she wore purple cat-eye gogs and a lot of mascara. As soon as her attention turned to me the person on her left got up and briskly moved toward the window, taking their drink with them.

"It's a betting machine," she said. "That's why I sit here. It's the only seat where I can get a drink and a ticket at the same time! You looking to make a bet?"

"I don't know how."

"Well, I would *love* to teach you. You want a drink? Call me Auntie. Ask me why."

"Why?"

"Because I always bet the Antifecta. You know what that is?"

The Antifecta. Nepheli had mentioned it when she'd told me about Calysta Chen.

"Sure," I said. "You bet on a breaker to blow."

Auntie Antifecta waved down the bartender and placed an order that I couldn't hear. Then she leaned in close to me so she could get to the machine.

"Now if you really want to turn some heads you can bet the Super Antifecta."

"What's that?"

"That's when *everybody* blows."

"Does that ever happen?"

"Not as much as I bet it," she said, wistfully. "It's so exciting though, it's like fireworks. Don't you think?"

"No," I said. "Bad odds and bad vibes."

"But *phenomenal* payout. Big enough to get your picture taken for the federal yearbook."

She pointed to a camera behind me, above a sign, which I couldn't help but read in Agent Somer's voice:

STAND HERE TO RECORD YOUR WINNINGS FOR TAXATION PURPOSES. THE INTERNAL EXCHANGE SERVICE THANKS YOU FOR YOUR COOPERATION.

"They like to keep track of all the high rollers." She handed me my ticket. The bartender placed our drinks in front of her. She passed me a coupe glass full of something purple, fizzing angrily.

"Put it on room three-twenty-seven," she said to the bartender. Then she turned to me. "Drinks on me. On my boyfriend actually. It's been *ages* since I've won an Antifecta, the coffers are running a little dry. It'll happen soon, though. I can feel it."

"Hello, Auntie," a voice said behind me. "Whose death warrant you got signed there? Mine?"

"Riley *Ortiz*!" she screeched. "I'd never bet on you. Wouldn't dream of it. You know it's all in good fun."

He stole a glance at her ticket. "You are betting the Super though, huh? On the Canaveral? We have different ideas of fun."

"I'm only betting the Super Antifecta because you're not racing. If you were racing I just know you'd squeak through, no matter what happens out there. And there's no prize for every breaker blowing but one. Not yet, anyway."

"What're the odds on Nepheli?" He peered over at her console screen.

"And if it *were* going to happen, dear, and I do sincerely pray that it never does, I would be beside myself. All my favorite breakers, gone in an instant? The payout would be my only comfort. Though for the Canaveral," she said to me, winking. "There's *quite* a lot of comfort."

"Uh-huh." I could tell Riley wasn't listening. He was distracted by something he saw on the screen. Auntie Antifecta glanced at me and then turned to the person on her other side.

"Can I borrow her for a second?" Riley asked, but Auntie Antifecta was already deep in conversation with the unsuspecting patron on her left.

I pulled Riley aside and filled him in on my encounters with the Church and Gomer.

"Escape?" he said.

"The Church thinks you're in danger."

"From Maurice?"

"Where's Deena?"

"She's taking Nestor, one of the other Mourners, out on Maria's yacht for a joyride, to keep him good and tipsy. She's got orders not to let me leave the hotel until Maurice gets here."

"Where is he?"

"Running around trying to get all the fogey Mourners back together, minus Maria. Deena told me exactly how much money Maurice still owes the Church."

"How much?"

He glanced back at Auntie Antifecta. "A hell of a lot. Half a million kiloDollars. Once everyone's here, I'm supposed to make a grand entrance and tell them all that my dad would want them to invest in the high-rise deal."

"What happens if you don't?"

"I didn't ask. But you say the Church thinks he'll kill me?"

"He tried it before. Deena rigged the gator to attack you."

"Why?"

"I think he killed Edgar too."

"What?"

"I told the agents I'd take you to their room when I found you. We can talk there."

"I got a better idea," he said. "Let's go to the Ortiz suite."

Riley took me to a special elevator that went all the way to the penthouse floor. He led me down the hallway and opened the door onto a huge living room, at least the size of the *Ghost*. There were just enough curated items of furniture and art to indicate extreme luxury. Red carpet and warm lighting on soft white walls. A hallway led to more rooms. The entire back wall was a window looking out over the sea, and it curved at the top to form a skylight.

I had never seen the yoreshore from this high before. This was the biggest structure that had ever been built up here, and we were at the very top of it. I understood, looking at that view, why someone might be interested in living here, after many years of living in a windowless dome. Especially now, at the end of the day, with the sun setting on the other side and turning the sky shades of pink against the blue. It was the kind of view that looked great on a marketing flyer.

There was an AutoBar in the kitchen and Riley made us drinks and I told him everything: the dive in Edgar's wreck, recovering the card, the open blue barrels that were to be used on Miami. And my own conclusions, that Maurice had found out and killed him, that he had taken the body and used it to frame Maria.

"So how do we stop him?" he asked, finally.

"We?" I replied. "We can't. That's my point. All we can do is escape."

"I'm not running away."

"We don't have a choice. I don't, anyway."

Something caught his eye, out of the floor to ceiling window that faced the yoreshore. He stood up, so fast that he spilled his drink, an R-Special, all over his shirt.

"What are you doing?" I asked.

"Come on," he muttered. "The angle's better in the old man's room."

He went down the hallway and pushed in the second door. I followed him. Edgar's room was the most cluttered room in the suite, the most lived-in, though the bed was made and everything was mostly organized. Riley went right to the window, stepping over a little pile of equipment at his feet.

"Is this where he kept his mix machine?" I asked.

"He kept all his equipment here."

I pulled off a wetsuit draped over a box on the floor a little smaller than the AutoBar. "Can't you smell that?"

"Sure. Where have I smelled that before?"

"Whatever your dad was breathing in that wreck smelled like that. But then, at Coral Castle, Kohl was covered in something that smelled like this too."

"Kohl?"

"I thought it was a plant or something, because then later, on the shore, when the two of us were talking to Nepheli, I could smell it there."

"I remember."

"Now I can find out what it is."

"How does that help us?"

"I'm not sure. But whatever it is, it wasn't the right mix. I was breathing it when I went into the wreck and it almost knocked me out."

I turned the mix machine on. I hadn't used one extensively before, but the readouts seemed pretty straightforward. Three dials, each displaying a different kind of gas. In Edgar's last setting, the first gas came up $O_2$, the second N, and the third . . .

Was blank. Empty. No, wait. I looked at the readout more closely. The machine knew it was a gas, it just couldn't identify what it was. I sniffed the nozzle. The smell was definitely strongest there.

"Smells like . . ." Riley trailed off.

"Dead flowers," I said.

Riley paused, and I convinced myself it was because he wasn't really paying attention to me. He was focused on what was outside the window. "Yeah," he said. "Exactly."

His reaction was strange, but before I had a chance to ask him what he meant, he suddenly pointed through the window and out to sea.

"Look," he said.

Nepheli's circuit barge, with *Bulls on Parade* still in tow behind it, had appeared on the horizon. Three boats, the same size as the gunboats that surrounded the *Marino*, had sped out to meet them, and were now escorting them into the hangar dock where Deena had pulled me off Maria's boat.

"Nepheli's too late," I said. "They won't make the race in time."

As if on cue, the race started, and a great cloud of collective smoke billowed out under the racing barge, a muffled roar bouncing off the windows and making them vibrate slightly.

Riley shook his head. "These are just the qualifiers. The Canaveral's tomorrow morning. I flew so well at Key West last night that the *Bull* prequalified. So Neph's still in it, thanks to me."

"Deena interrogated me when she got me," I said. "Tried to find out if I knew where Nepheli was."

"Well now they're finally here," said Riley.

"They're under guard," I replied. "Why?"

"Probably to keep Nepheli safe, away from the race barge," he said, but he sounded uneasy.

"That's not it," I started to say, but it was clear that he wasn't listening to me. He wasn't watching Nepheli anymore either.

He was watching the breakers, their exhaust obscuring the yoreshore in front of the Astro America. More gunboats came out to the circuit barge until it was flanked from all sides, but Riley's eyes were on the race in the background.

"You still want to race, don't you?" I said, standing up. "That's why you won't leave."

He blinked. "Well, yeah. I'm an atmo-breaker. That's what I do. And it *should* be me out there. I got us this far." He sounded guilty, like he'd been caught doing something worse.

The breakers rose slowly, almost as a unit. Some of them started to peel away from the rest.

"Haven't you been listening to me?" I said.

"Maybe if Maurice gets here in time, if I agree to help him, he'll let me back in. And then I can race, and we can find another way out. Or you tell the feds to hold off for a few hours."

"Riley, Maurice tried to kill you. You can't trust him."

"But now he wants something from me. He brought me all the way here, didn't he?"

"Aren't you . . ." I couldn't think of the right word. "Afraid?"

"Of what? Dying? Nah. I'm an atmo-breaker. I could die any time I go up."

"Aren't you afraid that if you help him it'll . . . it'll work? He'll get the money, and he and the Church will churn up the yoreshore. They'll churn up Miami. Exactly what your dad died to stop."

He watched the breakers shoot past the window, disappear into the sky. He was quiet for a long time.

"I'm not really going to help him," he said, finally. "I'll just say I will."

"Why risk it at all? It's just a race."

That hit a sort of nerve. He whipped around, and I realized only then, when it was entirely gone, that there was almost always at least a little trace of grin on his face. But now the party boy heir apparent had departed, replaced by the atmo-breaker. He focused the intensity of his entire self toward me like a laser or a bullet, his strange eyes reflected the dying light like hungry, golden embers.

"You want to know what I'm afraid of?" he said. "I'm afraid of dying for nothing, dying without understanding what I'm dying for. That gator drowning me? I won't go that way. At least if I race I know what the stakes are. I know what's coming to get me."

"Dying while atmo-breaking is dying for nothing," I said. "You don't even win."

"But you make a big payout for someone else," Riley said, trying, failing, to catch his smile again. "But nah. It is different. Once you reach the other side of the Karman and you're just floating, and you won, no one can get to you . . . it's the only time I feel . . . Well, it's like freedom. It's a feeling worth dying for, anyway."

"It's a selfish way to die," I said. I wasn't sure why we were still talking about death, when we could talk about escape, but if I followed him down this path maybe I could bring him around.

"Not selfish," he said. "Not since I started flying the *Bull*. You know, I wasn't even supposed to fly her in the first place? It was secret, just like Nepheli said. The old man kept separate lives. But when I found out about her I was so jealous I snuck out of this very room and flew her, right under my dad's nose. This was . . . I think it was last year's Tres Equis Classic. After that she was all mine. Even the old man agreed she listened to me best, even if his way of agreeing was to give me the cold shoulder.

"But Neph let me in. They told me their plan, what they wanted to build. I knew about their parents, I knew what it meant to them. If I blew with the *Bull*, at least I'd know that Nepheli was watching and collecting that data and they'd use it to make something safer, for the breakers that come after us. If I died doing what I was best at and making something better, well, that's not such a bad way to go."

"Stop talking about dying," I said.

"Think about it that way and it was actually sorta genius for the old man to rig it the way that he did. With the UltiMon card. To set it up so that when he went, something else would move forward, just a little bit. Something that could never move forward while he was alive. Yeah, that's the way a breaker dies, on the move."

"Moving the needle," I said, mockingly, forgetting that Riley didn't know what that meant. That's how Ermie had described how Eli had died, how an echidna fighter's supposed to die. He tried to make his death sound noble, when the truth was it was avoidable and pathetic. And even the lie was pathetic. Moving the needle? That was barely moving anything at all.

"So I ain't afraid of dying," said Riley. "It just sucks to die at the starting line."

"Then let's get out of here."

He contemplated this. The breakers had burst past our window during his speech, their plumes of smoke hazing the beautiful sunset that rich Consolidators would pay Maurice and the Church to see. I put my hands on the glass and watched them rise.

"Fine," he said, finally. "You win. I'll go."

"Really?"

He nodded. "In the morning. Tonight, I'm staying here. Nostalgia and all. Your feds said they're going to disable the fire alarm? There's a fire exit at the end of the hallway, I'll use that."

I was apprehensive. We had a plan. If we followed it, we'd get out. I felt the same way I did when Kohl convinced me to throw anchor at Key West. I should have kept moving then, I shouldn't have listened to him. But as much as I wanted to, I couldn't make Riley go.

"What about you?" he asked. "What will you do?" The question surprised me.

"You asked me that already," I said. "There are too many 'ifs' right now to say."

"I meant tonight."

I realized that he was looking at me, had been looking at me since I told him he was selfish. The breakers in the race had become little points of light in the sky. He was sitting on the edge of Edgar's bed and looking at me.

"The Church and the feds gave you a free night at the Astro America," he said. "It's the fourth most popular tourist attraction in the country."

"Third."

"Right," he said. "Niagara's got that weird smell now. Anyway, you got free reign here for one night. Fifteen bars, seventeen restaurants. Three spas, plus the good one on the roof. All for you. You can put it all on this room, if you want."

"Thank you."

"But you gotta tell me. What does Triss Mackey do with her one free night?"

He meant free, like gratis. But I heard the other kind of free, and realized that that was something I had never truly been, not since the moment I had dragged Eli into that 2C3 recruitment office. Just various loosenings and tightenings of the collar.

Even now, if I got out, if I got the *Ghost*, I was just as leashed to the Church as Kohl had been, as well as to the feds.

He was Riley Ortiz and even he wasn't free. The only moment he could ever pretend to be was when he was alone, in space, in some ways freer than anyone could ever hope to be, in other ways more trapped.

Maybe that was all that there was, anymore. Collars under cages under domes beneath the atmosphere.

In this room, though, I sensed that we could pretend. This was where Edgar Ortiz had hatched a plan to fund his own Third Way, and if anyone could find a way to do it, it was him. I could trick myself into believing the Church couldn't see us here.

I could even pretend I believed Riley when he said he'd come with me, ignore the little voice that told me, quietly, persistently, that if I left him now I would never see him again.

I wanted to escape with him. But, failing that, I wanted to hold on to him for as long as I could.

The sky was still a little pink, against a deepening blue, and his orange-gold eyes seemed to draw that failing light straight from the window toward them, and me with it. What would I do, with my one free night? I walked up past him, touching the top of his chair, brushing his hair with my fingertips, and then I walked out of the room and down the hall, where the scent of Edgar's tank was so faint I could only really smell the sweetness. I opened the door to the guest room and kept exploring, pulling myself through the suite like it was another shipwreck and the prize of my life lay somewhere in the silt.

One night, in this luxurious place. I'd slept barely at all in two days, just a quick nod-off into the realm of nightmares. Maybe this was just another pipe dream.

I flipped on the light of the bathroom at the end of the hall. It was bigger than the master stateroom on the *Ghost*, with white tiles and a showerhead wide enough to make a mini-hurricane.

"Honestly?" I replied. "I'm exhausted and I'm starving. I want to eat everything and do it lying down. And I desperately need a shower."

"Maybe your fed friends will get you a cot," said Riley. His voice was close. He had followed me down the hall. "And let you order room service."

"I don't think Somer will let me in without you," I said. "He doesn't like me very much."

"Well, I said already, I'm sleeping here. The guest room's got the hotel's only Lunar King bed, and I sleep like a starfish."

"That's funny," I said. "I sleep closed up, like a clam." I turned around. Riley was standing beside the open bedroom door. The other room, not Edgar's. I approached him. "I only need a little corner. Can you spare one?"

"At least one," he replied, grinning slightly. "I'm not that tall."

I disappeared through the door of the bedroom, into the pipe dream.

"Then maybe I'll open up a little."

## 12

I woke up late, in the center of an endless bed. I checked the time on the vintage clock on the bedside table. It was just inside the feds' fire alarm window.

I'd slept deeply all night, after we had finally tired each other out. I'd woken only once, and just long enough to recall Riley's steady breath on the nape of my neck, the twitch of his forearm under my side as he pulled the pillow closer. I thought he might have been awake, but I fell asleep again soon after.

I do not live a life that favors long-term romance, and I'm not much interested in one anyway. But I am quite curious about certain other people, and sex accelerates the satisfaction of that curiosity through its primal closeness. Sex reveals the inner wordless self, upon which we base all the stories we tell about ourselves.

So it was only through sex that I could glimpse the root of Riley beneath his somewhat contradictory behavior: this brash and needy deathsport racer, this wealthy New Daytona brat who had submitted to me, but stolen my boat, but showed me how to listen to her. Was he a taker who had learned to give a little as a tactic? Had he been taught to listen by someone that he loved? Or was he a natural giver who was just a little more accustomed than me to getting his own way by the trappings of his wealth and station? Or something else entirely?

What I learned that night is not for me to tell.

I also got a glimpse into myself—Knuckle-bound loner that I am—a reminder that sometimes, with certain people, I really can play nicely, and have the stamina to do so in the dark without my demons paying me a visit. That I am not so broken. More like a stubborn puzzle piece, strangely cut, who might stick to many but rarely the right way.

I fell asleep so quickly last night because against him I felt slotted into place. On one side at least.

But when I woke that morning he was gone.

The bed was so big I had to roll my way to the end of it. I slipped out from under the sheets, still in my underwear. The suite was silent enough that I knew already that Riley was gone, but I checked the rooms anyway. I wondered if he had gone to meet the agents himself, without me. But why wouldn't he have woken me up?

I knew that it was much more likely that he had abandoned our plan, gone to the big main lounge, the Waxing Moon, or somewhere else to meet Maurice and try to convince him to put him back in the race.

I was almost too late. There wasn't enough time for me to find him and still make the window. I would have to meet the agents without him. I'd left the other set of clothes that Gomer had bought me in the living room, the jumpsuit with a wildcat pattern. I ripped off the tags and put it on, dashed out of the suite, down to the fire exit at the end of the hallway. I paused with my hands on the handle, then pushed. Silence.

The fire stairwell for the penthouse floor was a straight shot down, no access at all to any other floor, perhaps to give special escape access to penthouse residents. When I pushed open the ground floor door I found that I was outside of the building entirely, next to a little path that led downhill toward the sea and then disappeared. I could see the very top of something bobbing up and down. A docked boat. I heard voices.

But to my left there was another door. It was wide open, and I could see the same cacophony of machinery I'd weaved through the day before.

The hangar.

Riley told me last night that he had snuck into the hangar before, the first time he had flown the *Bull*. He'd done it from Edgar's suite. Had he done the same thing just now, using the feds' plan for cover?

I had to check. The more I thought about it, the more sure I was. I walked through the door, with a rising creeping feeling that I was missing something terrible, and then, sure enough, I spotted Riley, pulling Nepheli toward the exit. Nepheli pointed behind them, to something out of the way. Riley looked where Nepheli was pointing. Neither of them saw me.

They argued, and then Riley shoved Nepheli to the ground, inches away from a breaker zooming over their head. I recognized *Bulls on Parade*. Riley leapt over a walkway, just before a different breaker came by. He was sprinting with the same long-legged dexterity he'd had at Key West, running through the water to catch the barge. His expression was different: where there had been glee was now grim resolve.

He wasn't wearing a flight suit, just the clothes he'd worn yesterday. Nepheli stayed down, and I ran over and pulled them out of the path of the breakers. Riley snatched a helmet from one of the other pilots in the circle, and leapt into *Bulls on Parade*, which seemed to tremble with excitement at his return. I saw him pat the dashboard, but then an incoming breaker blocked my view of him.

"He was trying to take me with you." Nepheli stood next to me, rubbing their side.

"With me where?"

"To escape with the feds. But I told him she was already set up, and I wouldn't leave her."

"So he took your place?" The terrible feeling was growing. He didn't want to compete? He wanted to escape with Nepheli? "Why?"

"Without either of us to pilot her she'd still try to fly the race on her own. It wouldn't go well."

"He doesn't want any of you to race? Why not?"

"I don't know, I didn't understand it. All he kept saying was that I wasn't listening. That I had my head up the ass of my diagnostics pad. Once he saw the *Bull* was already going, that's when he shoved me."

I remembered how Riley had looked when I reminded him where he'd smelled the dead flower scent before. He'd realized something then, something about *Bulls on Parade*. What could it have been? I'd told him about the mystery gas in Edgar's tank, how I'd smelled it on Kohl, and then later on the shore.

Kohl.

He'd been wet, when he'd come back to let me out of Ermie's cage. I thought the *Ghost* had tossed him overboard, but he'd said he couldn't even get close to her.

But the circuit barge was right next to her. And tied up alongside it in the water was the *Bull*.

The next time I'd smelled the dead flower smell I was near the *Bull*, too, with Riley and Nepheli. She was upright on the shore and all of her guts and valves were open.

"Nepheli," I said. "I think Kohl did something to *Bulls on Parade*."

"Kohl?"

"Is there anything he could have touched or tampered with?"

"Yeah," they replied. "Like several thousand things."

"Anything that has a particularly sweet smell?"

"I don't know," they said, annoyed. "I don't keep track of what everything in her smells like."

"Edgar had a diving tank that smelled the same. Not just similar, exactly the same. Riley said you looked at his equipment sometimes."

Their eyes went wide.

"Was there anything in his mix that—"

"It's fuel," said Nepheli, breathlessly. "Nitrous oxide."

"You're sure?"

"Kohl must have stuck his hand in the fuel tank."

"Did you check it?"

"The fuel tank? Check for what, sabotage? Why would I?"

"Because the *Bull* knew," I said. "She was trying to tell you something was wrong. Only Riley listened to her."

Nepheli stepped back onto the walkway and I had to pull them back out of the way before another breaker zoomed by and took their head off. On the other side the mover plucked the *Bull* and pulled her toward the waiting barge. The remaining pilots were staring at us.

"I don't understand," said Nepheli, helplessly. "Why would they try to sabotage her?"

"What could Kohl do with the fuel tank? Think."

They did. "Two things. Either he clogged it, to ground her. Or..."

"Or what?"

"Or he overloaded it."

I could guess what that meant.

"It doesn't make sense," they said. "If Riley knows she's going to blow, then why the fuck is he trying to fly her?"

I had no idea, except maybe he thought he could save her.

"We have to stop the race," I said.

"How? It's the Canaveral Cup!"

My mind raced. What was important to them? Blood and money, Nepheli had said. "If we tell them that Riley took the *Bull*... it'd mess up everyone's bets, right? They were betting on you to fly her. They'd have to stop it then, wouldn't they?"

"Maybe," Nepheli replied. "Or they'd just let him race and disqualify him after."

"It's worth a shot, isn't it? Where are the officials?"

"They're in a booth in the Waxing Moon Lounge. But—"

"Then let's go."

The movers were still pulling breakers around the space. I pulled Nepheli along, back to the elevator I had used the day before. The breaker barge gave a long blow of its foghorn, and then the doors closed.

The lounge was packed. There was barely any standing room. We were in the very center of it. Nepheli pointed to the booth all the way on the far side of the wall that was just a window that faced the sea. We started to push our way through the crowd.

We were near the bar seat where I'd met Auntie Antifecta, when I felt a hand close around my arm like a vice.

"Got you," said Deena. Then she saw Nepheli. "You. What are you doing here? You're supposed to be out there."

She looked at the barge, counted the breakers.

"Who's flying your ship?" she demanded.

A wild thought entered my head. "Is this your plan?" I shouted, over the din of the crowd. "Is this how you're going to kill him?"

"What? Who?"

"Your cargo."

"You mean . . . it's Ortiz out there? He's in the race?"

Her eyes went wide with fear and disbelief and I remembered something that punched a hole right in the middle of my accusation: Maurice had been the one to pull Riley from the Canaveral in the first place.

And Deena really was afraid, terrified even, and that increased my own impending dread. Her fear meant we were right, the *Bull* really had been sabotaged to blow.

Riley flying her just wasn't part of the plan.

Which meant that they'd been trying to kill Nepheli.

"What did you do?" I demanded, pushing her away. I kept myself between her and Nepheli.

"Wait right there," Deena stammered, fiddling with her gogs, trying to make a call, fending me off with her other hand. "Don't go anywhere. Don't *move*, or I'll—"

The countdown started, ignition in under a minute. The crowd crushed against us. Deena tapped her gogs and they frosted over. Nepheli grabbed my hand and pulled me away, through the crowd, toward the booth. Then they had to let go so they could use both hands to pull people out of the way. It was like wading through water, or running in a nightmare, so slowly that we might as well have been standing in one place, smoldering like the breakers on the barge.

We almost made it.

I could see the stairs that led to the little elevated platform. But the crowd pressed up against us once again and we hit the massive glass window and watched, helpless, saw the billowing cloud of smoke, heard the countdown hit zero, then ignition, the deafening roar vibrating the glass against my face. Through the haze the breakers levitated, impossibly slow for the amount of force involved.

Except for the *Bull,* who made her presence known immediately.

She danced around the other breakers. She was a fly flitting around them, gaining feet where they were gaining inches. She was a mountain climber, sprinting toward the summit. The breakers around her had no more life than the rocks that a climber deftly leaps to, like Riley leaping from pylon to pylon on Key West.

I had spent enough time with the *Floating Ghost* that certain mechanical qualities in the *Bull*'s climb manifested to me as signs of her rich internal life. She slowed suddenly and then sped up, and I saw exertion. Several bursts from her exhaust hinted at hunger. A lateral move that looked like an engine had faltered left me with an impression of yearning, perhaps for the sky above.

I grabbed Nepheli's hand and squeezed it, and they squeezed back. I had never seen anything, human or otherwise, so desperately alive.

The crowd saw it, too, I thought, though they did not understand it the way that Nepheli and I did. They were hushed, muted. They knew that they were seeing something special, something even rarer and more beautiful than the explosions whose promise had brought them all here.

I glanced up at the Jumbotron above us and found Riley's cockpit feed. His hands hovered above the *Bull*'s joystick. *You have to trust her,* he had said.

He had a helmet on, but no flight suit. The name below his feed still read "N. Guardini," so no one could know that it was Riley in there. He waved at the camera with his two empty hands, and

*Bulls on Parade* danced in the sky all by herself, well beyond the reach of even the next closest breaker. She was a bull on parade, charging through the sky.

I thought she'd make it. I knew she wouldn't. I hoped she'd make it high enough to be out of my sight, at least. If I couldn't see it maybe I could pretend she'd made it all the way.

Her nose touched the upper limit of the great glass window, and then she blew.

The crowd broke their hush with a gasp, a collective gulp of air. Except for one person, a woman, who laughed. I turned. Riley's cockpit feed was static on the Jumbotron. The woman laughing was Auntie Antifecta, and she was holding up her ticket. By the time the second-fastest breaker flew through that ball of fire it was a harmless white puff of cloud. The yoreshore in front of us sparkled, briefly, as if with falling rain.

Both my hands were pressed against the glass now, which meant that Nepheli had let mine go at some point.

I thought I heard them whisper. "Why?"

But they knew why. Maurice must have blown the *Bull* because he was afraid of what it could do.

Why did Riley do it?

"He saved you," I replied, breathlessly. "Only you can build another one. Without you it all stays the way it was."

He did it to move the needle.

When I turned around there was no Nepheli, only Agent Somer. His grip on my arm was just as tight as Deena's.

The feds' room on the third floor was less than half the size of the Ortiz suite. It might have been close to it in glamor if equipment wasn't spread out on every available surface. The bed was a storage space. A black-ops sort of telescope was set up on the balcony. On the right-hand wall were wires coming out of diodes attached to a pair of headphones. They were spying on someone here.

Another someone sat in a chair on the balcony, facing the sea, smoking a cigarette. I could tell from the door that it was Maria Feinstein-Reyes.

"You're the package," I said. She slid the screen door closed behind her.

"Where's the kid?" she replied.

I pointed to the remains of the race, the plumes of smoke that dissipating into the sky.

"What do you mean?"

"He raced," I said, simply, my voice breaking nonetheless. "Maurice rigged his breaker to blow. Now he's dead."

She accepted this with a nod, and silenced Somer with a hand when he tried to ask me follow-up questions.

"That's cold," said Maria. "Even for Thibodeux." She put a hand on my shoulder. "I told you breakers have a short shelf life. But that's not the way he should have gone."

"He wasn't supposed to be there," I said.

"So what now?" said Maria, to the agents. "Can we do this without Ortiz?"

"Maybe," said Somer. He turned to me. "Welcome to the Maurice Thibodeux fan club. Think you can pay the dues?"

"Paying my dues" meant, at first, listening to Somer give a lecture.

"Technically, the government still owns all of the yoreshore in South Florida," he said. "Thibodeux isn't allowed to build on it. Not yet."

"But he is," I said.

"Yes."

"So arrest him."

Somer sighed. "It's not that simple. We're in the middle of pulling out, and we don't really have the resources to stop him, at least not that way. But very soon we're going to start selling the yoreshore in parcels. There are a lot of interested parties."

"Yeah," I said. "Myra told me."

Somer nodded. "The problem is, in certain cases we're trying to return the land to the original owners."

"That doesn't sound like a problem. That sounds like what you should be doing."

"It's messy. Think about it: An individual has a deed saying that their great-grandparents owned a house built on a lot in a suburb in Coral Gables. The problem is, not only did the house get washed away, but the entire property line shifted over the years, and now it's submerged. The remains of that lot are underwater, and probably half a mile from where it was originally, and mixed up with all the other lots. So who owns what, and where? There's no standardized system. What if that individual's deed says they have waterfront property? What if they say that means they're entitled to dry land next to the water, miles away from where their original plot was, and still much more valuable? Multiply that one quarter acre lot times four and then times twenty million. It'll take decades to sort it all out."

"So just do what you feds always do," I said. "Make up a policy and force everyone to comply."

"We could," said Somer, ignoring my tone. "In my opinion, we should have. But there have been enough precedents in other yoreshores now that some powerful groups have developed a viable loophole."

"Precedents for what?"

"Using salvagia to . . . strengthen a yoreshore claim."

This had to be related to what Edgar had said, the last time Félix had seen him. And I had a feeling that this was what the Church had started to tell me about, back on Maria's boat. "How?"

"In lieu of any concrete standard of proof," said Somer. "The courts have been hearing . . . well, basically, tall tales: 'My great-grandmother owned an orange grove in Homestead that stretched from this creek to that Waffle House.' That sort of thing. If you happen to be in possession of salvagia that support that narrative . . . orange boxes, farming equipment, et cetera, it makes the argument more convincing. Extra points if your salvagia was dredged up in the lot you're trying to claim, but not required."

"Sounds easy to fake."

"Absolutely," said Somer. "And they do. We found out about a hedge fund buying up tons of sneakers, for example, because they're going to try and convince us that a beautiful little sandbar on the Gulf used to be the site of a warehouse where an investor's grandfather stored his shoe collection."

I gritted my teeth, remembering the Ked.

"It's all happening fast enough that everyone thinks they'll get away with it," he said.

"Will they?" I asked.

"Maybe," said Somer. "For now. That's why the IXS is so important. That's why we need to keep watch. Because there will come a reckoning, one day. And we'll need the receipts."

"It's a self-feeding system," said Maria, piping in. "Speculators are setting prices for plots based on how much salvagia might be there, which increases the value of the salvagia they find there. And salvagia is its own separate asset, which can be bought and sold and borrowed against."

"Interesting," I said, sarcastically. "But how does this relate to Maurice's high-rise plan?"

"We have two theories," replied Somer. "It could be one or the other or both. One, we spotted his construction titan roaming up and down the coast, churning up yoreshore."

"I know," I said, remembering Coral Castle. "He's setting down the foundations of his buildings."

"Yes. But remember, he doesn't own that land yet. So why is he already starting to build?"

"To get a head start," I said, after thinking about it. This was not an original thought, this had been Myra's theory back on the *Ghost*. "You said yourself that there are a lot of parties interested in the land."

"Maybe," said Somer. "But he still has to buy the site. And if he's cash poor, then he might get outbid. We think it's something else. We passed one of those sites on the way up. They're using a particular chemical. The damage to the ecosystem was . . . extensive. Unnecessarily so."

"I know."

"We think," said Gomer. "That he's churning up the sites on purpose to destroy any potential salvagia underneath it. So when it comes time to buy that land he can get it for cheap, because no one else wants it. And any existing salvagia claims around those sites might not hold up, if there's nothing there to corroborate them except black goo."

"So how do we stop him?" I said, finally losing my temper. "That's what we're all here for, right? To stop him? What's the point of knowing all this if it doesn't help us do that?"

The agents blinked. "Sorry," said Gomer. "I guess we forgot that civilians don't find this kind of thing as interesting as we do."

"If you can dive and get a sample of that black stuff for us," said Somer. "We can run it up to headquarters, get the FDA involved. They'll do an environmental analysis, and maybe we can get it banned, make it retroactive under the Act of—"

"That'll take too long," I cried. "That's your plan? If you don't have the resources to arrest him for building without a permit, you definitely don't have the manpower for that."

"My *plan* was to have Riley Ortiz and Maria convince the other Mourners to turn on him," said Somer. "Now I'm improvising."

"You said you had two theories. What's the other one?"

"Oh," said Somer. "That one's simpler. Thibodeux needs money. We're not sure exactly how much, but—"

"Half a million kiloDollars," I said. "Riley told me."

Somer blinked. Gomer whistled, low.

"Okay. So obviously, we thought that he'd be after a piece of salvagia to cover that spread. When we saw you there on Key West with Riley Ortiz, we figured that that's what they were hiring you to do. Was it?"

"Not for Thibodeux," I replied. "Not for this."

"For what then?"

"It's not important," I said. "But I do know that he had until this morning to pay the Church," I remembered. "Or there would be consequences. And he wanted Riley to stay and help him get all the Mourners back to the table."

"So maybe we don't have to do anything," said Gomer, hopefully. "Maybe it's already over. Without Riley he can't get the money together."

Somer shook his head. "According to our intel," he said, "the titan's still operating. It should have shut down by now. And they didn't make a deal—we saw Nestor Ortega leave the hotel after the

Canaveral and Maurice still hasn't shown up. So we have to assume he's getting the money some other way. We just don't know how."

The agents began to bicker over where Maurice's hidden money could be. They bickered about what to do with me, if threatening me with reenlistment would help me brainstorm. I remembered, actually, that Félix had said that he had developed the black stuff to use on the foundation of the Astro America and I could dive here for a sample, but at that point their fight had bled into their personal lives. It turned out their wife thought Somer wasn't letting Gomer take the lead enough, and while Gomer didn't agree he needed something to say when she asked and, well, maybe he actually did agree. They went onto the balcony and slid the door closed.

Maria sat in an armchair. She stared at me for a long time, the same sort of look she gave me when I met her for the first time on the beach. She looked exhausted. Her journey to the Astro must have been at least as harrowing as mine.

For my part, I would have left, if I had anywhere in particular to go.

"Do me a favor," she said. "Take down that smoke detector over there."

I obliged. She took out a pack of rejuvenating cigarettes and lit one. The smell of grease and eucalyptus filled the room when she sighed out the smoke. She relaxed a little more in the chair.

"I have a message for you," she said. "And a gift. The message is that your boat is free."

"Free?" I sat upright. "Is she safe? Where is she? Where's Myra?"

She held up a hand, for silence. "The gift is this."

She reached into her pockets and pulled out two little handles. They had been cleaned and painted matte black. When I saw my Knuckles, I almost didn't recognize them. But when I took them from her they fell easily back into my palms, like freshly oiled machinery. They were just a hair heavier, and they had two extra buttons each.

"How did you get these?" I asked. I slipped them on and triggered the batons. They slid out silently.

"These two found me after I fled the *Marino*," she said. "I agreed to give them information if they could sneak me into the Astro. I left my people and joined them up the yoreshore. Agent Afti went ahead. Yesterday he told us to meet up with a CabanaBoat on the way. They had an interesting story. One of them gave me this to give to you."

"'They?' So Félix, Ermie, and Myra, they're all together?"

"They're waiting for you somewhere called the Inner Boca Boatel. Your friend Myra said you'd know how to find it."

I smiled. Inner Boca was as myth, but it was based on a real site that just so happened to be a couple of miles south of the Astro. "I absolutely do."

"The old guy told me to tell you to get familiar with all the new features before you try to use them."

"I don't suppose he gave you an instruction manual."

"He did not."

The agents' bickering climaxed with an angry speech from Gomer, followed by Somer passionately embracing his partner. It was, in my opinion, very unprofessional.

"I'm sorry about the kid," Maria said. "You look like you're taking it pretty hard."

I ignored this. "I'm surprised to find you of all people working with feds" I said.

She shrugged. "Our interests appear to align for the moment. The Astro America belongs to Mourning in Miami. Maurice gave it to the tourists. He'll do the same with his high-rises. I'm going to do what Edgar couldn't. I'm going to take it all back."

"Why couldn't Edgar?"

"He negotiated. He was always negotiating. He didn't give up the cause. I used to think it got away from him. But your friends told me an interesting story about that, too."

The agents signaled for me to come out to the balcony, then went back to arguing. Maria grabbed my arm.

"Mourners loyal to me are making their way up the yoreshore right now," she told me, in a low voice. "They're in position at the Red Cigar. You know where that is?"

"I do." The Red Cigar was a partly ruined lighthouse, at the site where three rivers once met and spilled out into the ocean together. The rivers were gone, but the ghosts of their currents remained, swirling around the island like an old-fashioned washing machine. The light was gone and the red paint near the top had faded to gray, so it really did resemble a cigar with a deeply un-ashed tip.

"They're waiting for my signal," said Maria.

"You're going to assault the hotel?"

"You want to know a secret?" She nodded to the agents. "They don't really care about getting rid of Maurice. They only care about the money. They won't even take it. They just want him to know that they know it's there, come tax season."

"Why are you telling me this?"

"Because you're special," she said, pointing to my Knuckles. "I knew it when I met you. When the time comes I think you'll do some damage. Just trying to point you in the right direction."

"Which is where?"

"Away from me."

The agents returned. Somer dropped Gomer's hand and said that they had decided that they would sneak me out of the Astro America and I would dive the foundation for a sample of the black stuff. In exchange, they promised to delete my file.

The *Ghost* was safe. She was mine. And I would be free. I would have even played a part, however slight, however ineffective, in stopping Riley's killer.

What more could I hope to do?

Maria wished me luck. Gomer took the lead. We left the room with a cheap mask and diving tank, the same sort of federal issue that he used to rent out to me at the Hydrofluorocarbon Center.

We headed for the fire exit at the end of the hall. The door to the next room opened and a woman stepped out and headed for the elevator at the other end. I recognized her. Auntie Antifecta. She didn't notice us.

I glanced at the room number: 327. I remembered she had said that this was where her boyfriend was staying.

It just happened to be the room right next to the IXS agents, who had set up listening equipment against the shared wall between them.

"Gomer," I said. "Why did you set yourself up in this room?"

"Oh," he said. "Feinstein-Reyes told us Thibodeux was staying next door."

"I see," I said.

"Triss? Where are you going? It's this way. Triss, wait!"

# 13

I took the stairs, Gomer huffing behind me. We made it to the Waxing Moon Lounge just in time to see Auntie Antifecta walk through, and the crowd part for her like the Red Sea. She went to the big IXS sign, the cutout of feet near the ticket booth, with the label that read STAND HERE.

Two well-dressed people came out with a metal briefcase. They made a big, drawn-out ceremony of it, blocking my escape to the stairs. They stood next to Auntie Antifecta, one on each side of her, and she placed her feet on the cutout of feet. They all faced the same direction, away from us, toward a wall that must have had a camera or some kind of scanner in it. They pressed their thumbs to the briefcase and the latch clicked open. Auntie pressed her thumb on the briefcase too. The briefcase emitted a loud beep, presumably to indicate that her biometrics had been transferred.

"Triss," said Gomer. "We want to go out through the service entrance. It's—"

"What is she doing?" I asked him. "What's happening?"

"Must have won a big pot," said Gomer.

"How much?" I demanded.

Gomer shrugged. "The payout list is up there."

He directed me to the Jumbotron screen. It listed all the payouts for the various bets.

Auntie was collecting her payout for an Antifecta bet, on Riley presumably. I remembered I'd heard her laughing when he blew.

I found the line on the screen: "Canaveral Antifecta: 80,000 USkD."

Eighty-thousand kiloDollars. Not nearly enough. I stared at it. Maybe I'd just wanted his death to mean something.

But then I saw the line above it, and I remembered Riley's face when he'd looked over Auntie Antifecta's shoulder at her screen, and I figured it out.

He'd done it all on purpose. He'd done it to save not just Nepheli, but everybody, all the breakers.

Everyone except himself, and the *Bull*.

Auntie Antifecta opened the case and held it up in the direction of the hushed crowd.

It was stuffed with glittering stacks of real bills, holograms that shimmered in the light like rippling water. Like twenty stacks of Kappacop cards, a hundred cards a stack.

"Why is she doing this?" I asked Gomer.

"It's gotta be handed over in physical cash," he replied. "So we can see it."

I'd never seen so much physical money in my life. Auntie Antifecta herself looked overwhelmed. She was smiling, but her jaw was clenched, and her hands were trembling. After showing it to us, she turned back to the camera and held it up, until they told her she could close it. She did, without looking at it again, like the money was blinding her, and then she clutched it to her chest.

It was a box full of paper. A useless object. Future fish food, future mulch. But today, a hundred people's eyes including mine irradiated it with enough worth that I could feel its value pulsing from within it. Like the Ked, like good salvagia.

"What will the IXS do about it?" I asked.

Gomer shrugged. "Nothing right now, I guess. Tax her later."

"Will they trace what she does with the cash?"

Gomer shook his head. "No. We make them stand on that 'X' so we can get a real-time record of the transfer. Physical cash, physical owner. That's what the IXS is all about. Once she leaves here though she can do whatever she wants with it. If she's a person of interest, we keep an eye on her. Just like we're doing with Thibodeux."

Auntie Antifecta took the briefcase, blew some kisses, and then headed for the lobby.

"That's Maurice's money," I said to Gomer.

"What do you mean?"

"That's his plan. He told her that *Bulls on Parade* would blow, and she bet the Antifecta for him."

He furrowed his brow. "That briefcase can't be enough. You said he needed half a million."

"Yes," I replied. "But the Super Antifecta is a little over five hundred and forty. The *Bull* was supposed to blow early enough to take all the breakers out. Auntie settled for a regular Antifecta payout."

Riley knew how much money Maurice needed, and he knew that Kohl had tampered with the *Bull* on his orders. He knew the Super Antifecta bet was enough to cover Maurice's debt. And he knew that he was the only pilot that would let the *Bull* race as fast as she could. The only one that had a chance to save everyone else by flying fast enough to blow at a safe distance.

He found a way to die for something.

"She's leaving the Astro," I said to Gomer. "I bet she's going to meet Maurice right now, to bring it to him."

"But it's not enough."

"We could stop him, Gomer. Agent Afti. You and me."

"But Andy—"

"You wanted to take the lead, didn't you? You have a car here?"

"You really think we can stop them?"

I fingered the new buttons on my Knuckles and headed for the lobby without answering.

Gomer played his part well. We went to the parking garage and he distracted the two Mourners at the entrance long enough for me to get to his car.

I spotted Auntie Antifecta getting into a luxury sport vehicle. It had big off-road tires, the kind that could handle the crumbled asphalt of the non-printed roads. I caught a glint of peroxide blonde hair in the driver's seat. Deena.

Gomer's car, by comparison, was much more delicate, meant for traveling between domes and other federally controlled areas. He got in and pressed a couple buttons and began to program the car to follow the license plate of Deena's car. I switched the monitor off.

"She's not taking the printed roads," I told him. "Do you know how to drive off-road?"

"Sure," said Gomer, unsteadily. "I passed the written exam, anyway."

We followed them, crossing the bridge that led from the yore-shore of the Astro America to dry land. Just like I predicted, Deena turned off the printed highway to OrlanDome and down a maintenance off-ramp toward the old, unsanctioned roads.

"Follow them," I commanded. Gomer swerved off. The car shook over ruined, uneven asphalt.

I tried to examine the new buttons on my Knuckles, but Gomer's driving started making me carsick. I hit one by accident. The wheel of the car froze.

"Hey!" shouted Gomer

"Sorry!" I cried, and pressed the button again, just in time for Gomer to swerve away from the edge.

We drove that way, over bumpy roads for maybe half an hour, until we thought we lost them around a tight bend. Gomer had to swerve when we came around the other side and found her car blocking the entire road. He slammed on the brakes to get the carshare to stop in time, and even then it drifted a few dozen feet over the gravel.

Auntie Antifecta stared at us through the glass of the back seat window. Deena stood off to the side. She wore laceless black boots, a black tank top, and wide camo pants that changed colors when she moved through the brush. She actually reminded me a good deal of Kohl with that equipment. She pointed her gun at us, a sleek black pistol. Gomer put his hands up. I pressed the brand new button again. The car shut off.

My first surprise.

She gestured for me to get out of the car. I did, with my palms out, showing her my Knuckles.

"Oh good, you got your sticks back," she said, and pulled the trigger.

Nothing happened.

My knees were shaking, and to hide it I started walking toward her. She tried again. The trigger wouldn't budge. She smacked the gun, I heard the crack of carbon fiber on metal.

"Your gun has biometrics," I said.

"What did you do?" she hissed, betraying her anger and surprise.

I raised my left Knuckle, tapped the new button with my middle finger.

"Biometrics can be confused, if you know the right frequency. You should have brought something dumber."

I extended my batons then. She grimaced and tossed the gun into the brush. She took out a knife.

"Tricks like that won't save you," she said.

"No, probably not," I sighed, and bared the stunner in my left hand, daring her to close the gap.

The first sting from the stunner surprised her, and I got a good hit on her arm with the baton in my other hand. But she readjusted, keeping her distance and feinting with the knife. She had no range, but she could slash faster than I could swipe. It would take fewer hits, maybe only one, to take me out, while I was just trying to wear her down.

She stabbed and got too close again, and I brought the stunner down on her hand. She swore and jumped back before I could counter-attack, and shook it out.

"All I need is time," she said. "If you want that money, you're gonna have to come to me."

I took a couple of steps toward her, tripped over a loose rock, and stumbled. She didn't take advantage of it. She should have, she probably would have been able to kill me.

But, I realized, she thought I was baiting her. That trick with the gun had rattled her.

Ermie was right. It was good to have a few surprises.

I decided to try the other one.

I came in swiping, as close as I could. I even got within her range. She deflected my attacks easily and countered with a slash that glanced my left arm. I yelled. It hurt, but I leaned into it, really baiting her this time, and this time she pressed the advantage, moved me back, and just when she thought she had me, I brought my right Knuckle to my shoulder, aimed the stunner at her body and pressed its brand new button.

The stunner sprung out of the Knuckle entirely, and flopped to the ground, missing Deena's body by a foot or so. We stared at it.

Then something else shot out of the hole in the Knuckle. Spring-loaded, a puck the width of the handle. It was harder, it went farther. It hit Deena in the chest and stuck there. It glowed an angry red, and started beeping.

I scrambled back for cover.

She clawed at it with her free hand, tried to pull it off. She couldn't, and now it was stuck to her hand too. The beeping got faster. I was ten feet away from her. She pulled at her hand desperately. My foot hit the rock I'd stumbled on earlier.

When the beeping hit a crescendo it just became one long tone. Then it stopped. Deena froze.

But I knew what this was. This was a Void Warrant trick my Gamma had shown me once. A decoy.

The rock I threw at her head was real, though.

I ran at her. She flailed her knife and stumbled, but there was blood in her eye now and she didn't have a free hand to wipe it out. I hit her twice and she went down. I stomped on her hand until she dropped the knife and I threw it into the bushes.

Gomer had spent the whole fight turning his car around. I leveled a baton at Deena's head.

"Where is he?" I demanded.

She smiled and spat blood at me. "On his way."

I fished around in her pockets for her car keys.

"Where are you going?" asked Gomer.

I had to get to the *Ghost*. But I also saw how I could stop Maurice.

"He needs to bring the money to the Church," I said. "He needs to do it today. If he doesn't, the Church will pull out of the high-rise scheme."

"You think you can get away from them?" cackled Deena. "They're probably watching us right now."

There were lots of bugs already, and some of them were hovering around me. It was late morning, and I was already sweating. None of them took Deena's cue, though. If there were any drones from the Church here, they might be the ones on my side.

"I can't let you just take the money," Gomer protested.

I remembered what Maria had said, that the feds didn't care about stopping Maurice, they just wanted him to know that they knew that he had it. But Gomer had gotten a message to Myra. He genuinely seemed like he wanted to help me.

"By the time you turn your car around again you won't be able to catch me," I said. "But I promise, I don't even want it. I'll give it back to you tomorrow. You can trust me. I still need you to wipe my name off the Corps' record."

Gomer's front wheel squealed in the mud. He was stuck. He looked at me and sighed. "Tomorrow," he said. "Call us."

I left Gomer and Deena there and got into Deena's car. Auntie Antifecta cowered in the back seat, away from me. There was blood on my hand, and getting in I smeared some on her window.

The myth of Inner Boca was based on an idyllic little cove carved out of an old ruined waterfront suburb that Myra and I had happened upon one long weekend with the *Ghost*. It made it easier for me to picture all her Third Way stories when she told them. It was also the perfect meeting spot, and only a few miles away from my standoff with Deena.

I drove so fast over those pock-marked roads that Auntie Antifecta got carsick a couple times and I had to pull over. She did not try to escape. We were surrounded on all sides by thick swampland bush.

I parked in the remains of an old cul-de-sac and spotted the *Ghost*'s white upper deck peeking out through the trees that surrounded the boatel and felt relief. She was still there.

No one had followed us, but still, I hurried Auntie aboard the *Ghost*, who opened her glass doors for me and revved her engines in what I took for muted delight.

"Myra?" I called. No one answered.

I brought Auntie back out onto the deck. In the seaside distance I recognized the thin black prow of Fèlix's *Oystercatcher*, tied up a couple slips down.

"Friend of yours?" came a familiar voice.

Maurice stepped out of the blind spot on the deck, under the stairs to the sundeck. He held a small pistol, the stupid kind that folds into a thick card shape that you can put in your wallet. Only useful if you have enough time to assemble it. The end of it was just barely sticking out of his hand.

"Where's Myra?" I demanded. He ignored me.

"Are you all right?" he asked Auntie Antifecta. "Did she hurt you?"

"No," said Auntie. "I'm fine. I puked a few times."

"Poor girl. Let's get out of here. You," he said, pointing the gun to me. "Stay where you are, please. Hands up."

I obeyed.

"She attacked your secretary," said Auntie. "Your assistant? She beat her up. The feds got her."

Maurice nodded. He pointed to the briefcase.

"Anything happen to the money?"

"No," she said. "The feds almost got it. It's less than what you wanted."

"It's fine; I know. It's all worked out. Did you ever leave anyone alone with it?"

"I've had it the whole time."

"You should check it anyway."

"Check it?"

"Open it, just real quick. Then we'll get out of here."

Auntie Antifecta pressed her thumb against the case, and it clicked open. The noon sun caught its contents through the *Ghost*'s glass doors and made the kiloDollars sparkle, a multicolored holographic wonder.

Maurice saw, smiled, and fired.

# 14

The gun made a flimsy, plastic flapping noise when it discharged, like a piece of wood clattering to the deck. Not even loud enough to wake the neighbors.

Auntie Antifecta looked at the red spot blooming on her chest in surprise. Her eyes were wide, and she clung to the briefcase like it was life.

Maurice swore under his breath.

"Put it down." His voice was cold now, empty of false concern. She crumpled to the floor, but kept her hands on the briefcase.

Trembling, she started to close it again, seal it with her fingerprint.

Maurice closed the gap between them in three swift steps and stuck his hand inside the briefcase just before she closed it. She slammed it down anyway, desperately, she clawed at his hand, but he held fast and gritted his teeth.

Tossing his empty folding gun across the deck to my feet, he reached into his coat pocket and pulled out a single cartridge, which he tossed after it, and another, identical gun, which he pointed at my head.

"Load this," he said, in a calm, even voice, against the crunch of the metal on his hand.

It was horrible to watch. My hands shook badly. The gun was flimsy. It looked fancy, with a fake mother-of-pearl handle, but it was all cheap printed polymer, the kind of novelty gun you could buy at any gift store off the printed highway. When I finally got the cartridge in, it made a click. Maurice nodded.

"Now slide it back."

I hesitated for a second.

"Don't," he said.

I slid the gun back to him obediently. As soon as it left my hand he fired the gun in his. Auntie Antifecta made a gurgling sort of whimper and slumped over the briefcase.

In one fluid motion, Maurice tossed his empty gun over the side and picked up the one I'd kicked over.

"Now let's go back inside," he said. Was that his only gun now? They were small, he could probably fit five or six of them in his coat pocket. But if he did have more, he probably wouldn't have made me reload one.

He poked Auntie Antifecta with the gun, and then he pulled the briefcase out with his other hand. He opened it all the way. Angry purple lines crossed his palm and it was already swelling. He held open the door and moved the briefcase into the lounge with his feet, then gestured for me to go in and pick it up.

"Deena called to tell me you were on her tail," he said. "I called her back and she didn't pick up, so I stopped at one of those novelty junk shops on the side of the road. They didn't have anything small and quiet. I thought these might do the trick. Didn't really consider what a pain in the ass they'd be to reload."

"How'd you find me?" I asked, trying not to look down at the body.

"I debriefed the Church on the situation and they were helpful enough to tell me where your boat was. I guess they've been keeping tabs on you. I tracked Deena's car and it seemed pretty clear you were headed this way. Fortunately I was in the area anyway, so had plenty of time to get here and get comfortable. That's not the important question, though. You know what is?"

"Why shoot her and not me?"

"Bingo. I need to be somewhere, and I can't get this semi-sent tub to move. Figured you could."

"Where?"

"First things first. Put the briefcase down there." He motioned to the counter of the galley. I obeyed.

"Now," he continued. "Your weapons. Your sticks. Give them to me."

I removed my Knuckles and tossed them to him. He appraised them with mild interest.

"You killed Deena with these?" he asked.

"Just humiliated her, mostly."

He chuckled, and tried to put one on his free hand, but his fingers were swollen. He put them in his coat pocket. "All right," he said. "Let's get a move on. Keep your hands out to the side of your body where I can see them. If you move too fast, I'll fire. Clear?"

"Yes."

"Then go to the helm, please. Put in these coordinates: 26.1135 N, 79.8 W. Then step back and let me check."

I did as he said. I saw the route. It took us out of the yoreshore immediately, into the Gulf Stream and then due south. He checked my work and moved to input it.

According to the map, his destination was right off the coast of Little Lauderdale, a few miles out of the yoreshore from the marina where Edgar had drowned.

"The Church is still helping you," I said. "Do they know you don't have their money?"

Maurice laughed. "They know everything. This is more than enough to buy me another day. And their leverage is gone too, now. They were always threatening to replace me with Riley. Now they can't. We're stuck with each other. So long as I still have a chance at the full score, I'll be fine."

"Is that where we're going? To get the full score?"

"None of your business."

Maria had told me that an army of Mourners was stationed at the Red Cigar. That was an abandoned lighthouse about halfway between here and Bahia Mar. If we intercepted them, maybe I could get them to help me. Or at least, take care of Maurice.

But the Red Cigar was in the yoreshore and the most direct route was out of it, down the Gulf Stream, which hadn't been strong enough to significantly slow boats from running south in decades.

I was sure the *Ghost* had seen the Red Cigar before. It was a distinctive landmark, visible for miles, the only red lighthouse on that part of the yoreshore.

I hoped she would remember. I hoped she would listen to me.

"You know if you want," I said, stopping him from approving the route. "We can take the yoreshore route. Get you there faster. It's a little more fun."

"What's fun about it?" he asked.

"Theoretically more dangerous, she'll move less cautiously. You have to keep your eyes on the road a little bit more, which I'm happy to do."

"Figured you'd want to move at as leisurely a pace as possible."

"ETA is three and a half hours. If I can get you there in under three, you let me live. And you hire me to be your new Deena."

He chuckled. "Well, you can't be worse than the old one."

"So it's a deal?"

"Sure, go ahead," he said, stepping away from the console. "But the timer starts now."

I quickly flipped through the collection of marketing images that Riley had found to navigate her to Coral Castle.

"Almost done," I said.

"What are you doing? Taking pictures?" Maurice asked. His voice was calm, with a threatening undertone.

"Just asking about the weather," I said. I showed him the image of all the CabanaBoats, together like one little family on an idyllic afternoon. "Clear skies. Calm waters. And we're almost ready to go."

Finally I found what I was looking for: a stock image of a family at the top of a red lighthouse, a CabanaBoat tied up at its base. I fed it to the *Ghost*, then told her to move out, and prayed.

I felt the rumble of the *Ghost* pulling anchor and untying itself from the auto slip. Once we started moving Maurice seemed to relax a little bit, but not enough to keep the gun off me. We went onto the aft deck outside the cockpit and he rummaged through a nearby equipment locker and found a mesh salvagia bag, like the one that held the Ked an eternity ago. He switched the gun to his swollen hand so he could keep pointing it at me, but he also had to use that hand to hold the bag while he filled it with money from the briefcase. It was awkward, but he knew it, so he took his time. We weren't in a rush. I thought about making a move anyway. I thought there was a chance he'd fumble the shot long enough that I could get to him. If I had my Knuckles I would have gone for it. I felt so powerless without them. Beating Deena had given me a sort of contact high. Giving them to him made me feel naked and vulnerable.

Auntie Antifecta's shoes poked out on the deck on the other side of the cockpit. She was lying in a red pool that had stopped growing.

"Why'd you have to kill her, anyway?" I asked, while he stuffed the bag. I tried to seem calm and collected when talking about murder, the way I thought an improved Deena might.

"I don't like loose ends," he replied.

"Is that why you killed Edgar?"

Maurice laughed. "Why the hell would I do that?"

"He found out that you were going to demolish Miami."

"I was wondering about that. He'd been acting pretty cagey recently. But no, I needed him. If I'd known he'd found out about that phase of the plan I'd have talked to him first. Just look at how things have gone without him around. Keeping these Mourners together, it's like holding sand in my hand and trying to make a fist, everyone keeps slipping out. If Edgar were alive, he could have smoothed the whole thing over with a word, put Maria back in line."

"But you did take his body and chain it up under Maria's boat to frame her."

"Oh, that. I thought that in death he could still do what he excelled at in life. A little morbid, but. Desperate times and all. I told myself I'd make it up to him by keeping Riley safe."

"Was that before or after you sent a mechanical gator to kill him?"

"Riley's the one who kept sneaking away from me, talking to the Church behind my back at Key West. That gator was just to scare him straight, make him realize that only I could protect him.

I needed him to think that I was the only one he could trust. If *you* hadn't stopped it, he might still be alive."

"Hey, it went after me, too."

Maurice fumbled a stack of money and it dropped to the deck just as the *Ghost* made a turn and slid into the red pool by Auntie Antifecta. He swore. It took a Herculean effort for him to get up, walk over to the stack, pick it up, wipe it as best he could on the deck, and stuff it into the bag, all while keeping the gun on me.

He looked exhausted, suddenly. And it became clear how close to the razor's edge he was, how close to losing control.

"You know what my problem is?" he exclaimed, out of nowhere.

I shrugged.

"I think that everyone is as enlightened as I am. If everyone just thought about it logically, the numbers would speak for themselves. We are just inches from changing everything down here in Florida, and now, all of a sudden, everybody's getting cold feet. A thousand units of private housing rising up just in time for the feds to see them in their rearview mirror! A hundred thousand kiloDollars a unit, easily!"

This speech seemed to be just as much to himself as to me, a pep talk to revitalize himself, this close to the finish line. And I did have the feeling that it was this conviction alone that kept him going, and that if it ever wavered in the slightest, he would crumble and teeter like those skyscrapers on Sweeps Week.

"Excuse me," he said, once he'd shoved the last stack of money into the bag. "I have to make a call."

He moved down the deck to the prow, far enough away that I couldn't hear him but still close enough that he could keep the gun on me. He tapped his gogs.

We were moving at a good clip now, and, more importantly, we were sticking to the yoreshore. It was dredged and mostly clear around here, since we were still close to OrlanDome.

The *Ghost* was agitated. I could tell. This was a familiar route for her, she should be moving quickly, but she slowed down often to inspect the various hazards—two metal poles, one with a backboard, an old basketball court, a rusted mound of shopping carts that poked just above the water. She didn't slow down completely, she never stopped, like she knew that Maurice would get suspicious if we delayed for too long. But she definitely wasn't in a hurry.

I wondered how much she understood about what was happening aboard her. This was the second time in three days that violence had been committed on her deck. I remembered our trip out of Coral Castle, how I felt like I could tell how happy and relaxed she was, throwing a little mini-party in the lounge while Riley named the lost buildings of the Miami skyline. She was fulfilling her purpose then, and had barely stopped to examine anything at all.

Maurice wouldn't have told me everything he'd told me if he planned on letting me live. I was glad she took her time.

Maurice was still on the phone on his gogs. He walked past me, over to Auntie Antifecta's body. With a little effort, he nudged her body over the railing into the sea.

"Satisfied?" he asked, pointing the camera of his gogs to the open bag of cash.

"No," he said, to whoever he was talking to. "Don't you dare send one of your drones. I'm on my way now. I'll meet you at the titan. Yes; I know where it is. I know exactly where it is because I know when you disabled it. Once you give me back control, I'll give you the briefcase and be on my way. Then you get a line to Feinstein-Reyes so I can show her I'm serious. It'll work! Trust me.

We're done playing nice on this, now we play hardball. And I swear, if I see anything flying anywhere near me I'll eat these paper bills."

In the distance, off to the left, I could see the construction titan. When Maurice told the Church where he was going, he was facing directly south.

Toward Miami.

He would take the titan and demolish it *now*. Or threaten to, at least, unless Maria complied with his demands and got all the Mourners to agree to the deal.

He hung up.

"Problems with the Church?" I said.

"Crypto folks," he replied. "Can't give them an inch." He glanced at the titan again. "Speed it up a little."

"I'll get you there," I said. "Don't worry."

He looked at me skeptically but said nothing. He started pacing up and down the deck. Some tense minutes passed. The yoreshore had been almost like a river, with debris on both sides obscuring the view. We came to a little break, a channel that led out into the water.

The yoreshore path led to the Red Cigar.

The *Ghost* passed the inlet. She chose the yoreshore. My heart leapt. She was listening to me.

But Maurice saw the titan too.

"What's it doing?" Maurice demanded. "We need to go that way. Where's it going?"

"This is the fastest route," I lied, without any evidence. "She knows every hazard here, she's already charted it."

As if to prove me wrong, she cut her engines and started drifting toward a group of sandbars on her starboard side, the way she would when she wanted to investigate something without disturbing it. *No,* I thought. *Not right now.* Maurice glared at me.

"There'll be other places to cut through," I said.

"It keeps slowing down," said Maurice. "There's too much debris. Take us out into open water, now."

I shook my head. "In open water we'll be fighting against the Gulf Stream."

"The Gulf Stream's not strong enough to pull a tricycle. Double back and take me out."

"She knows this route better. It'll be faster, trust me."

We approached a crop of sandbars, and my heart sank as she got close to them, too close. Old habits, dying hard. I considered taking control of her again, the old way, running the emergency stop routine.

But she had listened to me about the route. And Riley had told me to trust her.

"You're fucking with me," said Maurice. "Turn this boat around now."

I wasn't paying attention. I was focused on the water behind him. There was something strange about those sandbars. Nothing obvious. For one thing, it wasn't clear to me what had formed them.

I experienced that feeling again, of being perfectly in sync with the *Ghost*. She crept up to a sandbar but kept her distance. Instead of charging it head-on like she normally did, she scoped it out.

Maurice only had his one shot. He leveled it at me again, but the *Ghost* swerved toward a sandbar and he lost his balance. She nuzzled right up to it, too close again, but in a different position than before. Normally she attacked it head-on, but this time she scraped her side up against it.

And I realized that she was looking for a spot where I could jump. She was trying to help me escape.

This sandbar was too rocky. She sped forward again to the next one and Maurice lost his balance again. I held on to the railing.

The next sandbar was perfect. Seductive, if a sandbar could be so—a tidy little island, ringed with soft sand and capped with a single palm tree. An incredibly tempting piece of beach. The sand was clean, fine, and white. Nothing in the yoreshore was that white, it looked imported. I couldn't blame her for wanting to get close to it, it was right out of her marketing materials.

It was too perfect. Unnatural.

Bait.

I startled Maurice again by running past him to the bow. I was oblivious to whether or not he shot, or gave chase. I reached the edge of the railing just in time to hear the gut-wrenching screech of tearing fiberglass, see the jagged metal barbs that lay hidden just offshore that perfect little sandbar. The *Floating Ghost* lurched to a stop and I went flying over the railing, my heart breaking at the proof that Reefer was worthy of his nickname.

I grabbed for the railing. My arm slipped through something rope-like. I looked up and saw the mesh diving bag. Clutching for the railing, I accidentally pulled it open. My feet were in the water. Loose stacks of cash fell out of the open diving bag, smacking me in the forehead before flopping into the sea.

Maurice had followed, and tumbled as well, though he'd stayed on deck and mostly upright. He had one hand on the bag and the other still on the gun. He pulled the bag back. The money stopped spilling onto my face, but he couldn't pry the bag free from me.

He leveled the gun at my head. My foot scratched for purchase on the deck. If he shot me now I'd go limp and maybe take the money with me over the side. I had to balance holding the money and keeping up the threat of pulling him into the water.

I kept waiting for the light clapping noise, the sound of that toylike discharge.

I got my other arm up and reached into his coat pocket, feeling for my Knuckles. I got a finger on a dial and turned it up, then another on the primer. I got my foot firmly on the deck, and I leaned in to grab it, but he pulled back. Now he was on the deck and I was the one leaning forward, my hand just out of his pocket, and the gun was still pointed at my head, only now I had no leverage.

"You're sinking," he said, and wrenched the bag of cash off my arm and fired just as I kicked off the deck. I felt the heat and a sting along my temple, then I fell, hitting the water back first and slicing something open on Reefer's reef.

The *Ghost* went down. I kept close to her, kept underwater, and pulled myself around her. It felt like wreck-diving, and I had a dark thought that that was what she was now, a shipwreck, even though she was still above the surface. There was still time to save her, if I could only find the leak.

Reefer's reef was made of twisted strips of jagged metal painted with something, some sort of camouflage, to conceal itself from the *Ghost*'s radar. The edges were sharp, cut into barbs, to tear and sink her. I gashed my arm on one, but hardly noticed. Blood was billowing from the wounds in my head and side.

She pulled back from the reef and now was revving her engines strangely, randomly. She was distressed, confused. She wasn't sure what was happening. The flow of water got stronger the closer I got to the prow, and I followed that current until I reached the wraparound window into the stateroom, and saw that it was hopeless.

The window wrapped around the entire prow. The reef had smashed it open. Water had already flooded the room almost to the height of the window.

I waded my way over the broken glass and through the room and limped back up the stairs.

Maurice wasn't in the lounge. I figured he was still scanning the deck, hunting for me, but I didn't see him through the glass doors either.

The *Ghost* was sinking. It wasn't very deep here, but she would probably go all the way under. Maurice had either gone to higher ground, or he had jumped, tried to escape.

If he was still here, that left the sundeck, on top of the cabin. There was no other place that made sense.

The water lapped at my feet, halfway up the stairs. I crept out of the lounge and looked up to the sundeck but couldn't find him. If he was standing at the edge on the side that I was on we would have spotted each other, but if he was standing in the very center, we wouldn't be able to see each other at all. That made the most sense for him. I'd have no way to get to him where he wouldn't have plenty of time to take his shot, and I wouldn't have any cover.

But he only had one shot. It took long enough to reload that he wouldn't take it unless he was sure he could hit me. I hoped, anyway.

I grabbed the side of the sundeck and pulled my head up for just a second, just to take a look.

Maurice was squatting over the money, the gun pointed right at my head. He was on his gogs again, making a call.

I landed hard. The wound in my side sent a sharp pain through my abdomen and I doubled up. I winced, and hobbled back around, taking cover by getting closer to the cabin.

"If you want this," he yelled. "You're going to have to come and take it from me."

Interesting. He thought I wanted to steal it.

I went back into the cabin, made my way to the galley, and opened Charlie's rum cabinet. It was barer than I'd expected, but I found four bottles still full enough for my purposes. Four chances.

Water was flooding the cabin by then. It was tough to find a dry piece of material. I ripped the curtains off the window and tore them into strips, then stuffed a strip into each one.

I walked back out on deck with all four bottles, and chose four different spots, one on each side of the deck.

Then I went back and used the galley stove to light the first one. The bottle was the lightest and thinnest. I thought it had the best chance, and I figured my first shot would be my best, since Maurice wouldn't be expecting it.

I took a deep breath. The water was starting to come up onto the deck. My bottles wouldn't last long in their spots unattended. It was now or never.

I tossed it. It landed pretty close to Maurice. I heard him grunt and maybe even shuffle out of the way. But I didn't hear it break.

"Thanks for the drink," he said, laughing.

I hurried back, lit my next bottle and hurled it, higher this time.

That one did shatter. It didn't catch, but Maurice didn't make a snarky comment, so I figured it must have scared him. I hurried to get the next one ready while he was still off his guard. I chucked it as high as I could. I felt good about it. I didn't even wait until it came down, I just ran over to the fourth bottle, picked it up, and pulled myself onto the sundeck.

I clambered up just in time to see the third one hit. It shattered right at Maurice's feet, and lit the space in front of him. I was behind him, the last bottle behind my back.

"Hey!" I shouted when I was less than five feet away. He turned and raised his gun. I threw the bottle at him. It struck him in his arm right when he fired, and the shot went wide. So that was good.

But the sundeck was blazing now. I had set the *Ghost* on fire, and Maurice had been smart enough to sling the mesh bag over his shoulder, two steps away from the flames.

He had no bullets; I had no bottles.

I kept walking.

"You know, maybe I was wrong about you," he was saying. "Deena was very skilled, a very tough woman. She didn't quite have your knack for improvisation."

"Nope," I replied, which wasn't very clever in terms of improvisation. He braced himself, raised his arms up to meet me, but I wrapped my arms around his body and embraced him. He returned the favor, crushing me to him, but I reached my hand into his coat pocket and pulled it so that it was closer to the front of his body, then I felt around for the Knuckle with the charged primer, twisted it into his abdomen and pulled the trigger.

I woke up choking, the smell of singed hair in my nostrils.

Maurice was on his side, groaning, and rolling around. His body was right next to the spreading flames, but he wasn't in them now and it looked like he'd get up in time to avoid them. The mesh bag was still on his back, but it was open and his back was to the fire.

I pushed myself up. There was a black dot on the horizon. A stealthy-looking drone, the Church's larger model. The kind that had defended the *Marino* from Maria's coup. It flew fast and sleek and straight, and by the time I was standing it was upon us.

It saw the money. It saw Maurice groan and move the wrong way. It saw the bills catch fire and Maurice come alive and shake the bag off.

I hobbled down the stairs to the deck and stumbled off the aft, into the water.

I swam out a little bit, then I turned around and looked back at my beautiful, burning *Ghost*. She was taking on water even faster now; it had swamped the deck. I hoped that it would put out the flames before they consumed her. She should be buried at sea, not cremated.

Maurice had climbed to the highest ground he could that wasn't on fire, the aft side of the sundeck. The drone hovered about twenty feet above him and over the water. They stared each other down. His shoulders slacked. His arms fell to his sides. He stared at the drone, the water surging at one side of him, the flames licking at the other. He had nowhere to go.

The drone adjusted itself, dropping altitude and retreating a few feet. Then a long few seconds of nothing. Then it flew forward and connected with Maurice's head, blades up. Slower than a bullet, but fast enough.

I treaded water with the *Floating Ghost,* until she sank so low the fire sputtered out.

# 15

What do you do when you find yourself adrift?

You tread water until your legs give out, while your blood mixes with the yoreshore murk. Only then do you find something to hold on to. Anything will do, even Reefer's reef, that crude and deadly weapon.

And then?

You come to the party. You stay late. When there's a lull in conversation, you make another drink, since you're afraid of what silence will coerce you to say. You lie awake and wait, and see who might be there to greet you in the dark.

Maria's Mourners found me on their warpath up the yoreshore to take back the Astro America. We passed Inner Boca again and I saw that the *Oystercatcher* was still there, and so they dropped me off. There was still no one aboard, and the IXS agents found me shortly after. I answered their questions, which were mostly about the money.

"Destroyed?" said Somer, aghast. I nodded. I'd left out the part where I had been the one to destroy it, since I was pretty sure that was a federal crime.

"I'm sure I don't have to explain this to you," said Somer. "But that wasn't our deal."

"She did good work," said Gomer. "She was the one who figured out where the money was going. She's the one who stopped the transaction." He looked at me. "We got a report that the construction titan that's been tearing up the coastline is heading back out to international waters."

"She disobeyed your orders," said Somer. "You are a federal agent, so that's a crime. Furthermore, she was supposed to gather evidence around the hotel, she was supposed to—"

"Andy," Gomer said, firmly. "Relax."

If anything, Somer tensed more.

"If you really want to toss her back to the 2C3," Gomer continued. "You're going to have to talk to Yousef in Personnel Policing. You know that, right?"

"So?"

"That means we have to have him over for dinner again. That means another three hours of listening to him drone on about his blue-ribbon hive mind pugs." Gomer looked at me. "Once you train one pug, training the rest of them is the exact same process. At least, it seems that way to us. Not to Yousef, though."

"So what," said Somer, through gritted teeth. "We just let her go?"

"It'll be much easier for her to pay us back in Florida than out on the lunar war front. Don't you think?"

"Yes," I said. "Wait. What? Pay you back for what?"

"There were eighty thousand kiloDollars in that briefcase," said Somer. "You know what tax bracket that puts you in?"

"Me?"

"By your own admission, you were the last person alive to touch it. In our book, that makes you liable."

"You can't be serious."

"Congratulations, Mackey. You get to stick around. You owe us a score."

Somer walked off. Gomer patted me on the shoulder. "We'll be in touch."

The *Instant Pot* appeared on the horizon shortly after. A smaller sailboat followed close behind. To my surprise, I saw that Myra was at the helm of the smaller boat, not so much turning the wheel as shaking it vigorously. She had never operated any sort of water vehicle bigger than a Jet Ski, as far as I knew. Félix stood nervously behind her.

The boat was small, barely thirty feet long. It was perhaps sixty percent rust and twenty percent mast. Myra scraped off a significant part of the rest on the auto slip, even with me waving her in. It didn't make much of an aesthetic difference.

"You're here!" she exclaimed, running off the deck and embracing me. The wound in my side made me wince. "You're hurt!"

"Where were you?" I asked. "What's this?"

"My new boat!"

"What do you need a boat for?"

Félix stepped onto dry land. He looked a little seasick. "She's joining the Flaco."

Myra took me aboard her boat. It didn't have a name yet. It was a fixer-upper, for sure, but bigger than it looked from the outside. There was a V-shaped berth above the prow, a little galley and saloon with couches that could be converted into extra berths, and a head in the back that you couldn't stand up in. It reminded me of Gamma's van. The layout was almost exactly the same.

"I like it," I said. "It's just like you."

"What, small?"

"Seasoned. Less than sentient."

"Speaking of," she said. She looked around. "Where's yours? I told her to stay put. Did Riley take her out? Now that I think about it, there was a juicy-looking pile of old shopping carts just sticking out of the—"

"She's gone," I said, cutting her off, collapsing, again, into her arms. "They're gone."

Our little armada sailed back to the old familiar place, right above the marina where Edgar Ortiz had drowned. Félix said that he'd found the name of the old marina on a map: Bahia Mar.

As soon as we threw the anchor, a mass of black dots burst out from within the shattered letters of the nearby Bahia Mar building and flew down to us, revealing themselves to be beautiful purple birds.

"Those are your parakeets?" I asked Sofia, who had joined us on deck.

"Sure looks like it," she said.

"Here's the scheme," said Myra. "I convince Nativitee to lobby the feds to protect this part of the yoreshore."

"So make it a wildlife corridor?"

"Almost. The Flaco would be allowed to work on it, clean it up, and live on it, so long as they improve it in such a way that it attracts a specific animal to return."

"What, panthers again?"

"No. Not panthers. A bird."

"These guys?"

"No, though I am warming up to them. Actually, Félix gave me the idea. Or his boat did, anyway. The name of it. *Oystercatcher*."

"Oystercatchers are birds?"

She nodded, sagely. "The American oystercatcher is like the panther of the sea. From a conservation perspective, I mean. In that they're extinct, but all the Consolidators really want them to not be. Hypothetically the yoreshore is actually the perfect habitat for them—coastal, undeveloped, kinda gross, with lots of little barrier islands like where the Bahia Mar is, and with the potential for oysters, obviously. So if I tell Nativitee I saw one, and that I'm working with a group to restore the oyster beds in the yoreshore, I bet I can convince them to lobby the feds, write me a check and leave us alone, at least for a couple of years."

"Years? You're going to live on this thing for years?"

"I don't have to *stay* here," she said. I caught her looking at Sofia. "Unless I really want to. The point is to give them time, for the boys to build up the Flaco and Sofia to finish her research on what kind of ecosystem these parakeets actually enable up here, and that hopefully will turn into something that I can pitch to the Consolidators that has the added benefit of being real."

"That's a big commitment."

She was still looking at Sofia. "They had a good pitch."

"Feels like it'd be easier if you'd found a panther."

"I did find one," she said, patting the back of her boat. "He's just a little toothless right now."

Myra was kind enough to let me sleep in one of the side berths in her newly christened *Florida Panther*, and we got to work.

I fell into a routine, helping Myra in the morning with all the various boat-owning tasks that she knew next to nothing about. I'd spent so much time studying how to maintain the *Ghost*. It was nice but bittersweet to put that knowledge to use for another boat entirely.

In the afternoon I dove the marina with Félix, clearing the rubble out of the shallows around the Bahia Mar building, diving Edgar's wreck and excavating the hazardous blue barrels. We weren't quite sure what to do with them, just that we'd prefer not to have to sleep over them.

When dusk fell and the day's work was done, we'd gather on the *Instant Pot* and drink cold, crisp beer and eat real, raw oysters obtained from Félix's spat provider. They were fresh and briny but small, lab-grown specimens with thin shells that were too round, too perfect.

Félix promised us that one day the oyster beds would be so high we could wade through them and it would look like we were walking on water. We could pluck whatever we wanted and eat as we went. I didn't even like oysters that much, but I wanted to believe him; he painted the picture so vividly.

But in the silence that followed the laugher, I looked out into the calm night and in a tall low cloud that touched the horizon I could easily picture the construction titan, on its way to devour the Flaco in an instant. I looked at Sofia and Myra and I saw Kohl just outside the glass, poised to kill and pillage. I saw the thousand ways the Flaco could die, and how woefully insufficient its defenses were.

I got another drink.

## SALVAGIA

They found me on a cloudless night, dozens of black dots bouncing against the moonlight shining through my little open porthole. I was already awake when I felt the familiar tingle in my inner ear.

"We're here for the salvagia," my old acquaintance whispered.

"We?" I replied. "Not 'I'?"

"There's only 'we.' We are aligned. Fetch it for us."

"What are you paying?"

It crackled in a way that seemed to imitate a laugh.

I opened the drawer under the berth and sorted through my meager possessions—spare clothes that Myra had brought me from her apartment, the wearable that Ermie had cobbled together with spare parts, my single Knuckle, which I had somehow held on to, while the other joined the *Ghost* in her watery grave.

The UltiMon card was near the very top, actually. Fèlix had handed it to me shortly after we'd returned to Bahia Mar, after a dive where we'd recovered Edgar's diving mask and tank, which I had discarded when Deena captured me.

I'd accepted the card, but I hadn't tried to sell it yet. Thanks to Myra, the Flaco didn't need the money anymore. Neither did I.

So I'd take it out and stare at it, hold it up to the light and watch the rainbow holographic colors dance. Sometimes I took it out of the case, and suppressed a strange urge to rip it in half, as one might suppress an urge to lick the paintings in a museum.

The card itself wasn't true salvagia, I decided. It hadn't been under for long enough, hadn't had the chance to decay. Just like Riley, who was vaporized in an instant. He would forever be exactly the way I knew him, in those final seconds, that final look at the camera.

If salvagia was the art of turning loss into beauty, then the salvagia of Riley's death was the payout, the briefcase of cash, which had been beautiful—stacks of perfect pretty bills, glinting holographic colors, just like the UltiMon card but infinitely multiplied. Riley's act of sacrifice transformed into something powerful, useful, the power of a hundred life-changing chances compressed into a single brick.

But that was gone, too. Destroyed by my hand. His death had led to nothing at all.

Except Nepheli's life. And mine.

And the card.

Once the flies saw it glint in the moonlight, they swarmed it. They tickled my hand and I jerked it back. The card hung suspended in the air, the flies buzzing along its chain. They pulled it out through the porthole and were gone.

I tensed, waiting for the prickle in my ear to either disappear or intensify into a burrow.

But it simply remained.

"Yes?" I said.

"Edgar drowned here, didn't he? Right here?"

"How do you know that?"

"This was where we fished you out."

"So what if he did?"

"You mentioned something about Edgar wearing this at the moment of his death. Do you have proof?"

"Yes."

"Give it to us."

"I will. On one condition."

"Oh, we love conditions."

"The people here are looking for a home. This is it. You should protect them."

"Why?" It felt like a rhetorical question, like the drone was a teacher giving a final exam.

And in a way, it was. All these nights I'd spent staring at the card, I'd been going over it all, trying to figure out Edgar's plan, why he had pinged Félix to come pluck the card off of his corpse. All the various ways that he had tried to move the needle.

Trying to figure out why the air in his tank smelled just like the *Bull*'s fuel.

But this particular lesson was related to the Church, who had hired Kohl to sabotage the *Bull* to blow, then told him to let us go at Coral Castle so that Nepheli could race and die and get Maurice his payout. Beings of little value, strung together to maximize profit, until the Church loosened my collar and I decimated that profit and eliminated Riley, their contingency. But they didn't mention that at all. Actual money was secondary to the hope of money. So was revenge. They'd killed Maurice not out of revenge, but because he'd become unprofitable, a cash crop that was sprouting into a weed. Now they wanted to see if I was a weed, too. Revenge didn't seem to be in their nature.

It was in mine, though. Or would be, someday soon.

For the moment I told them what they wanted to hear.

"You should protect them because it's in your best interest," I said. "If I understand correctly, the value of that card is tied to the death of Edgar Ortiz. He died here, below us, in a wreck in an old marina. Anyone who buys this land to develop it would destroy that marina, which would destroy that added value to the card. The Flaco is building a floating community. Floating, as in, on the surface. They will never touch that wreck. And no one can move in while they're there. Their existence protects your investment."

"What if some bigger fish comes along to chase them off?" asked the drone.

"Then it'll have to deal with me."

The drone did that little hiss-laugh that made my eardrum burn. "See? We knew you were more competent than the other one. Yes, so long as we have the card and the footage that ties it to this place, and so long as the site of his death remains intact, we have no incentive to disturb you. And we know how to protect our investments too."

"Then I'll send you the video," I said.

Another tingling wheeze. "It was a pleasure working with you, Mx. Mackey. Salvagia is the future down here. Our paths will likely cross again."

And the prickle vanished.

My new wearable pinged shortly after with an FTP link to a hidden server. I found Edgar's diving mask and put it on. Riley had set it to stay unlocked. I scrolled through the footage.

I stopped at a particular place and watched it very closely. Several times. Then I scrolled ahead and found the relevant clip and sent it to the Church.

I fell asleep that night, confident that I knew how Edgar Ortiz had died.

In the morning, I found that the Church had left me a surprise on Myra's deck—a loose pile of sodden, wrinkled, holographic cash. Many of their edges were singed, some of them were half-burned away and probably worth less than the paper they were printed on. As payment for a Series 1 Kappacop UltiMon card it was a rip-off, probably a little less than forty thousand kiloDollars of usable currency.

But as salvagia, it was remarkable.

I showed it to Nepheli, when I went back to the Astro America to dive the foundation for Maria and the feds. They opened the door to the Edgar Ortiz suite and looked at the open bag of wrinkled bills and stuck up their nose.

"What's this?" They asked.

"Seed money. To build a better breaker."

"I don't deserve it," they said. "The *Bull* told me what was wrong with her and I didn't listen. Her death is my fault. So is Riley's."

"They're not," I said. "And neither is Edgar's."

They blinked. "You're right," they said. "Edgar's line got cut. I didn't have anything to do with that."

"But you feel guilty about it anyway."

They hesitated. "What makes you say that?"

I walked past them, into Edgar's room, the room at the end of the hall. They followed. I pointed to Edgar's portable mix machine, and their distress upon looking on that machine confirmed my suspicion.

"Edgar was claustrophobic," I said. "At least, that's what Riley told me. But on the stream of his last wreck dive, Edgar pulled himself through the wreck without a problem.

"The thing is, if you're breathing regular air under really high pressure, like during a deep dive, you get something called nitrogen narcosis. You feel drunk, uninhibited. It's dangerous, but it also would have calmed Edgar down. The way I figure, he'd done a deep dive at some point, and when he realized it would help him get over his claustrophobia, he must have looked for a way to simulate narcosis while shallow diving, since he knew he would be in the yoreshore looking for evidence to take down Maurice.

"You told me that Kohl smelled like nitrous oxide, when we realized he'd tampered with the *Bull*. Down here on Earth nitrous oxide has a much more . . . recreational use. I won't say I've never done a whippit before, but the ones you can get outside the domes have fun flavors like sour cherry, to mask that dead flower taste. Anyway, turns out, on a shallow dive a little nitrous oxide in the mix feels very similar to breathing regular air on a deep dive. I should know. I pulled myself through the same wreck that killed Edgar, breathing from the same tank. It's the only way I didn't have a panic attack. But it almost killed me. I got so disoriented that I silted out in that wreck, and if Félix hadn't saved me I would have either torn my line or run out of air trying to figure out which way was up. My guess is Edgar wound up doing both." Nepheli was silent. I pressed on. "Edgar asked you to get the nitrous oxide for him, didn't he? And rig it up to his mix machine?"

"He owned the team," said Nepheli. "He owned all the nitrous oxide. Why would he need my help?"

"Because he had to cover his tracks. He didn't want Maurice or the Church to know what he was doing. He scrubbed the location data off his mask to hide it. But you knew, didn't you? On the stream, right before he dove down, he held up his tank. At first I thought he was saying goodbye to Riley. But he wasn't. He was showing it to you, to make sure he had the right one."

They sat down on the bed.

"I lied," they said, finally. "I lied to him. The night before, he told me to up the percentage. But it was already so high. So I kept it the same, but I told him I raised it. He must have realized and tried to increase it himself.

"After you told me about Kohl it got me wondering, how you had made that connection. When you brought up Edgar's tank . . . if you could smell it, then the percentage must have been . . . well, I just checked this morning. I can't believe how high it was. He must have been . . ."

"High as shit," I said. "I know I was."

That got them to laugh a bit, which opened the floodgates wide enough that some tears escaped, too. "I should have just done it when he asked. I wouldn't have set it that high."

"It's not your fault," I said, gently. "He knew what he was getting into. You couldn't have stopped him. Or Riley. I couldn't either."

"It's not about whose fault it is!" they cried. "It's about what happens when you stick your neck out. They were the Ortizes. They were the bravest and the richest and the best of us. And now they're dead, and everything's the same. The Flaco's gone. The *Bull* is gone! What chance could I possibly have to build anything when they couldn't?"

I didn't tell them I'd been asking myself the same question. If I did I'd have to tell them that I didn't quite believe my answer.

"You have their chance," I said. I tossed the bag of money onto the couch, and walked to the door. "They didn't lose it. They just kept it alive for you."

Though I'd told the Church that I would stick around, it was unclear to me what my role could be in an aquatic co-op. I still didn't really believe that the Flaco would go anywhere, despite the work that Myra and I had done to protect it. She had harnessed the First Way and gotten federal protection, and I had harnessed the Second Way. The Third Way, though, was a mystery to both of us.

"We want to make you an offer," said Ermie, one night. He and Fèlix were sitting at the dining table. Ermie had a screen up. It was displaying what looked like a yoreshore depth chart. "See, uh, I've been going over the blueprints for these old CabanaBoats. They have a lot of interior space that is not well configured. And it's got limited offshore capacity. We could take out these tanks here, move some stuff around, and fit a desalinator and a battery big enough to hold what we need to really take the Flaco to the next level."

I blinked. "The *Ghost* is gone," I said.

"Oh," said Ermie, scratching his head. "Yeah. Well first, we'd have to pull her up."

"What?"

"You remember where she is, don't you?"

"Sure," I said. "But there's a huge gash in her side. There's fire and water damage."

"Well, we don't like to waste things at the Flaco," said Félix.

"Have you ever done a recovery like that before?" I asked.

Fèlix and Ermie looked at each other.

"We'll figure it out," Ermie said.

"I can't ask you to do that."

"You could if you were part of the Flaco," said Myra.

"Me? But. I'm useless. I don't know anything about building or speculative urban planning or whatever it is you do." Or oyster farming or birdwatching or anything, except trying to stay unnoticed and failing.

"You sold that card," said Félix. "You got rid of Kohl. You're useful in a real-world kind of way."

"And," said Ermie. "You can teach Félix how to actually dive. That was probably why we kept Kohl around as long we did."

A couple of days later, Ermie raised anchor and we took the *Instant Pot* back up the yoreshore. It was bigger and less maneuverable than the *Ghost*, and much tougher to navigate through the yoreshore. One of the more narrow passes near the Red Cigar took almost an hour to get through, and we got pretty close to beaching on a sandbar half a dozen times.

Eventually, though, we found her.

I dove down to check her out, and to make sure that she was still there. I was afraid that she'd be gone already, washed out to sea or moved by Reefer. But there she was, nestled against the pile of junk that sank her, like den mates in hibernation. There was no sign of Maurice, except for a singed white linen jacket that still held my other Knuckle. I grabbed it and made a survey of the damage.

It was almost dark by then. Myra and Fèlix and I slept on Ermie's deck, under the stars, talking and planning.

We brought up drums of a foaming solution that Ermie'd acquired from somewhere, and the tubing they'd used for dredging around Coral Castle. The idea would be to patch up the *Ghost*, then pump the solution in her, which would foam up, push the water out, and raise her high enough to tow her back to Bahia Mar.

It was a pretty big project, but it could have all been done in a couple days. In the end it took closer to eight. We spent a lot of time fishing and not catching anything. We all took turns heading back to the Flaco to bring out more supplies. It was a peaceful stretch of yoreshore. No hope of salvagia, nothing of any value. Not a lot of people passed through. I knew the days of a yoreshore that was worthless in every way to everyone, save a happy few, were numbered. The tide was coming back in. But the happy few were the ones I'd found.

On the eighth day, we made the water boil. The sun was shining, but it was also raining, and thick drops rippled the surface. Myra slipped and steadied herself on the railing. Fèlix worked the pump, grunting with the effort.

The rippling around a certain patch turned violent. The water churned white. Ermie signaled for Fèlix to stop, and he leaned against the pump and watched.

They all did, in captivated, hopeful silence. I watched them. I was certain that it would go wrong, that the foam would burst her from inside, splinter her into a million pieces. The deck would collapse from the fire damage, the water inside her would deflate her like a balloon on the way out. I didn't want to watch her die again.

But when their faces changed, I knew that they had done it.

I wanted to live in that world, the one shaped by their looks of satisfaction. I wanted to believe in that reflection for as long as I could.

Stretch it out, Triss. Drink and laugh on a quiet, worthless stretch of yoreshore. Take shelter from storms and systems, and dream of how it could be.

Look a little less at how it is.

## Acknowledgments

It's been six years since I wrote the first draft of the short story, on which *Salvagia* is based, titled "One Free Night at the Astro America." In that time, I stretched it out to a novella, then to a novel, then rewrote it entirely more times than I care to think about. The essential idea remains mostly intact, and it's still a pretty good one, I think, but good ideas are cheap. Persistence is the real price; a long, hazardous time where the good idea is always in danger of becoming delusion or dissipating entirely. To stay the course requires constant encouragement. Those with the generosity and talent to provide it, across months and years and drafts, are irreplaceable. They are the sources of truth around which the work is cast into its best, most honest shape.

The following is an incomplete list of the people and texts that deserve the lion's share of credit for anything approaching quality or accuracy, and none of the blame for a lack thereof:

Bernie Chowdhury's book, *The Last Dive*, is a harrowing account of the dangers and thrills of technical diving. Mario Alejandro Ariza's *Disposable City: Miami's Future on the Shores of Climate Catastrophe* was indispensable for its insights into the history of Miami and the threats it faces in the present and near future. Jake Bittle's *The Great Displacement* and John Vaillant's *Fire Weather* helped immensely with the details of Consolidation and the

## Acknowledgments

logistics of the Second Civilian Conservation Corps expeditions in Wyoming.

Thank you to my agents, Joshua Bilmes and James Farner, for hearing my pitch at Boskone and sticking with me through lots and lots of drafts. You're the best in the biz, and I feel immensely lucky to be part of the JABberwocky family.

Thank you to my editor, Toni Kirkpatrick, and the whole team at Diversion, for championing this book and taking such good care of it, and for listening to me just the right amount. Thank you to Steve Thomas for his unbelievable cover art.

Thank you to the Smack (Clarion West 2019) for your advice and support, particularly Derrick Boden, Filip Hajdar Drnovšek Zorko, C.S. Peterson, and Kristiana Willsey (who by this point has noticed that the hive mind pugs have been mostly cut), who were kind enough to read early versions of this book and help me steer it in the right direction.

Thank you to Morgan Kane for taking my various panicked career calls and long texts; your advice is the tops and to have it on demand is a gift. I hope I don't abuse it too much. Thank you to her husband, Nathan, for his support, much less useful but no less cherished.

Thank you to John D. MacDonald, who not only inspired this book but taught me how to write it.

Thank you to my parents, who raised me on a healthy highbrow/lowbrow diet of Latin American literature, high fantasy, and spy novels.

And most importantly, thank you to my partner, Carrie, for a life of adventure and art.